Secret Second Chance Baby

A Small Town Medical Romance

Brandy Piker

Copyright © 2024 by Brandy Piker

All rights reserved. This story, including all names, characters, places, events, and incidents, is purely fictitious and created by the author's imagination. Any resemblance to actual persons, living or deceased, or real-life events is entirely coincidental and unintended.

No part of this publication may be reproduced, distributed, or transmitted in any form or by any means, including photocopying, recording, or other electronic or mechanical methods, without the publisher's prior written permission, except for the use of brief quotations in a book review.

Contents

Chapter One	1
Alex	
Chapter Two	9
Bryan	
Chapter Three	15
Alex	
Chapter Four	23
Bryan	
Chapter Five	31
Alex	
Chapter Six	38
Bryan	
Chapter Seven	48
Alex	
Chapter Eight	55
Bryan	
Chapter Nine	63
Alex	

Chapter Ten Bryan	71
Chapter Eleven Alex	76
Chapter Twelve Bryan	83
Chapter Thirteen Alex	91
Chapter Fourteen Bryan	99
Chapter Fifteen Alex	106
Chapter Sixteen Bryan	114
Chapter Seventeen Alex	123
Chapter Eighteen Bryan	130
Chapter Nineteen Alex	139
Chapter Twenty Bryan	145
Chapter Twenty-One Alex	153
Chapter Twenty-Two Bryan	159

Chapter Twenty-Three 　Alex	166
Chapter Twenty-Four 　Bryan	173
Chapter Twenty-Five 　Alex	183
Chapter Twenty-Six 　Bryan	190
Chapter Twenty-Seven 　Alex	197
Chapter Twenty-Eight 　Bryan	202
Chapter Twenty-Nine 　Alex	211
Chapter Thirty 　Bryan	219
Chapter Thirty-One 　Alex	227
Chapter Thirty-Two 　Bryan	235
Chapter Thirty-Three 　Alex	243
Chapter Thirty-Four 　Bryan	252
Epilogue 　Alex	260

Sneak Peek

    Grumpy Billionaire Single Daddy

Chapter One

♥

Alex

As I step into the courtroom, my eyes immediately lock onto Bryan Knight, the billionaire playboy doctor who once turned my world upside down. He's dressed in a dark gray tailored suit that shows off his hazel eyes—eyes that used to get me every time.

Despite the other people that fill the wooden benches of the solemn courtroom, it feels like it's just me and Bryan. As those piercing eyes follow me across the room, I feel the overwhelming urge to turn around and run.

The air suddenly feels hotter than usual, almost suffocating. My palms grow clammy, and my stomach churns with nerves. I feel everything all at once—anger, sadness, and a twinge of longing all mingled together, swirling like a turbulent sea inside me.

When I got the call from Bryan's lead attorney, Jim Porter, asking me to handle this case—due to my landslide victory with the highly televised negligence case for Dr. Graham Fuller last year—my first thought was *hell no*.

I later changed my mind for two reasons.

One, regardless of what happened between us, Bryan is a damn good doctor. One mistake shouldn't end his career and prevent him from saving more lives.

Two, I am a damn good lawyer myself, and winning this case will solidify my place at the firm so I can finally make a senior partner. Why should I pass up such an opportunity simply because my ex was a jerk?

I knew it would be tough seeing Bryan again, but presently, as I stare at him, it feels more like I'm experiencing the warning symptoms of an impending heart attack.

My chest tightens, and I struggle to steady my trembling hands as chills course through my body. For a moment, time stands still and memories flood my mind—both comforting and unsettling.

It's been almost six years, but he still has that calmness in his gaze that catches me off guard. I used to think he was always so calm because he was ten years older than me, and so he'd acquired more maturity and composure.

But now, I'm much wiser. At thirty-one years old, I'm no pushover—I won't be easily trampled on and thrown into the wild like I was years ago by Bryan and his family.

Which means that I can't let my emotions get the best of me. Not here. Not now.

He looks at me with an expression of shock etched into his features as I approach the defense table. I bet he never expected that one day one of his flings would be the one to help prevent the career he's spent years building from crashing down like a ton of bricks.

He looks furious as he whispers something to Jim. The older, nearly fully grayed man motions for him to stay calm.

Jim stands and extends his hand to me for a handshake. "Ms. Collins, we've been expecting you. You already know Bryan Knight."

Bryan Knight. The cream of the crop in this town and the unexpected lover I met by chance. I clench my fists, determined not to let him see how much being near him still affects me.

Everything that happened between us plays back in my head, and the memories—memories I spent a greater part of my weekend trying to convince myself didn't matter anymore—come flooding back to me.

When I got the call, six years ago, that the company funding my law school scholarship had declared bankruptcy and could no longer sponsor me and the ten other students in their scholarship program, it felt like life as I knew it was over.

That was the call that changed the course of my entire existence and led me to meet Bryan, the man who showed me how boring my life was and transformed it in ways I had never imagined.

Feeling down, and not sure how I'd be able to afford the rest of my degree, I had decided to dance my problems away. That night, I attended a party for the first time since I started law school, oblivious to fate's plans for me.

I decided on a short black satin dress. It was backless, stopped just over my knees, and hugged my curves in all the right places—and it paired perfectly with my favorite black-heeled sandals and some matching jewelry.

I was never one to go to parties, despite how many times Cara, my roommate, had tried to convince me to go. But, the news about my scholarship funds had loosened a screw in my brain. I made up my mind to go out with a bang, since I was certain I couldn't continue law school without a scholarship and would be forced to drop out.

The moment I walked into the crowded room, filled with drunk soon-to-be lawyers grinding against each other on the dance floor and making out in dark corners, I knew this wasn't my scene. But I had dressed up and come out for the night, so I figured I might as well try to fit in.

I walked toward the bar—since alcohol was one thing everyone seemed to have in common—and asked the bartender for a shot of tequila. I scrunched up my face as the alcohol hit the back of my throat on its way down. I honestly didn't understand how people enjoyed any of this.

After recovering from the shot, I scanned the room, taking in the exuberant crowds...until my eyes landed on a man walking toward the bar. He was tall—probably six foot three—and had brown hair that fell over his face a little. His jaw was so sharp I was sure it could cut through glass, and he had the most hauntingly beautiful hazel eyes I'd ever seen.

I tried to pull my eyes away from his. I mean, I really tried, but it was pointless. I could stare into those eyes all night and not tire of them. There was just something soothing about this man, and I was curious to find out what it was.

As he drew closer, I had to force myself to look away and pretend to be more intrigued by whatever was happening on the dance floor. He sat on the empty barstool beside me, ordered a scotch without as much as a glance in my direction, and then, when his drink arrived, he took a sip. Finally, he turned his attention—and those gorgeous eyes—to me.

Damn, was my first thought when I saw his lips, and I knew immediately I wanted them on mine.

"What's a beautiful woman like you doing alone at the bar?" he asked. His confident smile teetered on the edge of arrogance.

"Maybe waiting for you?" I smiled back at him, attempting to be seductive and lightly tossing my hair to reveal my neck—which I've heard is my second-best feature.

After some flirtatious banter back and forth, he asked me to dance, which we did until he whispered that he'd love to have a private dance with me and then proceeded to graze my neck with his lips before pulling away. He was a tease, but I somehow found it to be a turn-on.

This was just what I needed to help me forget all my problems for the night.

We danced a little more and he invited me back to his hotel room, his lips landing on mine as soon as the door clicked shut behind us. He was a fierce kisser with very soft lips, and it wasn't long before I let his tongue into my mouth, letting him taste me fully as his hands found their way to my braless breasts.

He broke away from the kiss, not breaking eye contact with me as he took off his shirt to reveal a perfectly toned chest. His lips found their way to my neck, making me hotter with each kiss, hardening my nipples as my head swirled with excitement.

His hands trailed around my back to untie the string that kept my dress on my body, and I admit I had a bit of fun as I let him lose his mind trying to undress me. He grunted in frustration. I knew he was seconds away from ripping the dress off me, so I quickly untied it and let it slip off, slowly, as he watched in anticipation, his eyes darkening with desire.

He carried me to the bed, kissing me all the way, and gently laid me on the soft bedspread before taking off his pants. Crawling on top of me, he swiftly took an erect nipple into his warm mouth while his hands slid down to remove my panties.

I let out a soft moan as his finger slipped inside of me, and my toes curled from the torrents of pleasure coursing through my entire body.

He started with one finger, and then added another, increasing his tempo to make me moan even louder. With his lips igniting fires between my breasts and matching the tempo of his fingers in my pussy, it wasn't long before my legs trembled and gave out as I came all over his fingers. Not waiting for me to catch my breath, his lips trailed down my body to drink up every bit of my juice.

Afterward, he tugged off his briefs to reveal the thickest cock I'd ever seen. Before I could gather my scattered thoughts, he rolled a condom over his steely erection and slowly entered me, allowing me to feel every inch of it.

I gasped, moaned, and groaned all at once. He was gentle but meticulous, his eyes locked with mine as he slid in and out of me slowly. It was the most intimate thing that had ever happened between me and a stranger.

Each of his strokes made me want to scream his name—but I didn't even know what it was. We hadn't gotten around to introductions.

As he increased his pace, I let out a loud moan and reached my peak, tensing around him, and in about three strokes he followed me over the edge, letting out a groan as his body went limp.

He rolled off me to remove the condom and when he came back, we both fell asleep almost immediately, our bodies intertwined. I can recall our first time so vividly because it was the most intense sexual experience I've ever had.

I woke up to see him staring at me, and he looked even more perfect in the daylight, with messy locks of brown hair falling over his forehead.

"Hi," I greeted shyly. I could feel my face turning red.

"Good morning, beautiful. I got you breakfast."

I looked over at the corner of the room and saw a tray on the table, full of delicious-smelling food. I politely excused myself to the bathroom to freshen up and then joined him at the table.

Now that I took the time to look around, I realized the hotel suite looked more like an apartment than a room. It had more rooms than the house I grew up in.

We ate in silence, occasionally catching each other staring. He looked as if he wanted to say something to me, but he didn't know how to let it out.

"May I ask you something?" he finally said, breaking the silence with the vaguest question possible.

"Yes, of course."

"Are you in a relationship?"

I kept quiet for a moment, contemplating my response. I couldn't give him an answer without knowing his reason for asking.

"Why do you ask?"

He went on to explain that he wanted us to form an alliance. His girlfriend had broken up with him for another guy—a guy he hated—and his parents had been on his back to show his maturity by settling down with one woman. If I would be willing to pretend to be his girlfriend, he would give me whatever I wanted.

"I don't even know your name," I blurted out, mentally beating myself up for not asking the night before.

He chuckled before replying, "It's Bryan. Bryan Knight. But I don't suppose knowing my name is your only request for this deal? You know I can make it worth your while." He smiled as my eyes widened in surprise.

Holy shit!

He was one of the elusive Knights, a billionaire family that owned one of the biggest hospitals in Woodvale. I'd heard Cara mention the name Bryan Knight like a million times since we started law school in Bright Sands, the town next to Woodvale.

According to Cara, he was quite the ladies man. Given our interaction the night before, and the fact that I was in a robe, wearing nothing underneath, in his hotel room, she hadn't lied.

I quickly composed myself, trying not to show too much excitement. I was happy to accept his deal. After all, what did I have to lose except two years of law school and my chance to become a brilliant lawyer? I was almost tempted to say no to him just to wipe the smug look off his face, but sticking it to the billionaire bad boy at the cost of my future wasn't worth it.

I pretended to think about it for a few days before telling him my part of the deal—he would sponsor me through my final year of law school.

That was how my life first got mixed up with Bryan's, and if I had known then what I know now, I would've run for the hills when we first locked eyes.

Now, back in the courtroom, I respond to Jim, avoiding eye contact with Brian. "Yes. We've met."

I settle down in my chair, ready to do the job I was hired for and then cut ties with Bryan Knight all over again.

Chapter Two

Bryan

In all my forty-one years on earth, I have never been this blindsided.

When I saw Alex walk into the courtroom, I thought surely she'd walked into the wrong room. That or the prosecution had somehow found out about our history and decided to torture me with her presence into admitting I was guilty.

Six years ago, she disappeared without an explanation and I haven't heard from her even once—I would very much like to keep it that way, but Jim just told me she's my new lawyer.

She looks more mature than she did a few years back. Her killer curves are more accentuated in her black power suit, her pristine black hair is up in a bun, and her dark brown eyes look as perfect as ever...but I can't help but wonder why on earth she's here?

Why did she agree to take my case?

Jim is sitting in the chair separating us, but her unmistakable lavender and lemon scent isn't letting me think clearly. Agitated, I get up and walk out of the courtroom. I can't fathom being in the same room as Alex without wanting to scream at her.

A few minutes later, Jim and my best friend and colleague, Mark, join me in the break room. We all sit in silence as they both avoid eye contact with me, knowing how furious I am.

Mark leans over to Jim, and I can't make out what they're whispering to each other, so I clear my throat until they both look at me. "Jim, can you tell me what's going on?"

He stays quiet for a moment as if he's contemplating what to say to me or how to say it. He knows I'm pissed—I hate when things are done behind my back.

"Can we talk privately?" His deep baritone voice goes even lower as his eyes plead with me.

"I would much rather we talk here."

"I contacted Ms. Collins a while back, asking for her help with the case. I thought we'd be at an advantage having her on our team."

Silence follows as I let his words sink in. I hate that she has to be the one to help me. After what transpired between us, I would rather keep believing that I'll never see her again, that she's dead to me.

When Alex walked into the courtroom, a small part of me leaped for joy. I've been hoping for years to see her again, even if I also loathe the fact that she still means something to me.

We shared so much in our pretend relationship that it felt more real than any relationship I'd had before her. But then, she was only with me for her own selfish interest. That's what she is—selfish.

That's it! There has to be a catch somewhere. The Alexandra Collins I remember would never do anything unless there's something in it for her.

"Bryan, we have to go back in," Jim says, looking down at his phone. "I was just informed that the judge is about to leave her chambers.

If we're not seated when she enters the courtroom, your case may be adjourned to God knows when."

"Fine." I straighten out my suit and button it. "I'll allow her to represent me for today's proceedings, and then you'll find me another lawyer."

"Fine," Jim says as we walk back to the courtroom.

Mark catches up to me and is about to say something, but I stop him. I need a little time to process everything before I can factor in his opinion.

We head back into the courtroom, and the proceedings begin. After Alex cross-examines a witness from the prosecution's side, she unexpectedly calls me to take the stand. Shocked, I confer with Jim, who seems hesitant but still advises me to oblige her request. As I get to the witness stand, I swear my oath and take my seat.

"Mr. Knight, I have just one question for you. Did you have a hand in the death of those patients?"

"What? Are you serious?"

"Mr. Knight, I ask the questions, not you."

I can't believe this shit. She puts me on the stand and this is the first question she decides to ask me? She might as well plant some evidence and send me to jail, too. Yes, things ended badly with us, but how can she even think I'm capable of doing something like that?

Still reeling in shock, my eyes dart over to Jim, who gives me a look as if to remind me to stay calm, so my gaze returns to Alex, who's still waiting for me to give her an answer.

"No, I didn't have a hand in their deaths."

"Were you aware that the nurse on duty had worked for seventy hours prior to her fatal mistake?"

"No. I wasn't aware of that."

She walks closer to me. "And why is that? Aren't you supposed to know everything that goes on in your hospital?"

"Is that a serious question?" I look around the courtroom to see if anyone else shares my view that her line of questioning is ridiculous.

She narrows her eyes at me. "Do I look like I'm joking?"

"Anybody who runs a huge organization like I do knows that one person can't possibly know everything. That's why I put other people in charge of various departments and sections of the hospital. Secondly, I wasn't even at the hospital when it happened."

"Where were you?"

"Does it matter?"

"Yes."

"Well, I went home to rest. I had just returned from New York, where I assisted in a major brain surgery to separate conjoined twins."

"No further questions, Your Honor."

"Does the prosecution have any questions for Mr. Knight?" the judge asks as Alex walks back to her seat.

They look as shocked as me as they ruffle through some files on their desks, sharing whispers, still trying to decide.

"We don't have all day," the judge snaps at them.

"No, Your Honor. No questions at this time."

"Then this case is adjourned." She bangs her gavel on the table and everyone stands as she exits the courtroom.

As I step down from the stand, I catch a small smile crawling onto Alex's lips, as if she had planned all this, and my stomach boils in anger. I walk up to her to confront her.

"What the hell was that? Are you here to defend me or throw me in jail?"

She turns, and her demeanor is as cool as a cucumber. "These are questions we could have gone over at your trial preparation, but Jim knows you're as stubborn as a goat and wouldn't have let me represent you if we didn't spring it on you like this. Besides, now I'm certain you're innocent, so...win-win."

She grabs her files and bags and starts to walk away, and I quickly go after her. "What do you mean by that? Did you really come into this court believing in the possibility that I did what they say I did?"

"Yes, that's what every good lawyer does for their client."

"So why represent me if you think I may be guilty?"

"Because—" She stops in her tracks and faces me. "I'm a professional, and it doesn't matter if you're innocent or guilty. The only thing that matters is that you're my client and it's my job to present you in the best possible light to the jury. Everything else is inconsequential."

"Well, I don't care if you're the best lawyer in the United States, blindside me like that again and you're fired."

"You know what—" She doesn't complete her sentence, just spins around and walks off in the regal way that only Alexandra Collins can.

"She's pissed," Mark says as he stands beside me. "What did you say to her?"

"Didn't you see what she pulled? Bringing me to the stand like that and questioning me like some common criminal? I told her I'd fire her if—"

"What? In case you didn't notice, this is the first time the prosecution has been left speechless since this trial started. She's a badass lawyer, man."

I take a long look at Mark. "But she's a terrible person. You know this more than anyone."

Only a terrible person would do what she did six years ago as soon as she got what she wanted out of our fake relationship deal. She graduated from law school and then disappeared a week later, without considering how I felt or admitting that we could have been something real. Of course, she disappeared—she didn't need my money anymore.

Mark places a hand on my shoulder. "But are you willing to let the past rob you of your future?"

I hate to admit it, but Mark is right. She did pull some badass moves just now, and that's the type of lawyer I need in my corner. "Let's hope she'll be back."

"I saw her entering the ladies' room, so if you hurry, you could still catch her."

"Thanks, man." I push through the courtroom door to apologize to the one woman I can't stand, to get her to agree to be my lawyer and help me win this.

Chapter Three

Alex

I'm talking with Tina, a lawyer I've worked with on a few other cases when I see Bryan walk out of the courtroom and immediately head straight toward us.

I say my goodbyes and try to walk away as quickly as I can.

"Alex, stop."

I hesitate for a moment, contemplating whether I have the time and energy to put up with his arrogance. On second thought, I do have some spare time to give Bryan Knight a piece of my mind.

Spinning around, I look into his eyes, which are still the most beautiful things I've ever seen. "I'm not a child who you get to threaten or control. Let's get this straight—I'm doing you a favor by being here, and if your fragile ego can't take it, then I don't have any business remaining your lawyer."

He's taken aback, shock written all over his face.

That ought to put him in his place for a while.

I can see the wheels in his brain turning, trying to decide what to say to me. I steal a little glance at his facial features as he frowns, my eyes tracing over every fine line, every corner. His face is like a song I've memorized that keeps replaying over and over in my head.

No matter how hard I try to deny it, I miss him and everything we shared.

"I want to apologize for threatening to fire you. I was just blindsided when you asked me to come up to the stand, and by your line of questioning."

Bryan Knight, apologizing? That's new.

If he can swallow his pride, I'll try to do the same. "I'm sorry you felt blindsided, but if you intend to still have a hospital to practice in after this, then let me do what I do best. It may not feel good sometimes, but it's for your own good."

"I understand." A little pause. "Can we go somewhere and talk?"

I take a deep breath. "Where did you have in mind?"

"The Corner Café, of course." There's a gleam in his eyes—not surprising because we spent a lot of time there back in the day.

Against my better judgment, I nod. "Alright."

We both get in our cars and drive to the café. When we get there, we walk inside together, and when I spot the booth that used to be our favorite, I intentionally choose the one farthest from it. That booth holds a lot of memories I don't want coming back to me. Not now, not ever.

Once we settle down, a waitress approaches us for our order.

"Black coffee for me, and some iced tea with a splash of vanilla for her." Bryan looks to me for approval, and I give the waitress an affirmative nod.

"You remembered, after all these years?" I ask him after the waitress leaves to get our drinks.

"Of course, I remember. I've never met anyone else who puts vanilla in their iced tea."

I try to hide the small smile that draws at the corners of my lips before he notices, but I know he's already seen it. "So, what really happened?"

"You really wanna know?"

I nod. "Of course."

He leans back in his seat. "Like I told you in court, I'd just come back from a trip to do a major brain surgery in New York, and I was so exhausted that I didn't go visit the active comatose patients in the hospital like I usually do. One of the nurses—apparently, she'd been working for seventy-two hours straight—mistook an opioid for a sedative that we give to the comatose patients every night to help them relax. This mistake suppressed their breathing, led to respiratory failure, and ultimately, the death of six of them. And now, the families are suing the hospital for negligence."

"Wow, that's awful."

"I found out the next morning, and...I do blame myself. If I'd gone to make my rounds like I normally do, I could have caught the error and they might still be breathing today."

I can hear the pain in his voice as he narrates what happened, and deep down in my gut, I have no doubt he's telling the truth. Bryan may be bad at relationships, but he's always valued life more than anything.

"My former lawyers offered to compensate the families with five million dollars each, but they turned it down. They asked for fifty million each, or they would sue the hospital and well, here we are."

The waitress returns with our drinks and he takes a sip of his coffee. "Be straight with me—is there any way the hospital wins this?"

I smile. "If there's a way, I'll find it. In the meantime, I'll get a meeting with the judge and get her to lift the ban on your hospital so you can start working again."

He sighs with relief. "I really hope it works. I know I asked you here to talk, but can I buy you lunch?"

My body takes a pause. The last thing I want to do is spend any more time outside of the courtroom with Bryan. I don't think I'm ready for that just yet.

"Come on, it's just two people with healthy appetites eating, nothing more," he adds as if he knows I'm about to say no.

"Sure. I'm starving anyway, so let's eat."

He signals to the waitress. "So, we'd like to order some lunch too. I'll have a classic BLT, and if I were to hazard a guess, she'll have a turkey and avocado wrap." He turns to me. "Am I right?"

"Yep." God, I hate that he still knows me so well after all this time, and I'm mad at myself for being so damn predictable.

"A young couple just took our booth." I can feel his eyes roaming my face, trying to figure out what I'm thinking.

"It's no longer our booth," I respond dryly, trying to sound as unaffected by this conversation as possible.

"I noticed how you specifically avoided sitting there when we came in."

"Yes, and so?"

He leans forward over the cool surface of the marble table separating us. "Do you still remember the things we did in that booth, especially on those nights when we would stay until there were only one or two customers left?"

I swallow hard. "Of course, I remember."

"Do you ever miss it?" He's staring deep into my eyes now, and I squirm uncomfortably at the intensity of his hypnotic gaze.

"Lex?"

"Don't call me that." The waitress returns at that exact moment. *Perfect*. "You know what? I'll take my lunch to go, please."

"Alright, ma'am."

"What? Did I say something wrong?" Bryan feigns ignorance.

"Nothing. I just think having lunch with you isn't such a good idea. We should try and keep things as professional as possible." Unable to wait for the waitress to come back with my food, I scramble out of my seat, pick up my bag, thank him for lunch, and grab my to-go box from the waitress on my way out.

Getting into my car, I drive off to pick up my son from school. Apart from the fact that I needed to escape Bryan—who apparently still knows how to make me feel like the helpless girl I was when we met six years ago—the realization that it was almost time for Cooper's school pickup was what really made me get out of dodge.

It's not like I could tell Bryan about Cooper anyway. He wasn't interested all those years ago, and I'm sure nothing has changed.

I pick Cooper up from school, and when we get home he changes into his regular clothes as I cut the turkey and avocado wrap into three equal parts and put one part on a plate for him.

Too tense to eat anything myself, I decide to change into more comfortable clothing and see if I can do some cleaning around the house that I've put off for long enough.

After changing, I come out to find an exhausted Cooper asleep on the couch with the last piece of food still in his hand. I pat down his dark brown hair—just like his dad's—and pry the food from his hand, carrying him to his room quietly. I don't want to wake him, plus I need the house to be quiet for a while so I can think and clear my head.

It takes me about forty-five minutes to clean up the entire house, and then I settle down to do some work. I bring out all the files Jim sent over about the case and start going through them carefully. I manage to stay focused until I stumble upon a photo of Bryan attached to a file.

I've always known that Cooper looks like Bryan, but I was reminded of their uncanny resemblance the moment I saw Bryan again in court today. Now, looking at the picture in the file, it's like I'm looking at an older version of my son. The oval-shaped face, the slight curve on the bridge of the nose, those beautiful hazel eyes. It's unfair how much Cooper looks like his dad.

I briefly wonder how Bryan would react if I were to tell him about our son. I still haven't decided if I want to. I'm not sure I want to bring that kind of complication into Cooper's life, and then there's the bigger question of whether Bryan even wants a son.

My mind wanders to the one time I jokingly asked him what his reaction would be if I got pregnant. He had answered seriously, and promised to give the child the best life. It was meant to be a light conversation, well before I found out about Cooper, but Bryan's reply had made my heart flutter.

That was one of the many things that had me so taken with Bryan back then. Yes, he had moments where he didn't seem to care about anyone but himself. But deep down, under the whole facade he shows in public, he's someone who cares a lot—too much sometimes.

He's a very selfless person when it comes to those who are important to him. He would go to the ends of the earth to make the ones he loves happy. But he has to be in control, too and never allows anyone to take him for granted.

Bryan asked me if I miss us, the *us* that would stay at that booth for hours, and the truth is that I do. We were happy then. Not just pretending to be happy, but actually happy being alone together in our own world.

"Mommy, who is that?" Cooper's little voice brings me back to reality. He's woken up from his nap, which makes me wonder how long I've been sitting here thinking about Bryan instead of working. Cooper is pointing to the photo in my hands.

Your father, baby.

"This is one of Mommy's clients, baby."

"What did he do?"

I chuckle at his innocence, stretching out my hands to lift him and sit him on my lap.

"He just has allegations against him and Mommy has to clear them all."

I'm sure his little mind doesn't quite understand any of that, but he still nods at me, his eyes fixed on all the files I have on the table.

"What would you like to have for dinner?"

"Pizza."

"Alright. We have some leftovers in the fridge I can reheat."

I carry him to the kitchen and place him on the kitchen counter, then I grab the leftover pizza and put it in the microwave.

"Can we have ice cream too?"

I glance up at him, batting his eyelashes at me to try to convince me, and I laugh.

"Please?" Cooper begs.

"Okay, baby. But after dinner."

"Yes! You're the best." He grins, stretching his hands out for a hug, and I hold him close to me. I didn't know how much I needed this hug until now.

The microwave dings and I pull away from the hug to bring out the pizza, after which we head to the dining table to eat.

If my older sister, Grace, were around, she would scold me for having pizza for dinner three nights in a row this week. It isn't my fault, though—work has become very stressful. Grace has even tried to convince me to allow Cooper to stay with her, but I can't bear the thought of not seeing my son every day.

Besides, I would drive myself crazy thinking of a million things that could go wrong. Not that I don't trust my sister, but we mothers worry—it's just what we do.

After dinner, I help Cooper with his homework, run him a bath, and we brush our teeth together before I tuck him into bed. After reading him a bedtime story, I head back to my desk to continue going through Bryan's case files.

I take pages of notes, looking for an angle to prepare my defense. After about an hour and a half, I am completely drained and decide to finally head to bed. The second my head hits the pillow, I drift off to sleep.

Chapter Four

Bryan

I've just gotten off a call with Uncle Tom, my dad's younger brother, who's been calling to check in with me after every court hearing.

He's currently on vacation with his wife Sarah and their kids Leo and Nadia, and yet he still found time to check in—unlike my dad, who called only once to tell me not to make him regret leaving the hospital in my care.

Just a few minutes after the call ended, the doorbell rings. I stroll over to open the door, and find my mom smiling at me from my doorstep. As usual, I had no idea she was coming to see me, which wouldn't be so bad if I weren't preparing to go to court.

She plants a kiss on my cheek as she walks past me into the house. Even though we have our differences, and Mom is far from perfect, she's always supported me and pushed me to be the best version of myself. It was a little hard to understand when I was younger, but now I thank her every day for everything she's done for me, and still does for me.

My dad and I rarely get along—he hasn't been very present in my life, not since he left Mom and remarried—so I'm glad I'm still close to Mom.

Of course, she wasn't too happy when she heard about the case, but she's been here for me while Dad has only expressed his disappointment in me.

I'd started making some toast and eggs before she got here, so I put them on two plates, placing one in front of her before pouring a glass of orange juice on us both.

"So what's the unexpected visit about, Mom?"

She looks up from her food and smiles as she brings a piece of toast to her mouth. "What, I can't visit my son anymore?"

"No, of course you can. It's just that I'm supposed to be in court in twenty minutes. I would have scheduled another day to hang out if you'd told me you were coming," I tried to explain to her.

"Then I'll come to court with you. It can't have been easy not having me there all this time."

Somehow, the thought of Mom coming with me to court feels odd, not that I don't want her to be there. It's just that she hasn't come along since the case started, so I can't help but feel she's forcing herself to do something she's not ready for.

"Mom, you don't have to if you don't want to. We can just reschedule for another day."

"Nonsense, I'd love to be there with you. I know I haven't been available to support you during this case so far, but I'm here now," she says, taking my free hand in hers.

Even with the gray hair, her face looks young for someone her age. I smile at her and nod my head. "Thanks, Mom."

I finish up my breakfast and head to my room to get ready while Mom washes the dishes even though I tell her not to.

The suit I picked out yesterday seems to stare back at me from the hanger, and I do a little breathing exercise before I put it on. It's a dark blue suit that I intend to pair with a black suede office shoe. I make a last-second decision to ditch the tie, grab my briefcase from the bed, and head back to the living room.

The second Mom sees me, she shakes her head in disapproval. "Where's your tie?"

"Decided to go without one."

"No, my son won't be one of those sloppy men who wears a suit without a tie. Go grab your tie."

"Your son is an adult who can make decisions for himself. Tie or no tie, it won't affect the outcome of today's hearing, so, no, Mom, I'm not wearing one."

My mom likes to think she knows what's best for everyone but once in a while, I like to remind her that she doesn't.

"Fine, if you want to go out looking like a pauper, suit yourself," she scoffs angrily as she walks out the front door.

I decide to drive my Porsche today. After Mom gets in and is properly belted, we drive off to court.

The music playing in the car is interrupted by a call from Jim just as we pull into the parking lot. I don't bother picking up since I can see him, Mark, and Alex waiting for me by the stairs. Getting out of the car, Mom and I walk toward the group.

"Who's the woman standing beside Mark? She looks familiar."

"That's Alex Collins, my lawyer. You may remember her from when we fake-dated a few years back."

Mom stops moving, and when I turn to see why, she looks white as a sheet. For a second, I panic. "Mom, are you alright?"

"Yes, of course. I'm fine. I just didn't expect to see her here."

"Me neither, but apparently, she's the only lawyer who has a shot at helping me win this case. She left Kurt Miller speechless yesterday after she questioned me on the stand, and I've never seen Kurt Miller speechless before."

"She put you on the stand?" she asks, ignoring all the other good things I said about Alex. "I thought Jim said it wasn't a good idea to put you on the stand."

"He did, but Alex had other plans—and frankly, it worked."

"She broke your heart, dear. Are you sure you want such a woman defending you in such an important case?"

"I was reluctant at first, but yes. I think she's exactly what I need."

"You go right ahead, and I'll meet you inside. I just remembered there's an important call I have to make."

"Alright, see you inside."

"Morning," I throw at my legal team and Mark as I approach.

Mark gestures with his chin toward Mom. "Is Mel coming inside with you?"

"Yeah, she just needs to make a quick call."

"Your mom is here?" Alex has this look of dread on her face when I turn to her, almost identical to the one I saw on Mom's face when she first saw Alex. But it quickly vanishes.

"Yes, she wants to be here to support me."

"Whatever. Let's head in before the judge does."

Whatever is a strange response to someone's mother coming to court to support them, but there's no time to get into that with Alex as we all head to the courtroom.

"All rise. Court is now in session. The Honorable Judge Maria Denver presiding," the bailiff announces as the judge takes her seat.

"I hope the prosecution came prepared to do their job today. Don't waste my precious time."

"We won't, Your Honor." Kurt looks over at me. He looks ready to tear me to pieces.

Halfway into the hearing, Mom walks in, looking better than when I left her earlier. She and Alex lock eyes and throw each other the same look.

A glare? I wonder if I'm seeing things. Maybe Alex is transferring her feelings about whatever went on between us to everyone related to me, which isn't fair. Mom had nothing to do with how things played out between us. On the contrary—she was there to help me get through what Alex did to me.

The more I think about it, the more confused I get. I can't imagine Mom and Alex even knowing each other well enough that they would shoot hateful glares at each other. I try to take my mind off it. I need to focus on the hearing today. I can deal with the drama when we leave.

The hearing is going well. The judge has agreed to decline the motion set by the prosecution to take away my license to practice medicine, which is a huge relief. Watching Alex argue against the prosecution is a sight to behold. She firmly stands her ground, tactfully dodging all the intimidation thrown at her.

After about two hours, the judge rules in our favor and adjourns the hearing to a month from now. This is the thing that pisses me off about this case—the next hearing is always set so far apart from the last, and my patience is rapidly wearing thin. I've never gone this long without working in the OR, and it's messing with my head.

As we walk out of the courtroom, I take the opportunity to talk to Alex. "Look, I'm sorry for bringing up the booth thing the other day. I didn't mean to make you uncomfortable."

She shrugs. "It's in the past now."

"Great."

I'm not ready to let Alex go just yet, so I offer to take everyone to lunch at a restaurant a few minutes away from the courthouse "so we can discuss strategy." I notice Mom's discomfort at the suggestion, though she reluctantly agrees to come along.

I decide not to say anything to her with everyone present, but when we get to the restaurant, I notice how Mom tactically avoids sitting next to Alex or opposite her.

All through lunch, they keep shooting daggers at each other. Eventually, Alex gets a text and informs everyone that she has to leave. I offer to walk her out, and I don't miss Mom's shoulders dropping in relief when Alex declines the offer.

Shortly after, Jim and Mark leave, too, leaving only Mom and me in the restaurant.

"So, what was that all about?"

"What?"

"You know what." She feigns ignorance. "The looks between you and Alex, the tension."

"What tension?"

"Mom, I noticed that you two didn't say a word to each other all afternoon, and I also noticed how stiff you were in her presence."

"Sue me for not being in the mood to exchange pleasantries with that gold digger."

"It was six years ago. At least try to be civil with her. She's helping us keep the hospital open, and helping me hold on to my license to practice medicine."

"I can't make any promises, but I'll try my best."

"Listen, Mom. Alex is helping me out and I'll prefer it if you don't do anything to piss her off okay. You have to promise to be nice to her, for my sake at least."

"Fine, whatever."

Mom grabs her handbag. "Let's go, I've lost my appetite."

"I'm not done with my food."

"Then I'll go on without you. See you later."

"How will you be getting home?"

"Already texted my driver to come pick me up."

"Alright. See you later."

After Mom leaves, a text message from Alex pops up and I catch myself smiling in excitement.

> Alex: *Thanks for lunch today and sorry I had to leave so abruptly.*

> Me: *It's no problem, you looked uncomfortable. Is everything okay?*

> Alex: *Yes, why?*

> Me: *Uh…the awkwardness between you and my mom. I noticed.*

> Alex: *I have to go. I'm really busy with something, but I'll talk to you later.*

I'm left even more confused than I was in the courtroom. I try to remember if they had an altercation six years ago, but I can't think of anything major.

The first time I brought Alex to meet my parents, they bombarded her with lots of questions about everything from her social status to her parents' jobs to her career path, and other areas that were frankly not their concern. Alex did a great job of only answering the questions she felt were important and politely declining to answer the rest.

Mom wasn't too happy about that. She wanted to know everything and anything she could about the girl her son was dating.

Mom expressed her displeasure about Alex to me once, after about two months of our relationship, and I told her to steer clear. She didn't say anything else to me about Alex after that, until the day it all ended.

I signal to a waitress and pay for lunch plus her tip, and then decide to drive myself to the gym where I know Mark had planned to work out this afternoon.

The gym is packed, as always. Mark is running on the treadmill as though his life depends on it, and it's fascinating to watch.

"What do you think the weirdness between your mom and Alex is all about?" he asks, slowing to a walk so he can talk to me.

"You noticed that too?"

"Of course. It was clear as day. So what's up with them?"

"I asked Mom—she claims she's just upset Alex broke my heart."

He shakes his head vehemently. "Nope, it's much more than that. Alex seemed angry with her, too. Wouldn't she be remorseful instead of angry?"

"I think you have a point. I'm not getting the truth from either of them, though."

"Then you'll have to figure it out for yourself."

Putting the drama out of my mind, I power up the treadmill next to Mark's and start my warm-up.

Chapter Five

Alex

As soon as I leave lunch with Bryan and the team, I head over to Cooper's school.

I'm a few minutes early, but it's better than going home and coming out again to pick him up later.

I didn't allow Bryan to walk me to my car after lunch because Cooper's booster seat is in the back. I forgot to take it out this morning and it would've been hard to explain to Bryan why I have a child's seat in the back of my car.

I'll have to come up with a better solution, though. I can't keep taking Cooper's booster seat out and then putting it back whenever I need to drop him off or pick him up for the rest of Bryan's trial.

Seeing Mel again today made me realize that I'm still hurt by what she did to me all those years ago. She still looks at me with disdain in her eyes, despite the fact that I'm now a lawyer—the lawyer who's helping her son out of the mess he's found himself in.

I vividly recall how she reacted like I was some trailer trash when Bryan told her my parents had passed away and I was in law school on a scholarship. Phil, his dad, wasn't too happy either, but Mel made it her mission to make sure I knew I was beneath her every time we interacted.

"Mean Mel" was my nickname for her, because she never said one nice thing to me, no matter how hard I tried to impress her. I stopped trying eventually, and got used to her antagonism and the way she bad-mouthed me to Bryan in an attempt to change his mind about me. She went as far as suggesting he return to his ex rather than be with me.

The ringing of the school bell pulls me out of my thoughts, and I look toward the school entrance for Cooper.

Soon I see him running toward the car, and I get out to hug him.

"Hey, sweetie. How was school today?" I ask as I help him buckle in his booster seat.

"So cool, we made paper airplanes and pop-up cards. I'll show you mine when we get home."

"I would love that."

When I pull into the driveway, I see my sister Grace sitting on the patio. I had totally forgotten she said she was coming over today.

She walks toward us and offers to carry Cooper, who has fallen asleep, into the house.

I grab my things from the car and follow her inside, grabbing a can of soda from the fridge.

After Grace drops Cooper in his room, she comes out to meet me in the living room, sitting beside me on the sofa and studying me.

"So you want to tell me what's going on?"

"It's just work, draining as usual."

"That look on your face is way more than work, Alex."

I don't want to bother her with my problems. For one, Grace had advised me not to take on Bryan's case in the first place. I also don't want to just dump my burdens on her. I do that a lot and I'm trying to be more independent and handle things myself rather than running to my big sister all the time.

"Today was just stressful."

She rolls her eyes. "Come on, spit it out."

I sigh, hesitantly drumming my fingers on the can of soda I'm drinking. "Mel came to court today."

Grace's expression changes immediately. She's the only person I know who hates Mel more than I do. She goes from shocked to angry to concerned all at once.

"First of all, are you okay?"

"Yes, I'm fine. It was just unsettling to be in the same room with her," I admit.

My sister moves closer to me and pulls me into a side hug, rubbing down my arms and resting my head on her shoulder. She begged me many times to let her talk to Mel on my behalf when I was fake-dating Bryan, but I never let her. There was no point proving anything to Mel, or anyone else for that matter.

"Understandably so. But I'll remind you that you can drop the case anytime you want. You make sure you're putting yourself first, okay?"

"I might actually consider that. Working with Bryan is more draining than I assumed it would be, and not just the work part, but just trying to get along with him. I mean, the first time I questioned him, it ended with us almost yelling at each other."

"Look, Alex, you don't have to prove a point if you're incapable of handling it."

"I know, but you know I'm not one to start something and not finish it."

She sighs in resignation. "Promise me this, then—if it gets too overwhelming, you'll choose yourself first."

I nod my head just as Cooper comes out of his bedroom, rubbing his sleepy eyes. The moment he sees Grace, he comes alive.

"Aunt Grace!" he yells, running over to hug her.

She picks him up and they play a little before she focuses her attention back on me.

"Why don't we have a movie night? You know, to relieve a bit of stress."

I think about it, realizing that's probably exactly what I need amidst this drama—a special Collins movie night. It's a tradition passed down from our parents.

I miss them, Mom, especially.

Grace insists on making Cooper a proper meal, so she puts together a chicken sandwich with some leftover chicken from the refrigerator.

As Cooper watches his favorite cartoon, *PJ Masks*, in the living room, Grace and I make popcorn and food for movie night. We notice that there's no avocado for our usual nachos, so she opts to run to the grocery store to grab some.

By the time she returns with the avocados, Cooper is with me in the kitchen and we have fun making the nachos together. When it's ready, we grab our homemade nachos and our bowl of popcorn and head to the living room.

A few minutes into deliberating the movie we want to see, we agree on *Frozen 2* since it's one of Cooper's favorites. We oblige him because he'll soon fall asleep anyway.

True to our prediction, Cooper falls asleep about fifteen minutes in, and after tucking him into bed, we decide to watch *Upgraded*, a rom-com on Netflix I've heard so much about. I'm enjoying it, but toward the end I start to doze off.

Grace announces that she's staying over, emphasizing that I need some company. I don't argue with her. I know she's right—I feel better when she's around. I give her my spare toothbrush and after we brush our teeth, we both crash almost immediately.

Opening my eyes to the ray of sunlight piercing in through my curtains the next morning, I reach for my phone to check the time. The first thing I notice is several calls from a number that isn't saved on my phone. I ignore it, concluding it could be spam or some company trying to sell me some crap I'll never use.

Since it's Saturday, I don't have to wake Cooper up early for school. I let him sleep as long as he wants, which gives me time to do some chores before he wakes up.

I quietly stand up from the bed so as not to wake Grace. She looks like she needs to sleep in too. I noticed she looked tired yesterday, but my sister is a martyr, always putting everyone else ahead of herself.

I start my cleaning with the dishes in the sink, and then I gather our dirty clothes from the week and head to the laundry room. After putting the clothes in the washer, I decide to put off using the vacuum cleaner until Grace and Cooper wake up.

Instead, I grab an old rag and start dusting off dirty surfaces. Halfway through my cleaning, the doorbell rings.

Anger fills me up as I open the door to find the devil herself.

Mean Mel.

So many thoughts are running through my head as I stare at her with indignation and confusion. What does she want, and how does she know where I live?

"Are you going to let me in, or are you just going to stand there looking at me?"

Frowning at the arrogant smirk she has plastered on her face, I resolve not to let her into my house. "You have some nerve showing up here. What do you want?" I ask, closing the door behind me to block her from seeing into the house.

"I see you're still as ungrateful and disrespectful as ever."

"It's amazing you think your words still have any power over me. I no longer care what you think, Mel, but knowing you as well as I do, you didn't come here to tell me that." She's going through her purse as I speak, and she removes an envelope, holding it out toward me. "What the hell is that?"

"In this envelope is half a million dollars." My eyes widen with surprise and she continues, "I know you need it badly, so take it!"

I shake my head to contain my fury. "I don't need your money, Mel. If this is why you came down here, please leave."

"You think you're so smart, don't you? I bet this is all a plan to get your gold-digging hooks into my son again. You think he'll be so grateful that you helped him win this case that he'll be gullible enough to let you back in. Well, let me save you the trouble—take this money and drop Bryan's case."

"What are you talking about?"

"I want you to tell Bryan you can no longer be his lawyer. You're not competent enough to help him win this case, and you're damn good at running away, so I figured you'd like this offer."

I stand there in shock, not wanting to believe what she's asking of me. Never in a thousand years did I imagine that I would be in a situation where Mel would try to pay me off to leave her son. She's crafty, alright, but I didn't think she would stoop this low.

I sigh, face-palming. "You can keep your money, Mel. Unlike you, I have self-respect. Now, if you will excuse me, I'm going back to my house. I expect you to leave, or I'll call the police and let them know you're trespassing." I make sure to slam the door—hard—in her face, which ultimately wakes Grace up.

"Is everything alright? You look white as a sheet," she says as she strolls into the living room.

"Yes, sorry for waking you."

"What's going on?"

I wait a little to make sure Mel has gotten in her car and driven away. If I tell my sister what Mel came here to do while she's still anywhere nearby, I'm afraid Grace will have less self-control than I did.

"Guess who was at the door just now?" I ask even though I know she won't guess right in a million years.

"Bryan?"

"No, the devil's spawn." She still looks very confused. "It was Mel."

"Mel, as in Mel Knight, Bryan's mom?"

"Yes, that same Mel."

She drops the mug in her hand, and I can see the fury in her eyes. "Is she still here? My fist would love to have a very short conversation with her face." *Called it.*

"She left after I threatened to call the police."

"Good. What did she want?"

"She offered me half a million dollars to drop Bryan's case."

Her eyes widen in shock. "What?" Then she pauses. "Did you accept it? What did you say?"

"What else? Told her to shove her money up her uptight ass. Not in those exact words, but now I wish I had used those exact words."

Grace lets out a breath through her mouth. "That woman never stops, does she?"

"Nope, she never does."

Chapter Six

Bryan

Six Years Ago

It's been a few days since I proposed the fake relationship deal to Alex, and she requested that I give her a few days to think about it. Even though we had great chemistry the first time we met, I'm still worried about her response. Mom has been breathing down my neck these past few days, and I'm running out of excuses to give.

Waiting has never been my strong suit, so I make up my mind to call her in the evening if she hasn't given me an answer by then. In the meantime, I busy myself with other things, deciding to read a book that's been on my study list for a while. I grab a cup of coffee and sit in my study, my journal open in front of me to take notes.

Thankfully, the reading helps to calm me, taking my mind off the matter at hand for a while. It's a book about the surgery of separating conjoined twins that I'm surprised I haven't indulged in before now.

As lunchtime comes around, I make a meal for myself. I rarely order takeout except on the days I'm truly exhausted. I prefer home-cooked meals. Settling on some Alfredo pasta, I prepare the ingredients and start cooking. Pasta is easily my favorite food, and I love cooking it because there are so many ways to prepare it, which makes it feel new every time.

I decide to take a nap after eating, and I'm woken up by my ringing phone.

"Hello?" I ask as I pick up the call, my voice still hoarse from sleep.

"Sorry, is this a bad time?" I instantly recognize the voice on the other end.

Alex.

"No, it's perfect timing. How are you?"

"I'm good. Can we meet at the Corner Café?"

The Corner Café is a restaurant in Woodvale, but it's close to Bright Sands so it's the perfect meeting place. "Yeah, sure. I'll meet you there in thirty minutes."

"Okay, see you there."

The call ends, and as I get dressed to leave for the café, my mind starts to come up with various scenarios, imagining what her response could be. Although I hate being told no, I need to accept that things might not go my way this time. I'll just have to hope for the best.

When I get to the café, I scan the room, and the lack of her presence tells me that I'm a bit early. Sitting in one of the booths in the corner, I order a cup of coffee while I wait for her.

"Hey." Her soft voice washes over me, and when I raise my head to look at her, her beauty catches me momentarily off guard.

"Hey."

"Hope you haven't been waiting long?" She takes her seat opposite me.

"No, I just got here a few minutes ago." Telling her I've been here for twenty-eight minutes and some seconds reeks of desperation. "Would you like a cup of coffee or something?"

"Or something. I don't drink coffee this late."

"Cool." I signal to a waitress and she comes over.

"I'll have some iced tea with vanilla, please."

I blink at her, my curiosity piqued. I don't think I've ever seen anyone pair iced tea and vanilla, but I let it slide.

"How have you been?" Alex asks, probably fishing for something to fill the silence, her hands clasped in front of her.

"Um, good. I've been a bit anxious to hear from you," I admit.

"I know." She chuckles shyly as the waitress returns with her drink. "I just wanted to make the right decision."

"I hope you do, for both of us." I don't care if I come off as desperate at this point. I really need her to agree to this.

Alex stays silent, keeping me in suspense as she sips her drink for what seems like an eternity. "I'm in."

At first, I think I hear the opposite, until her words register in my brain. I have the urge to jump up and hug her, but I keep my composure. "I'd like to take you out tonight to thank you and, you know, properly kick-start our relationship," I say, turning on my charming smile.

Alex smiles back, her cheeks coloring up. "Sure, let's do it."

Even though we haven't known each other very long, we've been in sync the few times we've interacted—the conversations, the sex. Everything with her feels different, in a good way.

"Then I'll get everything ready. Where can I pick you up?"

"I'll be waiting outside my dorm."

"I'll pick you up at six thirty. Is that okay?"

"It is."

"Alright. Maybe I can drop you off now?"

"No, I have somewhere else to go, but thank you."

I nod, pay the bill, and we walk out together.

On the drive home, I try to create a timeline of how long we should "date" before I can introduce her to my parents without rousing any suspicion. I come to the conclusion that about six to eight weeks is a believable timeline.

Two hours later, after calling the restaurant to make reservations, I take a shower, put on a gray long-sleeved shirt and black jeans, and then text Alex to let her know I'm on my way to her dorm.

After pulling to a stop in front of the building, I only have to wait a few minutes before an elegantly dressed Alex walks out. I didn't think she'd ever look more beautiful than she did the first time I saw her, but she's proven me wrong.

The burgundy dress perfectly compliments her skin and hugs all her curves in the right places. Her hair is in a loose bun with a few strands let loose, and her face looks as extraordinary as always.

Getting out of the car, I walk over to the passenger's side. Before I open the door for her, I take her hand in mine and plant a kiss on it. "You look beautiful."

"Thank you." She blushes, getting into the car.

We engage in a little chitchat as we drive back to Woodvale, and when we arrive at the restaurant, the host shows us to our seats and takes our drink orders before leaving.

"You stuck to your word about being at my dorm by six thirty. In my experience, people like you like to keep people waiting."

I raise my eyebrows. "People like me?"

"Rich, influential, handsome."

"You think I'm handsome?"

She laughs and it's like sunshine on a cloudy day. "I said three things, and that's the one you hear?"

I wink at her. "Yes, my charming good looks are my strongest weapon."

"I'm starting to see that."

"So, Alex, can I get to know you more?" I lean closer to the table, maintaining eye contact as we talk.

The host returns with two glasses, pours us some merlot, and after he leaves, Alex takes a sip. "What do you want to know?"

I shrug. "Anything, everything."

"There's nothing much to tell really." She exhales and looks like she's searching for something to say. "You already know my name, where I go to school, and what I'm studying."

"Surely you're a little more interesting than that, Alex Collins. What about your parents?"

Her face turns pale as the last word leaves my lip, and the atmosphere changes immediately.

"They've both passed away." There's no emotion in her voice when she says this. She just picks up her glass of wine, sips from it, and places it back on the table.

Damn it, wrong question. "I'm so sorry for your loss, and for the invasive question."

"No, it's fine. It's not your fault."

The waiter breaks up the awkward tension for a moment, taking our minds off the conversation for a bit as he asks for our orders.

Alex orders a beef Wellington while I go for steak and some mashed potatoes.

The awkwardness returns as I try to recover from my last question. I'm usually so great with girls, so why do I feel like I have to be extra careful with this one?

"And what do I need to know about you, Mr. Knight?" Alex moves to break the silence, lightening the mood with her smile.

I call the waiter to request more wine.

"Well, I guess you know about me and my family, so there's really nothing else to know apart from the fact that I'm a doctor."

"You don't strike me as the typical dating slash relationship type," she says, and I'm surprised that she's so upfront.

I nod in agreement. "That's because I'm not."

She has a look of pity in her eyes. "Almost everyone who claims not to be the relationship type is that way because of a broken heart, so who broke yours?"

I laugh a bit at her question. Despite her lack of knowledge about me, she's not wrong.

"Well, I wish you were right, but unfortunately, you're not. My ex broke up with me because she wanted to get married, but I wasn't ready to settle down. I don't blame her for breaking up with me, what pissed me off is who she left me for—Dr. Dylan Cole. She knows how much he hates me and my family and she started dating him regardless."

The waiter comes back with our food, places it on the table, and leaves. "So what exactly do you want from me?" Alex asks, cutting into her Wellington.

"Two things. One, I want to make Rose regret leaving me for that bastard. And two, I need to get rid of my playboy persona, so my parents let me take over as CEO of Knight Memorial Hospital. Any suggestions?"

She nods. "Well, people need to see us out in public…a lot. And we'll need to pack on the PDA."

"I can do that," I say with a mischievous smile.

After that, we slide into easy conversation, talking about anything and everything. By the time we're done with the main dish, we both request an apple pie crumble for dessert. We have good laughs and light conversation in between bites.

"I like spending time with you," I tell her as we walk out of the restaurant, waiting for the valet to bring up my car.

"Of course you do." She smiles smugly at me, trying so hard to hide the blush on her face. "It's my superpower."

My lips curve up to a smile as my car pulls up. I open the door for her and then get in on the driver's side.

"I'd like to take you out again. What times work for you?" I ask as we drive back to her dorm.

"I have to check my schedule, but I'll let you know."

About twenty minutes later, I park in front of her dorm. "There's a town festival tomorrow. I'd love for us to be there."

"There's no telling you no, huh?"

"I mean, true. Also, Rose and Dylan are gonna be there, so it's the perfect place to pack on the PDA."

"I hate that you're right." She opens the door and lets herself out.

"I'll pick you up by three tomorrow," I call out to her as she walks into the building. She just turns around to smirk at me for a second and then continues walking.

I drive back home, smiling so hard that my cheeks start hurting. This was one of the best dates I've ever been on—Alex is so fun to be around. Too tired to take a shower, I fall asleep the moment my body hits the bed.

• ♥ • ♥ • ♥ • ♥ • ♥ •

The next day can't come fast enough, and by the time I'm on my way to pick up Alex, I feel like it's been ages since I saw her. I take my bike with me, which, from the look of shock on her face when she sees me, Alex is not prepared for in the slightest.

Thankfully, her clothing is bike-appropriate, and all she needs is a little nudging and convincing before she gets on.

We drive to the festival, Alex gripping my waist firmly throughout the ride, screaming that it's her first time on a motorcycle and I should drive more carefully.

The festival is fun. Rose's eyes keep following Alex and me everywhere we go, watching us hold hands and steal kisses the entire time. She looks furious by the time she forces Dylan to take her home.

When the festivities come to an end, I make the bold move of asking Alex if we can continue the fun at my place.

"Well, since you asked nicely, maybe we should," she says, wearing a bright smile.

I chuckle and take her hand in mine as we walk back to my parking spot. We get on the bike and head home.

"Today was nice. You were nice," she says as I pull the bike into my garage.

She climbs off, and when I do the same, we're face-to-face. "I'm a lot of things, Alex, but nice is sure not one of them."

We walk into the house and I offer her a can of soda, since she doesn't drink coffee in the evenings.

"Your house is nice, but it's far too big." She does a spin while looking around. "Don't you get lonely?"

"I do, and I wouldn't mind if you made it less lonely occasionally." I draw closer to her until we're mere inches away from each other.

I feel her breath hitch as she manages to let out her next words. "Less lonely? Is that why you're standing *this* close?"

"No, that's because I want to do this." I lean forward and place my lips on hers, and she lets out a sigh of relief.

Just like the first time we kissed, her lips feel soft against mine, and the strawberry taste of her lip balm has my head in a spin. I move to deepen the kiss and Alex moans, kissing me back with fervor.

Wrapping my arms around her waist, I pull her closer and explore her lips until she's begging for her next breath.

She pulls away and starts to undo the buttons on my shirt, and I assist her to release them faster. As soon as my shirt is off, she raises her hands to let me take off her V-neck top and unclasp her bra.

My dick stirs in my briefs as soon as I see her gorgeous breasts, and my eyes remain fixed on them as she takes off her jean shorts—leaving one last piece of clothing on her body.

Finding her lips again, I lift her to wrap her legs around my waist as I carry her to my bedroom. Once there, I lay her down and slowly pull off her cream lace panties, sucking in my breath as her pussy comes into view.

Falling on my knees between her legs, I take her clit into my mouth, sucking and licking it until she comes, my name on her lips. I yank off my pants and briefs, grab a condom from my wallet, and roll it over my dick.

Positioning my solid-as-steel dick at her core, I drive in, desperate to recall the sweet sensations of her pussy wrapped around me. I'm not disappointed.

Her moans fill up the silence of the bedroom as our hands and bodies move like a well-practiced dance. My lips find her breasts and I suck on each of them in turn while driving in and out of her.

I quicken the pace, letting her feel every inch of me with every movement, her soft moans at every stroke like melodious music to my ears.

Intent on taking the pleasure further, my lips find her ear lobes and suck on them, making her body tremble with pleasure as she gets close to her peak. I trace my lips to her neck and down to her breast before going back up to kiss her mouth.

As her moans become louder, my thrusts become faster, and I know I'm seconds away from erupting like a volcano.

Suddenly her eyes roll back in her head, fingers digging into my skin like her life depends on it as her body shakes from her climax. I give a few more thrusts before letting myself go, arriving at a much-needed and mind-blowing release.

I can feel her body still shaking as I lie beside her, her breath uneven as she tries to calm herself. I pull her closer to me, kiss her shoulder, and hold her until we fall asleep.

Chapter Seven

♥

Alex

This court session is a lot more hectic than usual—the prosecution is trying to pull a trick on us, but thankfully we catch on early. Apparently, they're trying to present evidence that they haven't registered, and we're almost caught off guard.

It's not quite a good day, but we're making progress with the case. I filed a motion to reopen Knight Memorial Hospital in the meantime, but the prosecution came up with a stronger argument and the judge ruled in their favor.

I plan to refile the motion and keep refiling it until the judge either holds me in contempt or rules that the hospital be reopened. In the meantime, all the patients in Knight Memorial have been sent to Dylan Cole's hospital. I'm sure Bryan hates that.

"Are you okay?" The deep voice pulls me out of my thoughts, and I look up to see Bryan looking at me curiously.

"Yeah, I am. Why?"

"I noticed you were a bit off today, that's all. Are you sure you're good?"

If only he knew what I was thinking of, but I'm still not sure if I should tell him. Ever since his mom appeared on my doorstep, I've tried my best to keep it to myself.

"Yeah, I'm good. We've made progress, even though the judge ruled against us today. I'll keep trying until she has a change of heart."

"I know you will. Thanks for fighting this hard for me, Alex."

"No need to thank me. It's my job, after all."

"Can we grab something to eat?"

"Uh…I'm not sure if that's a good idea."

"It's not just a leisurely lunch—I want to go over some things that have to do with the case."

I give in. "Okay, fine, let's go then."

We go to the same restaurant we visited the day his mom came to court, which makes the urge to tell him about her unexpected visit even stronger. Thankfully, it's just the two of us today, so there isn't any more awkwardness than usual.

After we place our order I lean back in my seat. "So, you wanted to go over the case? What parts of it?"

He shakes his head. "Oh, that was just the lie I told so I could get you here."

I sigh and shake my head. "Why am I not surprised?"

"Because you know me too well."

Our eyes meet briefly. "I do. Or at least I used to."

"So, what do you do when you're not working?"

I like that he doesn't try to dwell on the past.

"Mostly just rest and relax after the stress of my job."

Of course, I can't tell him I'm taking care of the son he doesn't know about, who I hang out with and who takes up most of my time.

"Rest and relax? That sounds boring—you used to be so much fun back in the day."

"Oh, I was never fun. I guess you brought out the fun side of me and I reverted back to my old ways right after our..." I trail off, and the waiter coming back with our food at that moment saves us from the weird turn this conversation was about to take.

"You know, they say a problem shared is half solved. You looked distracted in court today."

"Well, it's just— Actually, never mind." I quickly stop myself from telling him about it. There's no point in creating any family drama. The case will soon be over, and we'll go back to living our separate lives.

"Alex..." he chides.

"Fine, I'm just worried about the case," I lie.

He looks concerned. "Why? Is it because of today's loss?"

I nod in affirmation. "I feel a little like a shitty lawyer."

"Alex, you're a lot of things but a shitty lawyer isn't one of them. Even as a doctor, sometimes I do my best and still lose some, and many times we learn from those losses and do better."

My face breaks out into a smile.

"What?" he asks, clearly uncomfortable.

"It feels good to see you like this."

"Like what?"

"All motivational and positive."

My phone alarm beeps and I realize it's time to go pick Cooper up from school.

"Thanks for the food, Bryan, and for your concern. I appreciate them both, and next time I'm paying."

"So there's gonna be a next time, huh?" he asks, grinning from ear to ear.

"We'll see. Bye."

"Bye."

Walking out of the restaurant, I get in the car and drive to my son's school.

"Hey, Coop."

"Hi, Mom." His mood—usually enthusiastic when I come to pick him up—is low.

"What's wrong, little man?"

"My best friend Emily wasn't in school today, and I was all alone," he says in his cutest, saddest voice, the one that melts my heart.

"I'm sorry about that. What can I do to make you happy?" I already know the answer, but still decide to ask.

"Ice cream!"

"Alright then, you got it."

On our way home we stop at the grocery store and get some vanilla and chocolate ice cream before heading home. I give Cooper a quick bath and give him his educational iPad before whipping up some chicken and veggie stir-fry for lunch. Grace would be proud.

As Cooper eats, I decide to scroll through the channels and see if anything good is on TV. As I flip through, the news catches my eye. Bryan's case is trending, which is a bit odd because before today we haven't had any media coverage on the case.

I flip through the other news channels and realize they're all the same, leaving me surprised and confused.

Something just doesn't feel right with this news being circulated on almost all the channels, almost like they were paid to air it. But then again, the Knight family is really famous in these parts, so it's very possible the media has finally decided to catch on.

Not that I'm scared we aren't going to win, but the coverage just seems to be a little over-the-top.

"Mommy, isn't that the man in the picture?" Cooper asks. I didn't even realize he was watching.

"Yes, it is."

"Why is he on TV?"

"It's about the case I'm working on, baby."

"But you're not on TV."

"I don't have to be, it's not always a good thing to be on TV."

"Does that mean he's in trouble?"

"No, he's not."

"But how do you know you're not on TV?"

"I just know, sweetie. Mommy knows a lot of things, remember?"

"Yes."

"That's how I know it's time for your nap. Alright, chop-chop."

He finishes his food and goes to his bedroom to sleep, so I decide to look through one of my favorite law textbooks to see if I can find any solutions to my legal dilemma.

As I search through my books, I stumble upon something that I didn't think I still had. It's a photo album I made when I was still with Bryan, and it has tons of pictures from our time together.

The first page is a group of photos we took in a photo booth at an arcade we visited once. After competing in almost all the games at the store, I thought it would be nice to take some pictures. He thought it was silly, but I convinced him it would be fun.

The rest of the pages are filled with pictures that were taken throughout our relationship. Flipping through the book brings back so many memories—mostly good—that make my heart swell.

We were so happy together, but then everything happened and I had to leave. Still, I can't help but reminisce about all the things I didn't realize I missed about Bryan until I saw him again. His smile, his laugh, his eyes, the way he looks at me like he's staring directly into my soul...the way he loved me even though we tried to convince ourselves it wasn't real. Deep down, we knew how we both felt for each other.

The day we made the album, it was raining heavily and we couldn't go anywhere, so I suggested we put the album together. Bryan had other bedroom activities in mind.

We struck a deal that if we did his thing, we would do mine afterward, and he agreed immediately, only to grumble half the time when the high from his orgasm had worn off.

I eventually made it more fun for him by suggesting we play a game. For each page we completed, he got a kiss. That lasted only five minutes and we ended up making love again.

As I notice my body heating up at the memory of Bryan ravishing me, I decide that's enough of the past and proceed to fish out the textbook I came here for.

I'm not sure how long I read or when I fell asleep, but the screams of *Mommy, Mommy!* wake me up.

I open my eyes to see my son standing in front of me. It looks like he woke up not so long ago and came to find me.

"Hey, I'm awake, Coop."

"I'm hungry," he complains to me. "I want food."

Since there's not enough time to cook, I decide to order some pizza since the delivery is fast and it's one of his favorite foods.

As soon as we're done eating, we work on his homework assignment.

"Can I go to Sam's sleepover?" he asks as I prepare him for bed.

"I'll have to discuss it with his parents first."

"Okay, but he invited me."

"I'll talk to his parents tomorrow, okay?" I tuck him into bed and read his favorite bedtime story, and he soon falls asleep.

I try to do some work, but my mind keeps going back to the photo album I found earlier.

I put on some music to take my mind off it, but it doesn't work. Finally giving up after about an hour of trying to work, I head over to my room, take out the album, and flip through it until I fall asleep.

Chapter Eight

♥

Bryan

Six Years Ago

I wake up that Friday a little late. Alex has already left for class, and I'm home alone, so I decide to stay in bed a little longer today since I'm not doing anything serious.

After a while, my stomach grumbles and forces me to get up and make breakfast for myself. As soon as I'm done eating, my phone starts to ring, and I'm a bit hesitant to pick up since there's no caller ID.

"Hello?" It's odd that a strange number is calling me.

"Hey, Bryan. How are you?" The voice is far too familiar for me not to remember.

"Rose?"

"Yes, how've you been?"

"Oh wow, how did you get my new number?"

"Um, your mom..." It's like I was expecting that answer and not expecting it at the same time.

"Cool, what's going on?" I ask, trying to sound calm, unbothered even, but it's very hard. Maybe my fantasies about Rose calling to tell me how much she misses me and begging me to take her back are finally coming true.

"I don't know how awkward this might sound, but I want to invite you to my engagement party next week."

Engagement party?

It's been barely two months since we broke up, and she's already engaged? This is the last news I expected to hear today. The relationship with Alex was supposed to bring her back to me, not this.

"Hello? Are you there?" she asks when I don't say anything.

"Yes, I'm here. Congratulations, Rose."

"Thank you, Bry. So...are you coming?"

"I might. Are plus-ones allowed?"

"Of course."

"And Dylan is okay with this?"

"He encouraged me to invite you."

Of course, he did, that fucking asswipe.

"Then, I'll be there." I hurriedly end the call and try to calm myself down.

Everything has to look perfect at this party. I just have to make it clear that Alex and I are in love and make sure Rose notices how perfect Alex is compared to her. Moments later, my doorbell rings and the mailman hands me Rose's invitation to the engagement party.

Typical Rose, already sending out the card before asking me because she was sure I would say yes.

When Alex comes back from school really tired, I decide to let it rest—I don't want to stress her any further. It'll be better to tell her about it tomorrow since it's the weekend, and she'll be more well-rested too.

"Good morning." I kiss Alex on her cheek as her eyes flutter open the next morning.

"Good morning. How long have you been staring at me?"

"Only since I woke up." I chuckle and give her a kiss on her forehead.

"You know that's creepy, right?"

"I'm not sure if it is, but do you have plans for today?"

"Not really. It's the weekend, so I just want to rest."

"I have a better plan. Why don't I take you shopping?" She looks really surprised that I offered. "What? Why do you look so surprised?"

"Does 'I hate shopping, it's just walking around, picking out clothes, and trying them on for hours on end, I'd rather get shot in the head' ring any bells?"

"Yeah, okay, I said that. But maybe you've changed my mind."

She shakes her head vehemently. "I don't think that's it."

"It's not polite to look a gift horse in the mouth. Do you wanna go shopping or not?"

"Of course I want to. I've betrayed the sisterhood worldwide if I dare say no."

"Great, let's do it."

Alex is still curious about the entire drive as to why I suddenly decided to take her shopping, but I don't think it's necessary to tell her the main reason just yet.

We visit a few different boutiques, and I let her choose what she wants, but I suggest a few pieces I know are going to make her stand out at the party. Also, I advise her against a few things, keeping my mom and her criticism in mind.

"What are all these clothes for?" Alex asks me as we get to the third store of the day.

"Just for whatever you want, wherever you want to wear them to."

"I think the first two stores have given me plenty of options. Is there some big event we might be going to? Because that would be the purpose of most of the dresses in this store."

"Well, we don't know when we'll have to attend an event. I think it's better you just have them on hand."

I know she isn't happy with the answers I'm giving, but since I'm not sure how she's going to feel about the engagement party, it's best I don't tell her yet.

"What do you think of this?" She has on a wine-colored dress that compliments her skin perfectly. It's low-cut in the back, and has a slit up to her knee, and it's so beautiful.

"That's perfect, babe."

My eyes catch the shocked expression on her face as the last word leaves my mouth. This is the first time since we started fake-dating that I've called her *babe*, and it caught me off guard too.

"Sorry, I didn't mean that." That sounds worse. "I mean, I didn't mean *babe* as in my girlfriend or something, I just meant…you know what, never mind."

She's clearly amused by my confusion, so I decide to move on. She tries on a few more dresses, some shoes, and then I gently nudge her to get some jewelry to complement the dresses. We're both exhausted after the shopping, so we stop over at our favorite spot to grab lunch.

"You've been awfully quiet since we left the jewelry store," I say as we settle into our booth.

"I have? It's nothing."

"That doesn't sound like nothing."

"I don't know what you want me to tell you, Bryan."

"I want you to tell me why you seem annoyed after we just finished shopping."

"I'm not annoyed."

"Well, what is it then?"

"Don't yell at me."

"I'm not yelling at you. I'm just trying to figure out what's going on."

"Me too, Bryan. I've been asking you why you decided to take me shopping today, and you've been jerking me around. Also, you called me *babe* for the first time, which I don't think is normal."

"Alex, I'm being honest with you, there's nothing going on. Can you believe me, please?" I don't understand why I can't seem to tell her the truth. *Am I afraid she'll think I still want Rose back?*

"Alright, if you insist. I believe you. And thanks for today."

"You don't need to say that, it was fun for me too." She finally has a smile on her face, and I'm convinced she's let go of whatever doubt she had.

We finish our food and head home to rest since we're both tired. I decide to stay downstairs and read a book while Alex goes up to arrange the new clothes. I end up falling asleep after reading for a while and wake up to the sight of an angry Alex.

"What is this?" She drops the invitation to Rose and Dylan's engagement party on the table.

I stay stiff, racking my brain to try to figure out how she got her hands on it, because I'm sure I hid it before she got home yesterday. Or maybe I didn't...I can't remember.

This is not how I expected to let her know. After hiding it from her throughout the day today, I was going to make it seem like it arrived tomorrow so she wouldn't be suspicious or feel bad.

"Alex, I can explain."

"I asked you several times, and you told me that nothing was up. Why did you hide this from me?" Her face is red from anger.

"I just didn't want to hurt your feelings."

"And so you chose to lie to me?"

"I'm sorry."

She doesn't reply, but grabs her purse and heads out the door, refusing to acknowledge me calling her name, begging her to come back so we can talk about it.

I try to run after her, but by the time I'm up and out of the house, her car is gone, and she disappears into the night.

Deciding to let her be for a while, I head back inside and wait for her to come back. I know she doesn't want to be around me, so it's best to give her some space.

But I start to panic when it's close to midnight, and she still isn't back, and her phone is switched off, so I can't get through to her. Fear starts to creep in, worst-case scenarios filling my head. I decide to go looking for her.

I go to the café, but she isn't there. I check her dorm, but her roommates claim she isn't there either.

Out of places to look for her, I drive around a bit before heading home, still trying to reach her phone.

As I walk back into the house, the first thing I see is Alex in the kitchen making something, probably her dinner. I breathe a sigh of relief.

"Alex—" I try to talk to her, but she plugs in her ear pods to shut me out.

I understand she's angry, but she's taking it too far. What if something bad had happened to her when she went out, or she had an accident or something?

After she's done cooking and eating, she finally decides to talk to me.

"That was not a nice thing to do, Bryan. I know we're in a fake relationship, but I thought we were at least honest with each other."

"I'm sorry for what I did, but don't you think you're overreacting?"

"Overreacting? You blatantly lied to my face throughout the day, that's not part of our deal."

I know she's right—we've been very honest with each other from the beginning so as not to complicate things, and I've broken that trust.

"I'm sorry, Alex. I don't understand why it was so hard for me to tell you."

"This relationship only works on trust and honesty, and right now, I don't think we have either of those things."

Hiding the engagement party from Alex might just cost me the whole fake relationship, along with the chance to make Rose jealous. I feel stupid having this conversation, knowing I could have easily avoided it.

"I know I messed up big time, but I just didn't want to hurt your feelings. I didn't know how you'd react if I told you the entire truth."

"You didn't even tell me half the truth. You just lied to my face." The argument is getting more heated by the minute, and I know I have to find a way to calm it down.

"I know, you're right, and I'm truly sorry. I won't force you to go with me to the engagement party. It's up to you."

"Are you serious? Why would you say that?"

"To apologize for my behavior today."

She rolls her eyes. "Making your ex jealous is the main reason for this relationship, and you told me that from the onset. We go together because that's my part of the deal, but moving forward, I just want us to be more honest with each other."

"I'm deeply sorry about today and how I made you feel."

"Stop apologizing, it's over. And I apologize for leaving like that."

"I was worried for your safety."

"Thank you for worrying."

We talk for a bit before I go up to bed, and she stays up to read before calling it a night.

Chapter Nine

Alex

I wake up feeling refreshed and much better than I did yesterday, which is good because it's going to be a fierce day in court.

Since it's a school day, I wake Cooper up really early to get him ready for school. As the trial is getting more and more heated, I've decided it's best that he take the school bus in the mornings so I can be ready in time and prepared for the tough day ahead.

As soon as the school bus drives off, I take a quick shower, throw on my deep green blazer and black pants, and head out.

"Hey, where are you? I just arrived at the courthouse," I say to Bryan when he answers my call.

"Come inside the building, we're all right outside the courtroom."

"Alright, I'm on my way."

We're supposed to have a brief meeting before court starts, so I'm already late. Quickly, I get out of my car and walk as fast as possible to meet with Bryan and the team.

"Sorry I'm late," I say when I finally reach them. "Do you have any idea how it happened?" We've discovered that a lot of information about the case that was supposed to be top secret had been leaked to the media, and Jim, Mark, and Bryan all confirmed that they haven't spoken to anyone. I knew this media coverage would turn around and bite us in the ass.

"No, I'm surprised too," Bryan says, folding his arms across his chest.

Jim scratches his head. "Could it be a move by the prosecution? They are very tricky."

I shake my head. "No. Kurt may be a son of a bitch, but he'd never stoop this low." I look at my wristwatch. "It's time. We'll have to tackle anything else inside the courtroom, but don't worry—they won't get us easily."

I try my best to calm our nerves before we enter the courtroom, though mine are still very much unsettled. I hope Bryan is doing better than me.

"All rise." We all stand up as the judge enters the court and sits down.

"The prosecution has made a new discovery that we would like to present to the court, Your Honor."

"Objection! The prosecution did not inform us of any new discovery, Your Honor. This is the same nonsense they tried to pull the other day."

"Your Honor, it was only discovered this morning by our paralegals who searched all night, so we didn't hide anything from the defense."

"Yeah, right. As if the whole of yesterday wasn't enough for them to fabricate it and present it to us," I fire back.

"Order." The banging of the gavel stops us from throwing further banter at each other.

"Approach the bench, both of you."

The judge asks to see the evidence and then hands it to me to go through it. It's call logs placing Bryan in the city at the time the incident happened, showing specific cell towers where his device was pinged, in a call with someone close to his hospital.

"Your Honor, this is not right."

"Do you have sufficient evidence to prove that it is fabricated?"

"Not right now, Your Honor. We were not prepared for this."

"Your Honor, I assure you that this is not fabricated, and if you allow it, my witness will confirm it."

I scoff. "Let me guess, a new witness. Your Honor, the prosecution is purposely entering new evidence and witnesses now so that we're not able to vet and verify them." I'm hanging on by a thread, hoping the judge will not allow it.

"I'll allow it, but if I sense foul play, then I'll strike everything from the record."

Those are the words I'm dreading. I know the prosecution will make something of this evidence that could possibly affect us, but I try to remain positive.

Maybe Kurt *would* stoop low enough to leak information to the media. After all, this is a career-defining case for him.

Sitting back down, I inform the team of the situation but also advise them not to panic. If we're careful, maybe we can beat them at their own game.

"We would like to call in our first witness, Your Honor," the prosecution announces.

A middle-aged man walks into the court and makes his way to the witness stand, where he takes his seat after taking the oath.

"Do you know him?" I whisper to Bryan. He shakes his head.

"Can you tell the court what you told my team this morning, please?" the prosecution prompts the witness.

"On the sixteenth of October 2023, I visited Knight Memorial Hospital, and I was attended to by Bryan Knight."

"Are you sure he was the doctor who attended to you?"

"Yes, he was. The hospital was a bit busy, and he was the only available doctor."

"Do you see him in this courtroom today?" The man nods. "Point to him, please." He points straight at Bryan. "No further questions, Your Honor."

After carefully going through the measly file the prosecution handed to us during their questioning, something stuck out to me. Hopefully, it will be enough for the judge to disregard the new witness and evidence.

"Why did you go to the hospital, Mr. Williams?"

"Uh, I was having some serious chest pain that I needed to check out."

"And what medication was prescribed for it?"

"I really can't remember."

"And how long had you been having the pains?"

"For about six months at that time."

"And were you already taking medication during those six months?"

"Yes…but occasionally, I change them."

"That's not part of my question, I just need a yes or no," I remind the so-called witness. "And how has your chest been since then? Have you been using the same medication?"

"Yes, but…"

"And you cannot remember the name of the medication?"

"Objection, Your Honor, irrelevant line of questioning." The prosecution stands up to object, and I can tell I'm onto him.

"Sustained. Ms. Collins, please get straight to the point."

"Your Honor, the questions that I asked are not irrelevant. The prosecution brought on a new witness who claims that he doesn't remember the medications he's been taking for more than six months now, but somehow he remembers seeing my client once, five months ago?"

Kurt gets up. "The witness is a middle-aged man with health issues, and his family members help him purchase his medications. It is not imperative for him to know the name."

I scoff. "From his medical records, it seems that if he doesn't take that medication, he could die. So you're telling me your witness doesn't know the name of a medication that keeps him alive?"

"Enough, Ms. Collins. Any further questions for this witness?"

"No, Your Honor."

"Then the witness is dismissed."

After the witness leaves, Kurt gets up again. "Your Honor, the date provided from the testimony of the witness, along with the call logs we discovered, place Mr. Knight in the city at the time of the incident, which is contrary to what he testified in court."

"Objection, Your Honor, insufficient evidence," I argue.

"Overruled. Is there anything else any of you would like to add?"

"I ask for some time to confer with my client, Your Honor. I'm sure there's a reasonable explanation for this mix-up."

"You have forty-eight hours. The court is adjourned."

I feel defeated as the court hearing comes to an end. We all file out of the room, but Bryan invites us back to his place for a cheer-up party. At first, I try to come up with excuses as to why I can't come, but everyone insists, so I soon give in.

Once we've had a few drinks, Jim leaves, and shortly afterward, Mark follows. I can't tell if this was planned, but it feels like they're deliberately leaving to make sure Bryan and I get some alone time.

I should've probably come up with an excuse to leave after Mark did, but I find that I can't get the words out. After Bryan shuts the door behind Mark, he comes to sit beside me on his living room couch, the same couch where we shared many intimate moments together in the past.

Bryan fixes his eyes on me. "Can I ask you a question?"

I could hug Bryan for bringing me back to the present. I'm not sure what my train of thought had in mind with that one. "Sure."

"Why are you representing me? After everything, why did you agree to do this?"

Since the beginning of this case, I've been expecting this question. I thought I had my answer ready, but now that he's asked, I'm nowhere close to having a response.

I deflect. "I know today didn't seem like a good day, but trust me, I'll follow up on this new witness and evidence. We will beat this, I promise."

"That's great to hear, Lex, but that's not what I asked. I need to know why you're doing this."

"Is there a reason you think I shouldn't?"

"I mean, with everything that happened between us, I didn't expect us to be here. I never thought I'd see you again, much less that you would be representing me in a court case."

I sip on my rum and coke. "I don't know what you want me to say. If you're uncomfortable with me being here and don't want me to represent you anymore, just say the word."

He grinds his teeth and I can tell he's getting frustrated. "I'm not complaining, but there has to be a reason, isn't there?"

"I'm a lawyer. I don't need to have a reason other than a client needs my services to help them. I don't understand why you have a problem with it."

"I don't have any problem with it, Alex. You're a phenomenal lawyer, and if I had any doubts left about that you cleared them up today with the way you handled yourself in there. But there are other cases you could've taken on. For a lawyer as good as you, I'm sure there's a plethora of cases for you to choose from, so why did you choose mine?"

"Because it's right up my alley. Didn't you hear about my landslide victory with Dr. Graham Fuller's case a few months ago? It's precisely why Jim reached out to me to handle this case."

He sighs and leans back into the couch. "Alright, since you insist you're here merely because it's your job—why did you believe me when I said I didn't know the witness?"

"Was I not supposed to? You're my client, and I believe we've established the kind of relationship where we don't lie to each other. I'm inclined to believe you, since I know you wouldn't want to implicate yourself either."

He chuckles dryly. "God, you're such a lawyer. But it's been six years, and the first time we see each other after all that time is in a courtroom with you as my lead counsel. Forgive me if I'm skeptical about all this, but if you were in my shoes, wouldn't you be?"

He's right. I'd certainly be skeptical if the roles were reversed. "First of all, I know you didn't lie about not knowing the witness because my doubts about your innocence were cleared the first day when I put you on the stand. Secondly, I know how hard you've worked to get where you are now. You're excellent at what you do, and I believe you deserve the best lawyer you can get, which undoubtedly is me." He's staring at me, and I can tell he's taken aback by my response. "I'm on your side, Bry, and I promise to do a better job than I did today."

Bryan's intense stare holds me in place. Something in his eyes shifts—a warmth I haven't seen in years. My breath catches in my throat, and I feel a familiar flutter in my stomach. Memories of stolen kisses and whispered promises threaten to surface.

I quickly break eye contact, my heart racing, and reach for my glass. "I should—"

My hand fumbles, and before I can stop it, my rum and coke spill across my blazer.

"Shit!" I curse under my breath, jumping up.

Bryan quickly grabs a towel from the coffee table, offering it to me with a half-smile. "Here, let me help."

"No, no, it's fine," I insist, flustered. "I should go clean this up in the restroom."

As I hurry out of the living room, I can feel the heat rising in my cheeks and the weight of his gaze on me.

It's a much-needed escape from the overwhelming tension between us. Once in the restroom, I splash some cold water on my face and take a deep breath, trying to compose myself. But a tingle of unease ripples through me, and I have to remind myself that this is just business. Yet, a small part of me wonders if maybe, just maybe, there's still a spark of something more.

After a few minutes, I gather myself and head back to the living room, hoping the awkward moment has passed.

Chapter Ten

♥

Bryan

When Alex returns from the restroom, I'm still sitting on the couch, my expression thoughtful. I notice she looks a bit flustered, and a pang of concern hits me.

"Is everything okay?" I ask, trying to gauge her mood. "Do you need anything?"

She shakes her head and offers a small, somewhat strained smile. "No, I'm fine. Thanks."

This is the first time since Alex started representing me in this case that I've been rendered speechless by her. Okay, maybe the first time was when she put me on the stand without prior knowledge, but this is definitely a close second.

Hearing her admit that she doesn't doubt my innocence means a lot to me. I honestly think she took on this case just for the money—and to be fair, we are paying her a buttload of it—but she actually believes in me. I don't think Alex still thinks highly of me in any way, and I don't realize her opinion still matters so much to me until now.

There's a brief pause between us, the silence heavy with unspoken words. It feels like the air is charged with the tension from before.

"You're unusually quiet," Alex says, snapping me out of my thoughts.

"To be quite frank with you, I wasn't expecting that answer."

"What answer did you expect?" She tilts her head as she waits for my response.

"Definitely not that, but I am happy with it."

"Now that you've asked me your question, can I ask one of mine?"

"Anything. And I promise not to jerk you around before giving you a real answer." Her face breaks into a smile and a warm feeling spreads through my body.

"Why did you let me stay? I mean, you could've just as well insisted on me not being your lawyer."

"Jim and Mark insisted, so I didn't have a choice."

She raises an eyebrow at me. "Bullshit! The Bryan I know doesn't do anything because he's told. You promised not to jerk me around."

It's harder to be honest with Alex than I thought it would be, but I did make a promise. "Fine. You're right, I could've stood my ground, and Jim and Mark would've had to deal with it. But I guess a part of me was excited to see you again and wanted you to stay. Of course, now I know that you're the perfect person for the job. Maybe I always did, but I was just too hurt to admit it. Since you were brought in on the case, I feel more positive than ever about actually winning this thing."

She shakes her head. "That must've been very hard for you to admit. The great Bryan Knight isn't great at vulnerability."

"That's true, but there's just something about you, Alex Collins, that opens me right up."

Our eyes are buried in each other's now, and it's as if a magnetic force is pulling me toward her. Without pausing to overanalyze it, I move closer to her. When she doesn't spring up from the couch, but looks at my lips and gives her bottom one a gentle bite, I take that as a sign that she wants me to kiss her as much as I want to.

As my lips draw closer to hers, she whispers my name, her voice soft and quiet, but she doesn't stop me.

We both want what's about to happen. Maybe I want it more, but her eyes are saying everything her mouth isn't, her shaky breath telling me how much I still affect her.

Her breath just about stops as my lips meet hers, soft and—

"Bryan!" An all too familiar voice jolts us back to reality.

Alex quickly pulls away from me and stands up. "I better leave."

"Alex, please wait. Mom, what are you doing here?" I'm sure I locked the door after Mark left, and I didn't hear the doorbell ring, so I can't help but wonder how she got in.

"What is she doing here?" Mom fires back at me.

"I'm his lawyer, in case you've forgotten." I can hear the bitterness in Alex's voice, and I don't blame her. Mom had no right to barge in on us and question Alex.

"Then you should see him in court, not at his house."

"You don't get to dictate where I see my clients!" The animosity between them is clear as day, and I still don't understand why they have so much hate between them.

I get in between them. "Stop it, both of you."

"I'll be leaving now. See you later, Bryan."

"Yes, leave—we don't want you here," Mom calls out to her as she walks out, leaving me standing in disbelief at how childish she's being.

I wait until Alex is no longer within earshot before turning to Mom. "What the hell was that?"

"That was me protecting your interests."

"I don't need you to protect my interests, I'm not a child anymore. How did you even get in here?"

"I have a spare key."

I raise an eyebrow suspiciously. "Spare key? I don't remember giving you one."

"I made one for myself so I can surprise you from time to time. Is that a bad thing?"

I throw my hands up in the air. "Unbelievable. You took the key to my house and made a copy without my permission?"

She drops her Chanel bag on the center table. "That's not what you should be concerned about—you should be more concerned about why Alex is trying to force herself back into your life. First, she magically becomes your lawyer, and now she's coming to your place?"

"What? I invited her here."

"So you still like her?"

"What?"

"You were in the middle of kissing her when I walked in, Bryan. I think you're making a mistake getting involved with her again."

That's when I see red. "Mom, enough. Who I like, kiss, or want to be with is none of your business. I've had enough of you telling me what to do and trying to control me. I know you've always had it in for Alex, but I really don't care what you think of her anymore. We are adults, and whatever happens between us is between me and Alex, and has nothing to do with you."

"What if she's playing you again, or she has another agenda? Your focus right now should be on the trial and nothing else."

"Do you think this Alex is the same woman you intimidated and looked down on in the past? She's her own woman now, and she's a very successful lawyer. Besides, I don't really care about any of your concerns. You should find something else to worry about." I walk over to the built-in liquor cabinet and she follows me.

"Bryan, I'm just trying to look out for you. Why are you acting like I'm the enemy?"

I pour myself a glass of scotch and spin around to face her. "If you're really trying to look out for me, you'll tell me the truth about what happened between you and Alex."

She looks away. It's just for a second, but I see it and that's how I know the next words out of her mouth are not true. "Nothing happened between us. I'm looking out for my son so that a woman who used him in the past doesn't do it again." Her tone is softer now. "Everything I'm doing is for your own good, whether or not you believe it."

"All you've done since Alex resurfaced is tell me to trust that you have my best interest at heart, but then you continue to hide things from me. If you want me to trust you, then you have to be transparent with me. Trust works both ways."

She eyes me for a bit and grabs her handbag from the table. "Fine, suit yourself. But don't come crying to me when she hurts you again."

"Mom," I call to her as she walks away. She turns to face me. "I don't want to be rude, but can I have my spare key back?"

"Not a chance in hell."

"Then I'll be changing the locks."

"You can do whatever you want."

She storms out.

With my glass of scotch in hand, I settle into the couch, which only reminds me of what almost happened before Mom walked in and denied me the pleasure of remembering what Alex's lips taste like.

Fuck!

Chapter Eleven

♥

Alex

I can't believe I almost let Bryan kiss me. What the hell was I thinking?

Have I suddenly forgotten all the pain and heartache from the last time I got involved with him? Six years may have passed, but it's not nearly long enough to have forgotten, seeing as it affected me so much I've not been in a relationship since then.

Thank God for Mel.

That's something I never thought I'd say, but her timing was impeccable. She saved me from doing something that I know I would've regretted, so, for once, I appreciate her meddling nature.

Yes, kissing Bryan last night would've been a mistake, so why do I feel this sense of loss that we didn't get to finish what we started?

It's a Saturday, and Cooper's still sound asleep. I should still be asleep, too, catching up after waking up at half past five to prepare him for school every day. Yet here I am, lying in bed, staring at the ceiling and thinking of Bryan.

Knowing that fighting it is pointless, I open my bedside cabinet and pull out the photo album. As I open it, two pictures fall out and I pick them up. My mind immediately drifts back to that day, and I'm shocked at how vivid the memories still are.

The photos are from the day Bryan's ex had her engagement party.

· ♥ · ♥ · ♥ · ♥ · ♥ ·

The fight we had after he kept her engagement from me really threw us off our game. That entire week was crazy, but by the day of the party I reminded myself that whatever Bryan and I had was an arrangement, and he didn't owe me anything. I decided to suck it up and do what I was there for.

He had gone out earlier that morning and I didn't see him when I woke up, so I decided to make myself some breakfast. While I was eating on the kitchen counter, he came in all sweaty.

"Hey, where'd you go?" I asked, taking a bite of my toast.

"I just needed to clear my head, so I went to the gym. Sorry, I left without telling you."

"It's fine." He looked like he had something on his mind, so I prodded him. "What's going on?"

"Nothing important. I just wanted to confirm that we're still good for tonight."

"Of course we are. Is there any reason why we wouldn't be?"

He opened the refrigerator and grabbed a bottle of water. "Things have been off between us all week, so I thought you might bail."

He seemed nervous about something, probably the engagement party we were going to later that evening. It was understandable since this would be the second time he would see his ex in person since we got together, and it wasn't really the ideal situation. "Don't worry, I'll be right beside you the whole night."

"Alright, I'll be in the office."

At seven that evening, we started getting ready. It took me about half an hour to choose the perfect dress for the night. I debated between a long red sparkly gown with a thigh-high slit and some cleavage, and a stunning velvet black dress that also showed some cleavage.

If I was going to be the hot new girlfriend who was there to make the ex jealous, I had to look the part. I wasn't really into the color, but I knew the red dress would make me look hotter.

I wore the red dress, straightened and put a product in my hair, and did my makeup, after which we left for the party.

The drive there was an awkward one. We barely spoke two words to each other, and by the time we pulled into Rose and Dylan's driveway, the tension in the air was unbearable.

"Look," I said to him after we emerged from the car. "Let's just leave all this weirdness between us out here. You probably had your reasons for not telling me Rose got engaged, and I got maybe a little too upset, but the bottom line is that we got into this to make her regret leaving you, so let's do that tonight."

He smiled. "I'm happy to hear you say that."

"By the end of tonight, she'll wish she never left you for that douchebag fiancé of hers."

We walked into the house together, and Bryan grabbed two drinks and handed one to me. "Cheers."

"Cheers."

Sipping on my drink, I looked around the banquet hall, but Rose and Dylan were nowhere in sight. I'm sure she wanted to make a grand entrance. From all the things Bryan had told me about her, she seemed like a drama queen.

As we waited for the couple of the hour, Bryan started chatting with some people who I assumed were his colleagues. In order to give the impression that I belonged here too, with all these rich people, I struck up a conversation with some of the women around me.

It didn't take long for my prediction to come true as a very bright light suddenly came on in the center of the room. Out of nowhere, Dylan and Rose started performing a very sensual dance that I'm sure they'd spent weeks practicing.

The entire room came to a standstill as we watched them perform their dance. Finally, after what seemed like hours, the dance ended and everyone applauded them.

After a few activities that Bryan didn't really seem interested in, it was time for a few friends to give their toasts while Bryan and I made side comments about how boring their speeches were.

Just when we thought the torture was over, Rose—who was obviously a little tipsy—stood up and took over the microphone. Bryan had told me that she didn't know how to handle her liquor, and from the way she was giggling, I could tell it was true.

"I don't know where to start, but I want to thank you all for honoring my invitation. Even those of you who had other engagements but chose to be here, thank you for coming to celebrate with me and Dylan. I can spot some of my exes in the crowd, jealousy written on their faces. Well, sorry guys, you weren't the best men, so you couldn't get me. Bryan knows what I'm talking about."

Everyone in the room turned in our direction, like they were expecting a reaction from Bryan, so I decided to give them what they wanted and reduce Rose's ego in the process.

"Joke's on you—you weren't the best woman either, because he's mine now."

"Oh, please. Bryan is clearly trying to overcompensate after losing me by dating...what are you, a freshman in college?"

I chuckle. "Bold of you to assume he lost you, when you lost him."

Dylan grabbed the microphone from Rose. "Alright. That was a wonderful toast from my fiancée. Thanks for coming out, everyone."

In all this time, I didn't think to check in with Bryan, and when I looked over at him, he was clearly furious. His mom, who was also present at the party, came up to him, and they immediately left without looking at me. A few minutes later, my phone buzzed with a message from him, asking to see me outside. I didn't understand why he looked so angry. Rose was clearly being condescending, and I had to put her in her place.

When I got outside, Bryan was pacing back and forth, fists clenched.

"What was that, Alex?" He pulled me toward him, lowering his voice so he wouldn't draw more attention.

"Look, I won't apologize for standing up to that bitch. She was clearly trying to insult you, and I had to say something. Maybe I drew a little bit of attention, but it was worth it, right?"

"I could care less about the attention—I'm used to it. Why did you have to say those things? I never asked you to defend me."

"She was clearly trying to mock you. What was I supposed to do? Sit there and listen to her say whatever she wants about you?"

"Yes, Alex, that was exactly what I expected you to do, not get down on her level. You acted childish and petty. No mature woman would react that way."

"Oh, wow." Okay, I had expected a different reaction from him—a happy one. I was only trying to defend him, and he was getting all defensive and mad.

"Do you know how you made me look?"

"No, Bryan. I don't know. Why don't you tell me?"

"Like a desperate guy still trying to win her heart. You completely embarrassed me in there."

"Wow, that was unexpected. I apologize for making you look like that. Maybe I shouldn't have come after all."

"Yeah, maybe."

"I should go. Wouldn't want to embarrass you any further." I turned around and walked out of there with what little was left of my self-esteem.

"Alex—" he called out to me, but Mel was quick to encourage him to let me leave, and he did.

I went inside, grabbed my purse, and returned to my dorm.

I knew that it was really Mel talking through Bryan. The moment she had come up to him, I knew something was about to play out, but I didn't expect her to convince him to the point of him scolding me like that.

She brought out a part of him that he didn't like, but I was done making excuses for a grown-ass man who let his mother push him around. After I got back to the dorm, I waited for him to call or text me to say he was sorry, but he never did.

・♥・♥・♥・♥・♥・

Now that I think about it, from the way Bryan stood up to his mother yesterday, I can tell she no longer has the driver's seat in his life. But she's clearly still in the car, and I'm not willing to be another passenger on that crazy ride again.

Pulling myself out of my head, I try to dispel the thoughts of him from my mind, a place he has occupied ever since we almost kissed.

I'm glad when Cooper knocks on the door and pushes it open, still rubbing his eyes.

"Hey, baby, you're awake." I open my arms and he hugs me, which makes all my tension and anxiety melt away. "What are you hungry for this morning, baby?"

"Pancakes. The strawberry ones."

I flash him a broad smile. "Strawberry pancakes it is. Let's get that ready, okay?"

"Okay."

Chapter Twelve

Bryan

It's been about three weeks since Alex filed another motion to lift the lock on the hospital, and the judge still hasn't ruled for or against it. It's starting to bother me since the last few court hearings have not been going our way.

My life lately has consisted of going to the gym, trying to avoid my mom, who is hell-bent on fixing me up with a "nice girl," going to court—which is by far my favorite since I get to see Alex—and trying to apologize to the families affected by the incident at the hospital. My apology tour, which Alex strongly advised against, only made them think I was apologizing to get them to drop the case.

This morning, I decide it's best to hit the gym since I've been confined to my home these past few days. Unfortunately, Mark is in Chicago visiting his sister, who just had her first child, so I have plenty of solo workouts these days.

As I walk over to my car, my phone buzzes with an incoming call. When I bring it out of my gym bag, the name displayed on the screen makes my stomach churn. It's my mother, probably calling to tell me she met another girl who's just perfect for me.

I contemplate not answering, but I know she'll keep calling, so I might as well get it over with.

"Hey, Mom."

"Hello, Bryan. Are you home?"

"No, just got to the gym," I lie. If I say I'm in front of my door, she'll suggest I wait for her. I changed the locks in my house as I told her I would, but that hasn't stopped her from coming over anytime she feels like it. In fact, she's become even more relentless, like she's trying to punish me for taking away her key.

"Do you remember Kelly? Paul Macbeth's daughter, the nurse, not the dancer."

I nod as though she can see me. "Of course, I remember her. Why, what's wrong?"

"She's in town for her sister's wedding and I was hoping the two of you would connect."

"Mom, what did you do?"

"I gave her your number, so expect her to call you."

"Mom! I told you in no uncertain terms that I'm not looking to get into any relationship."

She scoffs. "Except when it involves Alex, then you certainly don't mind."

"You know what? I have to go, and I'm certainly not going to take Kelly's call. Bye."

I end the call and then call Alex immediately. I'm hoping we can meet to discuss the reopening of the hospital, my license, and how to move forward. If I'm being honest, I know we could discuss those things over the phone, but I just really want to see her.

Despite seeing her in court for every session, my desire to be around her is getting worse. Ever since we almost kissed, I haven't been able to get her out of my head. I'm getting pretty good at making up excuses to spend time with her, like the one I'm about to give her.

"Hey, good morning." She answers almost immediately.

"Hey, how are you?"

"I'm good. What's going on?"

My phone connects to my Bluetooth speaker as soon as I get in the car. "I want to discuss something with you. Can we meet today?"

"I hope there's no problem?"

"Not at all. I just wanted to go over something in respect to the case."

"And we can't talk about it over the phone?"

"It's a really sensitive issue, so I think it's best we meet face-to-face."

"Alright. Where do you want to meet?" she asks after a little pause.

"I was thinking maybe the park—the town park, at around four?"

"Let's make it five. There's something I have to do by four."

"That works fine, I'll see you then."

"Okay, see you then. Bye."

Around half past four, I shower, quickly get dressed and head over to the park. By the time I get there, it's already a few minutes past five, but Alex is nowhere to be found. Children are playing and running around, and a few of them are playing with their dogs, too, and their parents are screaming at them to take it easy.

I smile to myself as I walk over to the quietest spot in the park. I'm hoping no one else has discovered it, and even if they have, that they're not there right now.

When I get there, the tucked-away bench is empty and I sigh with relief. My phone rings and it's Alex. "Hey, I'm here, and I can't see you."

"Come over to our usual spot behind the swings. You'll see me once you get there."

"See you in a minute."

I wave at her as she approaches the bench where I'm sitting. As she comes closer, I can't help but wonder how she looks equally beautiful when she's in power suits, dinner dresses, or even when she's wearing something as casual as a wine-red T-shirt and faded blue jeans like she is right now.

"Hey, hope you didn't wait long?" she says, sitting beside me on the otherwise empty bench.

"Not at all. I just got here five minutes ago."

"Great. So you said we needed to talk?"

"Yes, I wanted to find out what exactly could be delaying the lift of the ban on my hospital. So far, I've lost four of my best doctors to other hospitals, and the rest are getting tired of waiting, too. I have a feeling the judge is delaying this case on purpose and I can't seem to figure out why."

"I'm really sorry about your doctors leaving, that must suck. I think the judge is just being extra careful about making decisions because the media has caught wind of the case. She's probably trying to avoid censure caused by reopening a hospital that's currently under such heavy scrutiny. Which is why lawyers try to avoid the media as much as possible when they have active cases."

Clasping my hands together, I put them on my knee. "I'm tired of just waiting around with the hospital sitting empty—there are lives to be helped and saved, and I feel useless not doing anything about it."

She nods in agreement. "I understand you. I'd go nuts if something happened and I suddenly couldn't represent people anymore. But you need to keep your head up, and you need to be totally honest with me throughout this whole process."

"I can assure you I'm not hiding anything from you. I've told you everything that happened, and I'm hoping the truth will prevail."

"That's good. I need a hundred percent from you."

"When have I ever not given you all of me, Alex? Even now, I still find it difficult to keep anything from you." I look straight into her eyes, and her cheeks redden but I refuse to look away.

"You mean other than the time you kept Rose's engagement from me, and we had that big fight when I found out?"

"Oh wow, you still remember that?"

"Of course I do. How's Rose doing these days?"

"Last I heard, she and Dylan got divorced."

Her eyes widen in surprise. "Really? That's too bad, they seemed perfect for each other." I squint my eyes at her mischievously. "Okay, fine, you caught me. I don't feel bad for them, not even a little bit."

We both laugh and when we get serious again, I reassure her that I'm being completely honest with her. "Would you like to grab a bite? Sorry for not asking earlier."

She shakes her head. "No, it's fine. I'm good."

I look around and smile. "Remember when we used to come here?"

She follows my eyes around, too. "Yes, I remember. It's still one of my favorite memories from our time together."

I'm kinda surprised she would admit that an activity from our time together is one of her favorite memories, so I decide to ride the wave. "I remember how happy you were going down those slides over there. I liked watching you be so carefree. The way your eyes lit up every time you went up and down on the seesaw, how beautiful you looked."

She looks away from the slides and back at me. "You sure remember a lot, don't you?"

"More than you think. It's difficult to forget someone like you." She squirms uncomfortably, so I decide to lighten the mood. "I saw some cute kids selling lemonade when I was coming in, maybe I could grab us a drink?"

"Alright, I could use a cool drink right now."

"Be right back." Two minutes later, I hand her the drink. "Here you go."

"Thanks." She opens her lemonade and drinks a significant amount.

"I bet you still want to go down the slides, huh?"

"No, I'm a no-nonsense lawyer now. Going down children's slides isn't befitting for my new status." Her answer is laced with hearty laughter that tugs at my heart.

"We can very much bring back carefree Alex. Don't worry, your reputation is safe with me."

"Yeah, right."

"Do you remember the 2017 winter break?"

"*Pfttt*, how could I ever forget?"

"You kept saying you wanted to go skiing but somehow forgot to mention that you didn't know how to ski. You were so bad at it, and it was almost impossible to teach you because you were so paranoid about the snow cracking and giving way beneath you."

"If I'd known you were gonna bring up one of my least favorite moments, I wouldn't have come."

"It may be your least favorite, but it's one of my favorite memories of you. You were so scared of going on the ice that even after days of trying to convince you, you still preferred to just watch me. The day you finally decided to try it, you got stuck in the ice, which was your biggest fear from the beginning."

"Yes, I remember. I felt like all you'd done those few days was lie to me about how really easy skiing was to learn. I honestly thought I was going to die that day, and you just kept laughing like it wasn't a big deal."

"I mean, it was a normal thing for first timers. It didn't really mean your death, but it was so fun watching you think that."

"It was not funny, and that was not nice what you did. I'm glad I survived after everything and, of course, finally learning how to ski."

"You're welcome." I give a cocky bow and tip my imaginary hat.

"I wasn't thanking you, you asshole." We're both laughing hard at this point.

"I definitely regretted teaching you—one week later, you were doing tricks I couldn't do after three years of skiing."

"And the student becomes the master." She gives her own cocky bow.

"Who's the asshole now?" I say, sending us into another fit of laughter.

"I'm glad you taught me to ski, it really came in handy when I was teaching Cooper." She sips her lemonade.

"Who's Cooper?" I ask, and I guess her lemonade went down the wrong pipe because she goes into a coughing fit. The cough finally stops after she drinks more lemonade to calm herself. "Sorry about that."

"It's fine, I'm the idiot who let lemonade go down the wrong pipe." She takes out her phone and looks at it. "Shoot! I gotta go. Need to pick up some things from the grocery store for dinner."

I'm not ready to leave yet, but I know I can't keep her any longer, so I walk her to her car.

"I've missed these types of conversations with you. It feels good to have them back," I say, stopping her from closing the door.

"I've missed them too. And don't worry about your case—I'm confident things will start looking up soon. Thanks for the lemonade."

"Anytime, Ms. Collins." I shut her door and she drives off.

I don't know why, but I suddenly get the feeling she's in a hurry to get away from me. Regardless, as I get into my own car, I can't help but smile.

Today was a good day, and I'm not ashamed to admit I wish it didn't have to end so soon.

Chapter Thirteen

♥

Alex

The unexpected smoothness in my relationship with Bryan has been a pleasant surprise. Initially, I didn't think we'd get past the animosity of the first day I saw him in court, but now I catch myself looking forward to seeing him at every court session and days like yesterday at the park.

The memories from the park, from our skiing trip...the way we talked like we did six years ago...the way he still makes me laugh. And then I almost ruined everything when Cooper's name slipped out.

If not for my coughing fit, I would've been forced to lie to Bryan about who Cooper is, as if taking out his booster seat anytime I go to meet with Bryan isn't enough sneaking around already.

The doorbell rings and when I open it, it's Grace bringing Cooper back from her place. I managed to convince her to spend the night with us after bringing him back home. I've tried to convince Grace to move in with me so many times, but she always turns me down gently, saying she wants her own place for when she meets the right guy. And then when I ask her, "What if the right guy wants you to move into his place instead?" she always responds, "Then he isn't the right guy."

I'd moved in with Grace in the city after things between Bryan and me turned sour. However, when I was offered a job here in Woodvale which would be great for Cooper's future, she decided to move back with me. My sister hates change, so the move was tough for her, but she couldn't leave me to raise Cooper alone. She's just two and a half years older than me, but she always acts like it's five.

"Hey, sis, we're starving," she says the second she and Cooper walk into the house.

"I knew you would be, so I ordered some pizza while waiting for you guys. It's on the dining table."

After we eat, I bathe Cooper and he goes straight to bed. Grace and I decide to indulge in some ice cream. I grab the pint of ice cream from the freezer and we sit down to satisfy our craving and watch some trashy reality TV.

"So, how was your day? What did Bryan want to see you about?"

"He wanted to discuss the case."

"And you couldn't discuss whatever it was over the phone?"

"He insisted we see each other in person."

"Hmm, I'm worried about you, Lex. It seems like you're starting to warm up to Bryan again. I thought you said this was strictly professional? If you're not careful, you could cross a line you won't be able to uncross."

I decide not to tell about our almost kiss, or that I slipped up and said Cooper's name while we were at the park.

"I'm warming up to him again, but not in the way you think. It's best for me as a lawyer when I'm on good terms with my clients. That way, they trust me, which makes my job easier."

She doesn't seem convinced. "There's a thin line between work and play, especially in this case where you have history with your client. Just be careful is all I'm trying to say."

"Okay, Mom," I say, and she rolls her eyes at me. "So how are things going between you and Darius?"

"Meh. Turns out he doesn't want anything serious."

I roll my eyes. "Men these days never do. They want the milk without buying the cow."

"Yep, they want the honey without the bee sting."

"His loss. If he didn't realize what a gem he had in you, he's an idiot."

Grace smiles. "Thanks for saying that, Lex."

・♥・♥・♥・♥・♥・

The next day is a Sunday, and Grace decides to take Cooper on their usual Aunt Grace and Cooper's day out. When they first started the tradition, I was jealous. These days, I can't wait to get Cooper out of the house and have a little peace and quiet.

Around noon, Cooper and Grace leave and I decide to take a relaxing bath. I've just started filling the tub with water when my phone rings. It's Bryan.

I stare at the name across my screen for a while, contemplating whether to answer or hit ignore. Of course, I answer. "Hey, Bryan."

"Hey, hope I'm not interrupting anything?"

I look at my half-filled tub. "Not at all."

"Um...so...I wanted to make some pasta, and I accidentally cooked the whole pack, and now there's pasta everywhere and I was wondering, you know, since you've always loved pasta, that you could maybe come help me eat some of it?"

I chuckle. "Accidentally, huh?"

"Totally. I didn't deliberately cook way too much pasta just so I could call you to come help me eat it. So, will you help a man out?"

Say no, Alex. Tell him you have other plans. Hell, tell him you're going on a date. Anything but yes. "Yes, okay. I'll be there in twenty."

"Great. I can't wait to see you."

Fuck.

I quickly empty the tub and take a quick shower instead, and then I catch myself picking out my black lace bra and panties.

What the hell am I doing? Am I expecting anything to happen between me and Bryan this afternoon? *Come on, Alex. You're not a child. You know what Bryan wants, and deep down you know you want it too.*

Instead of listening to the voice in my head telling me to text Bryan that I can't make it, I text Grace instead, telling her I'm going to hang out with a friend. I put my phone on *do not disturb* to avoid any follow-up questions.

After a few minutes of flipping through my work clothes, I finally find a stretchy black dress that I haven't worn in ages because I don't have anywhere to wear it to. I finish up my look with my only pair of white ankle boots and gold studs.

Satisfied with the finished look in the mirror, I leave the house and drive over to Bryan's.

As I walk up to his front door, I spend a few minutes telling myself that this is just dinner between old friends and nothing else. Then I ring the doorbell.

The door opens and Bryan and I come face-to-face. He's wearing a polo and gray sweatpants—*uh-oh*—and I suddenly feel overdressed.

"Hey, Alex. Come on in."

I walk past him into the house, and as he leads us to the kitchen, I can't tear my eyes away from his leg muscles accentuated by the gray sweatpants. "You weren't kidding about the pasta."

"I wish I had been."

My heart sinks. I thought maybe he'd just come up with the pasta thing as an excuse to see me again, but looking at the pot filled with pasta on the gas cooker, I see he was telling the truth.

He dishes the pasta onto two plates and hands me one, and as we walk into the dining room, I quickly realize I was right all along.

The ambience is romantic. Scented candles, rose petals, a bottle of wine on ice, and dim lights. He pulls out my chair for me and sits in the one opposite me.

"So…while you were accidentally cooking too much pasta, you accidentally lit some scented candles and accidentally spread the rose petals too?"

He grins. "Yep, honest mistake."

I shake my head as he opens the bottle of wine and pours it into both our glasses.

He looks even hotter in the dim light of the dining room, his hair falling over his face in the most sexy way. His eyes, which have been on me since I entered his house, are still as captivating as the first time I saw them.

"So how was your day?" he asks as he settles down to eat.

I sip some of my wine, and I can't help but notice how good it is. "It was pretty basic—I just did some chores. How was yours?"

He drops his fork onto his plate. "Well, I woke up this morning upset that it was yet another day of not going to the hospital, but then

I remembered our day at the park yesterday and I immediately knew I wanted to see you again. Then I spent a better part of the morning trying to come up with an excuse to get you to agree to spend more time with me."

"Wait a minute, so you mean to tell me you spent the entire morning thinking about this, and the best you could come up with was *I made too much pasta*?"

"You're here, aren't you? So I'd say it worked."

I shrug. "True."

"So, how's the pasta?" His eyes are locked with mine and I shift uncomfortably in my seat.

"Great. You always knew how to make a mean pasta."

"It's the only thing I can cook, so I had to perfect it to have an excuse to invite beautiful women over for dinner."

I feel a twinge of jealousy. "And here I was thinking it was just me you cook for."

"Of course it's just you. I don't show off my culinary skills for just any woman."

I blush. "Liar."

We finish up our food over some light conversation that mostly consists of us reminiscing about the past. I take the last sip of my wine and stand up, picking up both our empty plates.

"What do you think you're doing?" Bryan asks, standing up too.

"Going to wash these. You cooked, the least I can do to thank you is wash the dishes."

He moves closer to me until I can feel his breath a few inches from my face. Just when I think I'm going to drop the plates, he takes them from me and puts them back on the table. "I can think of a much better way for you to thank me."

Am I a racehorse who just got off the tracks? Because my heart is pounding furiously right now. "Oh yeah, what's that?"

He grabs my arms and pulls me close, my breasts crushed against his rock-hard chest. My breath catches in my throat as he leans in closer to me and my eyes trail down to his lips, begging him to put them on mine.

He makes as if to kiss me, but stops when he's a hair's breadth away from my lips and rubs his nose against mine. "Have I told you how beautiful you look this evening?"

I nod without hesitation, eager for him to get on with the kiss. He lingers, his eyes buried in mine as if trying to make sure this is what I want, so I make the first move.

Standing on my toes, I press my lips to his. I take his lower lip into mine, slowly teasing him. His hands, previously on my arms, trail down to the small of my back, and as he pulls me against his groin, I can clearly feel his dick, stiff in his sweatpants as he rubs against me.

It always excited me how hard Bryan got whenever we started kissing, and today is no exception. Now that he has my express permission, he takes charge, deepening the kiss, taking my lower lip into his, nibbling and sucking before moving to the upper one.

Bryan was always a good kisser, but right now, as his tongue slips into my mouth to explore every corner, it feels like I'm kissing an entirely different man. As his tongue does some exploring, his hands follow suit, grabbing my ass and squeezing gently.

He moans when I pull my lips from his and find his neck, gently biting and trailing kisses all the way down to the bit of his chest exposed by his V-neck polo.

"Alex," he pants, breaking off our kiss, "are you ready to go all the way with me? Because if you keep kissing me like that, we're going all the way."

His eyes are red-hot with desire, so I know he means every word he just said. "I don't think I'm ready, but I really don't want to stop kissing you."

He groans. "Me neither. I guess I'll just have to test how far I've come in the self-control department."

He lowers his head to mine again, and this time, we allow ourselves time to explore each other, free of every other expectation.

Chapter Fourteen

♥

Bryan

Today is a pivotal day for both me and Alex.

It marks the final court hearing that will determine my fate and the fate of my hospital for the rest of my life. I'm a nervous wreck, and I can only hope Alex is more confident than me. I know she must be because, winning or losing, she's always a beast in the courtroom.

Just like I predicted, when I arrive at the courtroom, she is way more composed and confident than I am, and she assures me that the case will go in our favor, which I find very hard to believe.

The press is huddled outside the courtroom, hovering around like vultures waiting to eat up a carcass, which, in this instance, will be me if we don't win.

"All rise." The judge enters the court and takes her seat before we do, and the court session commences with a hushed intensity.

"Your Honor," Alex begins, "I would like to put the defendant on the witness stand again."

Kurt jumps to his feet. "Objection, Your Honor."

"On what grounds, Mr. Miller?"

"It is the day of judgment, what more could the defendant have to say to sway the court ruling in his favor?"

"Are you here to dictate to me the exact day that I'll pass judgment over a case in my court?"

"Of course not, Your Honor."

"Then sit down. Please, Mr. Knight, make your way to the witness stand."

This time, Alex prepared me for the possibility that I would be taking the stand, so I walk up there confidently.

Before swearing my oath, I make eye contact with Alex, who reassures me with a firm nod.

"Mr. Knight, what is it that you would say you love doing the most?"

"Objection, Your Honor—relevance?"

"Maybe if you let me get two sentences out, you'll see how relevant this line of questioning is to the case."

"Overruled. You may continue, Ms. Collins."

"Thank you, Your Honor. Please answer the question, Mr. Knight."

"I love helping people."

"And how many people would you say you've helped since you became a medical doctor?"

"Countless. Through the hospital, for as long as I can remember, I have been obsessed with lending a hand any way I can. There's no other time I'm as happy as when I'm in the hospital, offering solutions to people who think they don't have hope—it's something that brings me the utmost joy."

Kurt chuckles. "Your Honor, need I say anything?"

"Ms. Collins, today please."

"Now, Mr. Knight, the first time I placed you on the stand, I asked you a question that I am going to ask again: Did you have a hand in the deaths of those patients?"

My eyes fall to the ground. "Yes, I did."

The entire court gasps, including Jim and Mark, who look at me as if I've completely lost it.

"Can you tell the court what you mean by that?"

"This tragic incident happened in my hospital, so I'm responsible. I should've known that my nurses ran a system where you could cover as many shifts as possible for as many people as possible, just so you'd get a day off to attend an important event, which was why the nurse was so exhausted on that day. I'm responsible for the two doctors who work for me who were on duty that night, and who would have caught this had they bothered to do their jobs properly. In many ways, I'm responsible. But if what you're asking is whether I am in any way directly responsible for those patients dying the way they did—then no, I am not. And I don't think all the other people who I help through my hospital should suffer for something that is no fault of theirs."

"No further questions."

"Would the prosecution like to ask the witness anything?"

"No, Your Honor."

"Then you can give your closing arguments. Over to you, Mr. Miller."

"Your Honor, the defense will have you believe that Mr. Knight, who is the owner of Knight Memorial Hospital, is totally innocent of all accusations coming his way, but why would an innocent man meet our clients one by one to apologize for something he refuses to take the blame for? Every piece of evidence we have presented points to Mr. Knight's involvement, and his suspicious movement supports our belief that he was involved in the deaths of the patients.

"Now you may ask, what motive did he have? Well, I believe the need to be relevant was his motive. Ever since his parents handed the hospital over to him, he hasn't been trending in the news like his contemporaries, so he decided to create a scandal. Who would miss patients who've been in a coma for months on end, right? Wrong." He points to the aggrieved family members. "All these people here miss their loved ones, and they are here to get justice. Thank you, Your Honor."

During his speech, I noticed that Alex was jotting down some key points to use against him, so I can't wait for her closing argument.

"Your Honor, I would like to point out a particular statement made by the prosecution—he said the defendant acted as he did because he wanted to be relevant and to matter in society. But here is a compilation of Forbes most influential men from five years ago, and it clearly shows that Mr. Knight has never struggled to be relevant in society. His hospital's patient intake may have fluctuated after he took over, but that's normal, and will continue to happen until people trust him enough as a doctor to entrust their lives to him.

"Your Honor, you have seen how deeply my client cares about helping others. No one throws away their passion and reputation for something they don't need, and I believe that is enough proof that Mr. Bryan Knight is innocent. The prosecution also stated that my client has been apologizing to the families of the deceased. If you ask me, it takes a bigger person to apologize for something he had no hand in while trying to clear his name."

And with that, Alex comes back to sit down. The judge announces that she'll make her final decision in an hour, so the court is on break until then. We all head to our private break room. Tension is evident on Mark's face, and Jim's, while Alex remains composed and unfazed by the situation. My mom didn't come to court today because she was sure we would lose and her poor heart couldn't take it. Her words exactly.

"Alex, is there something you're not telling us? Did you bribe the judge or something?"

"What do you mean?"

"You seem so calm and self-assured like there isn't a possibility that I'm losing everything I have today."

She smiles at me. "At the beginning of this case, I told you my job was to win the case, and that's exactly what we're going to do today. Today is the best day of this case, because it's today we win. Trust me. The prosecution's closing statement was weak, and they were casting nets in the wild without any concrete evidence."

"Wow, you know what? You're right. We are winning today," Mark says, and Jim backs him up.

Eternity passes, but finally, the hour the judge needs to make her decision elapses, and we head back to the courtroom to hear her judgment. She steps back into the courtroom, and it's so quiet you could hear a pin drop.

"Will the defendant please stand up?" the judge says.

"After very careful consideration of all the facts, evidence, and transparent proceedings of this court as witnessed by everyone present, as well as the arguments made by the counsel, I have reached a decision in this matter. For the charges of second-degree murder, I find the defendant not guilty."

I release the breath I didn't realize I had been holding.

"I hereby decree that the ban on your hospital is lifted, but you're on a four-week probation. Until the Arizona Medical Board concludes its investigation and declares you free to practice medicine in Woodvale and anywhere else in the world, you can't practice for now. In addition to my ruling, you are required to compensate each family with one million dollars each."

I don't think I heard anything else after the judge declared me *not guilty*. Alex was right—we won. Everyone, including me, had been so unsure until this moment, and it still feels surreal to know that I can go back to being a doctor once again. I stare at Alex in disbelief. She has a huge smile on her face, and my team is as shocked as I am.

Finally, it's over. After all these months, I'm free to go back to the hospital, and my name is cleared. I don't mind compensating the families at all—I know it's the least I can do after all they've been through.

"Thank you so much." I hug Alex after the judge leaves, then Mark and then Jim.

"You did it," I say to Alex as we walk out of the court.

"You're damn right I did. I told you we would win, didn't I?"

I have to mentally put myself under lock and key to stop myself from kissing her right then and there, the only thing I've been dying to do since our last kiss.

As we walk out of the courthouse, I contemplate asking her to meet me later in the day to celebrate our win. As I'm about to ask, the press rushes toward us.

"Mr. Knight, how does it feel to finally be free?"

"Mr. Knight, do you blame the families for their false accusations?"

"Mr. Knight, what do you plan on changing in the administration of the hospital going forward?"

Alex steps forward and addresses the press.

"We are grateful that the court ruled in our favor, and my client has been completely vindicated. We are also going to compensate the families as soon as possible, as well as send our utmost condolences for their loss. As for the hospital moving forward, as soon as the State Medical Board clears Dr. Knight, he hopes to continue saving lives and helping the community as a whole. Thank you."

With Jim and Mark's help, we finally cleared enough room to move through the press and get to my car. "How about we go out for drinks later on to celebrate? Actually, I'll be hosting at my place, and I would love for you to come. After all, you're the reason I'm a free man."

"I don't know. I mean, you're inviting your family, right?"

"Yes, why?"

"I don't think I want more Mel drama in my life. Besides, I don't want to be the reason why you won't invite your mom to celebrate with you, so have fun."

"Oh, come on. I don't care what my mom says or thinks—you are the reason I'm here, and she's going to accept that whether she likes it or not. Plus, you'll get a chance to rub it in her face since she didn't think you'd be able to do it."

"Fine. Any opportunity to rub anything in Mel's face is one I'll always take. When?"

"My place, three hours from now."

"I'll be there. Thank you for the ride."

As I get into my car to leave, the excitement of seeing her later keeps a huge grin on my face.

Chapter Fifteen

♥

Alex

Six Years Ago

After a week of hectic academic stress, my roommate, Cara, and I decide to unwind by throwing a sleepover with our friends—we'll eat some popcorn and ice cream, drink a lot of alcohol, and of course binge watch movies until we fall asleep.

As we plan the night's activities, arguing over which movies to watch, the background music playing via my phone is interrupted by an incoming call.

"It's Bryan," I say to Cara, and she gives me a thumbs-up. "Hello?"

"Alex! Guess what?" A high-pitched voice hits my ear and it takes me a second to realize it's actually Bryan, as he's never sounded this pitchy.

"What's going on? Are you okay?"

"I'm more than okay—the best thing just happened."

"What?"

"I just did a medically difficult surgery on conjoined twins, and it was successful. Both of them are alive, and their vitals are normal. I did that, Lex."

"I'm so proud of you." I'm already nearly as excited as he is—his passion for being a doctor always intrigues me. Sometimes I feel like he's more passionate about being a doctor than I am about becoming a lawyer.

"Thank you. Can you come over to my place to celebrate? I've missed you these past few weeks."

"Of course. I'll be there in an hour. Bye."

"Hey, Cara, can we put a pin in our plans? I have to go see Bryan."

"Of course we can. I still can't believe you're dating Bryan Knight, you lucky bitch."

"Fake dating," I correct her.

"Whatever. Not many of us will have the chance to fake date a billionaire, even if we're given two lifetimes."

"It's not exactly a bed of roses, you know. It can be quite challenging sometimes."

She rolls her eyes at me. "Yeah, right. Which part? Being driven around in luxury cars? Shopping in places where even if I sell an internal organ I probably still can't afford to buy a pair of earrings, or the privileges you get just from being seen as Bryan's girlfriend?"

"It's not always that glamorous."

"Please, feel free to switch places with me anytime. Besides, it's clear that you've actually started falling for him."

I spin around to look at Cara. "No, I'm not."

"Oh really? You need to see how your face lights up whenever you get a call or text from him. You talk about him incessantly, and look how giddy you are now because you're going to see him."

"You don't know what you're talking about."

She chuckles. "If you say so."

As I prepare to leave for Bryan's, I can't help but notice that I'm more excited than usual. We haven't seen each other for about two weeks, since I was busy with midsemester tests. I've even been sleeping in the dorm again so I can focus on studying.

Just as I'm about to leave, I get a text from one of the teaching assistants, saying that we all did really badly on one of our tests, but because we're in our final year, the professor is giving us one final chance to redeem ourselves with another test in an hour's time.

Completely forgetting to text Bryan, I change the course of my movement. I pick up my books and laptop and head to the library to get in a bit of reading before the test starts. I run into a bunch of my classmates at the library, and we end up studying together before the test.

After about forty-five minutes, we head to class for the test. Thankfully, we are more than prepared for it, as most of the questions are from what we just read at the library.

Half an hour later, we're done with the test and I decide to rest a little before heading over to Bryan's.

I'm woken up when my phone rings. I look at the time and sit up quickly. It's Bryan, and I'm sure he's calling to find out what happened to me since it's three hours past the time I told him I was coming over.

"Hey, sorry, something came up but I'm on my way now," I say as soon as I pick up.

"You could've at least sent me a text or something, I was worried."

"I'm sorry. It was kind of an unplanned test, and I had to put my phone on silent."

"It's okay. Are you sure you can still make it?"

"Yes, I'll be right there."

"Okay, then see you soon."

"Yeah, bye."

It's almost six by the time I leave my dorm and head to Bryan's house. I decide to take a cab—even though it's more expensive, it will be faster.

We pull up to his house, I pay the cab driver, and he drives off. I open the white picket fence and walk toward the oak doors. As I walk up the polished wood floating staircase, I notice that the hammock swing chair on the porch is dangling, as if someone was just sitting there.

Just as I'm about to ring the polished brass gold-and-black doorbell to let Bryan know I've arrived, the door opens and I come face-to-face with my worst nightmare—Mel.

"Hi, Mel," I say, attempting to brush past her into the house and avoid any unpleasant exchange. But she shuts the door behind her, blocking me from entering the house.

"What are you doing here? Who asked you here?"

"Bryan called and asked me to come over," I say, making another attempt to get past her into the house. She uses her body as a wedge, firmly blocking me from reaching the door.

"Where do you think you're going?"

"Inside to see Bryan, my boyfriend."

"Don't you ever call him that, you gold-digging brat?"

"I'm not a gold digger, and I don't appreciate you calling me that whenever you see me."

"I will call you whatever I want to call you."

"Mel, please. I'm really tired and just came here to celebrate Bryan's wonderful achievement at the hospital. I don't want any trouble, so please let me go inside."

"Or what?"

"Why do you always have to be this mean to me? What have I ever done to make you hate me so much?"

"I hate you because I know you don't really care about my boy, you're a leech, and you're only here to suck on my poor, unsuspecting Bryan until you dry him out like leeches do, and then you'll probably move on to the next rich guy. I know your kind, and I'm not going to let my son be your next victim. You don't have any business being here, just do yourself a favor and leave."

I shake my head in wonder. "If it wasn't a crime, I'm sure you'd probably marry your own son given how desperately you want to keep him under your control."

The moment I say that, her expression goes from disgust to fury. "What did you just say to me?"

"You heard me."

Her entire body is trembling with anger, but she pulls herself together enough to spit out her next decree. "I am Bryan's mother, and I will never accept you. Get out of here before I call the police."

"And tell them what? That I came to visit my boyfriend in his own home?"

Bryan comes out at that moment, stopping me from literally pushing past Mel into the house, consequences be damned.

"I heard voices, what's going on?" he asks, looking from me to Mel for an answer.

"Nothing is going on, Bryan," Mel lies. "I was just telling Alex here how you helped separate those conjoined twins. I couldn't wait for her to hear the details from you because I'm just so proud of you."

"Thanks, Mom. Come on, babe, let's go inside."

When we get inside, there are a few people in the living room. Mark, his best friend, waves at me. Bryan notices how uncomfortable I am, and suggests we go to his room.

"Hey, are you okay?"

Honestly, I'm not, but I try to calm myself down before responding. "I'm better now."

"I'm sorry about whatever my mom said out there."

I turn to him, furious at his response. "You're sorry? That's all you can say? Look, Bryan, I have tolerated your mom's hatred for me ever since we started...whatever this is we're doing...but if you don't get her to stop, we're done. After all, Rose is engaged and your mom hates me, so what's the point of this arrangement? Maybe we should call it off and go our separate ways."

He takes my hand in his. "Hey, calm down, let's not make any rash decisions right now. I'll talk to my mom, okay? I'll get her to stop, I promise."

"You better."

"I will. Besides, I just got off the phone with my dad, and guess what he said?"

"What?"

"That Alex girl is a really good influence on you, son. Don't let her go."

My face breaks into a smile. "He really said that?"

"He did, and you know what that means? Having my dad on my side means I'll still get to take over the hospital whether Mom likes you or not."

I suddenly have a bitter taste in my mouth. Oh my God! Cara was right, I have started falling for Bryan. Why else would I be so upset that this is obviously still just a business deal to him?

"Come on, let's go back to the party. I'm sure everyone is wondering where we are."

I try not to sound as heartbroken as I feel right now. "You go right ahead, I don't really feel like being around all these people right now."

He gets up. "Are you sure?"

"Yes, I'm sure."

He kisses me on the forehead. "Alright, join us whenever you feel like it."

After he leaves, I bury my head in his pillow and scream my lungs out. How stupid could I be to fall for Bryan Knight? Cara told me again and again that he's a playboy, and he made it clear from the start that this is a business arrangement. Once it's over, we'll go our separate ways. And now I've gone and messed everything up by falling for him.

I end up not going down for the party, and when the last person finally leaves, Bryan comes up to find me. I pretend I'm asleep. He gently wakes me up and I feign a smile. "Hey."

"We missed you at the party."

I rub my eyes. "I guess I underestimated how tired I was, I must have fallen asleep."

"It's okay, I understand. Are you sure there's nothing else bothering you?"

Yes! There is! I just found out I have feelings for you. "Not at all. I'm just tired."

"Alright. Well, my mom has ruined the story about the conjoined twins for me. I really wanted to tell you myself."

I scoff. "Of course, she didn't tell me about the conjoined twins, that was just her way of covering up what she really said."

He tries to take my hand in his again, and I pretend that something is itching behind my ear. I can't bear to make any sort of contact with him right now.

"I'm really sorry about today."

I wave it away. "It's fine, give me the details about the conjoined twins."

He sounds really excited as he talks about the process of separating them, and it's all truly fascinating, but the only thing I can think is, *What the hell am I gonna do about my feelings for Bryan?*

Chapter Sixteen

♥

Bryan

I'm not a fan of cooking in the slightest, but I do enjoy a good barbecue. The meat in front of me sizzles and pops, looking delicious already as I flip a juicy steak on the cast iron grill, sweat beading on my forehead despite the thermostat being set to sixty-eight degrees in the kitchen.

The family has gathered to celebrate the reopening of the hospital. Through the kitchen doorway, I hear the familiar roar of Mark wrestling with Uncle Tom over the thermostat. Mark has been coming to my family functions since we were in third grade, so he's like part of the family now.

"Jeez, man. What the hell are you cooking? It's freaking hot in here," Mark bellows as he walks into the kitchen.

"Really? I hadn't noticed," I shout back sarcastically, dodging a stray onion ring Tom's wife Sarah tosses at me. Mark picks up the onion ring and tosses it into his mouth. Yes, he's disgusting like that. "I mean, if you're feeling hot here, what'll happen when you get to hell?"

"Oh, fuck you, man. I'll be sure to take you along with me," Mark retorts.

Sarah ushers Aunt Agnes, who has just arrived, into the kitchen. I prepare myself to get an earful since the woman could judge a barbecue from across state lines. She sniffs the air suspiciously and looks at me.

"Bryan, dear"—her voice is dripping with concern—"are you sure we shouldn't just order some pizza or something? Are you guys sure it's safe to eat? Remember that time you tried to make a soufflé?"

My face flushes. "That was years ago, a learning experience, Aunt Agnes! This time, I'm following a recipe…loosely."

Mark stifles a laugh. "Loosely? Like a pirate follows a map, or more like a blindfolded squirrel?"

I throw a playful glare at my best friend, simultaneously giving him the finger and whispering, "Fuck you."

Aunt Agnes gives me one of her infamous glares. "I'm old. I better not spend any of my precious time on a toilet seat because of your barbecue."

"You won't."

"Don't worry, Bry," Uncle Tom says after Aunt Agnes leaves, grabbing a bottle of wine from the rack, "they only tease you because they're secretly jealous of how amazing and fun these little cookout sessions turn out to be."

I snort. "I don't know about that, man, I just feel like they don't even like me sometimes, you know. They just come here for the free food and all."

Mark chuckles. "Exactly. That's what families are for." He gestures at the bubbling pan on the stove. "Is that…fondue?"

My smile falters slightly. "Uh, yeah. I'm experimenting with a little Swiss flair."

Mark raises an eyebrow. "Swiss, huh? Or are you trying to recreate that mystery cheese incident from college?"

I wince. The incident in question involved a very memorable food poisoning episode.

"Hey, what do I have to do for you to forget that ever happened? Jesus! You have the memory of an elephant. Besides, I'm a different man now, a better cook if I dare say."

Ours is such a close-knit family. Despite the teasing, there's a warmth to the atmosphere and a comfortable camaraderie.

The whooping and hollering reach a fever pitch as I slide a sizzling platter of hot steak onto the counter. Just as I'm about to declare myself "The Steak King," a well-aimed dart ricochets off my backside.

"Hey!" I yelp, swatting at the air. Across the living room, my eight-year-old cousin, Leo, grins cheekily from behind the couch, a plastic blaster clutched triumphantly.

"No rough play in the house, Leo!" Sarah calls out from the kitchen, her voice strained as she wrestles with a particularly stubborn jar of pickled onions.

The whole scene presents like something out of a family television soap. In the corner, a fierce foosball match rages between Mark and Uncle Tom. Their shouts of victory and defeat mingle with the frantic commentary of my dad, who's glued to a rerun of the baseball game, yelling at the screen as if the players can hear him.

Leo and his sister Nadia, under the watchful eye of Aunt Agnes, are sprawled on the floor, constructing an elaborate city out of Legos while she holds court at the dining table, regaling everyone with a story about her prizewinning marmalade—a story I suspect I've heard at least a dozen times before.

I survey the scene with a tired but satisfied smile before grabbing my phone from the counter to check the time. A missed call notification blinks accusingly—my mom. With a sigh, I call her back.

"Hey, Mom, just checking in. Everything alright?"

"Bryan, honey, I'm so sorry." My mom's voice is laced with frustration. "I was at the supermarket trying to buy a gift that will upstage the bicycles your father bought for Leo and Nadia."

I wince. "It's not a competition, Mom."

"It became a competition the day your father decided to leave me for that little tramp, Chloe."

"Mom! Language!"

"You're a big boy. I hope he didn't bring her?"

"So you can call her a tramp again? No, he didn't."

"Great."

"Drive safe, Mom."

"I will, honey. Give everyone my love. And, Bryan?"

"Yeah?"

"Make sure you save some of those lamb chops for me. I haven't had a decent meal all day."

I chuckle. "Consider it done, Mom. Love you."

Hanging up, I rejoin the fray. Just then, a loud cheer erupts from the foosball corner. Mark has scored a seemingly impossible goal, leaving Uncle Tom slumped over the table in defeat.

"I don't accept, man. I demand a rematch!" Uncle Tom bellows, already reaching for the ball.

Sarah, ever the peacekeeper, intervenes. "Alright, boys, how about a break? Let's give Bryan a chance to breathe before he collapses from heatstroke." She flashes me a sympathetic smile.

I indeed feel like I'm melting. I grab a beer from the cooler, taking a long, grateful swig. As I wipe the sweat from my brow with the sleeve of my shirt, a sharp rap on the door cuts through the noise.

"I got it!" Leo, ever the eager beaver, practically races me to the door. Before I can protest, he flings the door open, and the scene that follows will forever be etched in my memory.

"Oh my God, Bryan. I think an angel must have come down from heaven." Leo is looking at the person on my doorstep in childlike awe. Standing there is a vision—a woman with hair dark as night and a smile that could launch a thousand ships—or at least a thousand catcalls from Mark, who's looking at her like she's a plate of lamb chops.

A collective groan rises from the living room as every guy in the vicinity seems to instinctively adjust their posture, smooth nonexistent wrinkles, and generally try to appear ten times cooler than they are.

"Hey, little man. How are you doing?" Alex is smiling widely from her cheeks. "I'm here to see Bryan."

I wipe my hands and head to the door, and there she is, a vision in red.

"I'm eight, you know," I hear Leo say.

"What?"

"Earlier, you called me *little man*, but I'm eight and Mom says I'm not all that little anymore."

"Oh my," Alex says in the most resigned and apologetic fashion. "I am so sorry. I will keep that in mind."

As I walk to the door, I brace myself for the incoming onslaught of questions. I shoot a warning glance at Mark, a silent plea that could be translated as, "Don't. Even. Think. About. It. Man. You. Better. Behave."

"Alright, Leo, I'll take it from here and attend to our guest," I say, tousling my cousin's shaggy hair and sending him off. But he finds it difficult to leave. He, too, must be entranced by the vision before him. Alex really is a beauty.

Alex goes in for a hug and her jasmine- and lavender-scented fragrance hits my nose, sending me whirling back. I, on the other hand, smell of meat and smoke, so I opt for a kiss on the cheek instead. Taking a deep breath, I usher Alex inside. "I'm sure you all remember Alex."

The room goes silent. The air crackles with a tension thicker than the fondue bubbling on the stove. My playful, teasing family has morphed into a pack of territorial wolves, silently sizing up the intruder in their midst.

Alex, oblivious to the sudden shift in atmosphere, offers a friendly smile. "Hi, everyone, it's nice to see you all again."

The silence stretches on, punctuated only by breaths and the growing sense that I might have just single-handedly ruined a perfectly good dinner by inviting Alex here.

A chorus of mumbled greetings echoes back, rather forcefully if you ask me, and not in the least bit genuine.

I look around the room, taking in the scene—Sarah glaring daggers at Alex from across the kitchen counter, Aunt Agnes scrutinizing her with narrowed eyes, and my uncle momentarily forgetting the baseball game to give Alex a once-over that could curdle milk. Even my dad isn't left out as he looks at Alex like a school principal about to dole out her punishment.

I sincerely do not appreciate the way they're treating Alex out of some misguided notion of loyalty to me. They've built up these false ideals of her in their minds and now they're letting it get the best of them and acting nastily instead of treating her with the respect that she deserves.

I need to say something. I can't let them just be rude to Alex and get away with it, then what kind of man would I be? What would that say about me?

I grab a glass and ring it with a spoon and everyone looks in my direction.

"Hey, everyone. May I have your attention, please? I don't know what you must have heard about Alex, but I need you to disregard whatever it is because it probably isn't true anyway. Alex is not only my guest, she's also responsible for keeping me out of jail and I would appreciate it if all of you are on your best behavior." I pause for dramatic effect and continue when I see that I have their undivided attention.

" And if any of you are uncomfortable with her being here, the door is just behind you. I will not tolerate any sort of animosity. Not today, not ever. Thank you."

I don't need them to fall in love with her, damn it, I don't even need them to like her. I just need them not to be assholes. Alex doesn't deserve their hate. It's been far too long, and frankly, none of their business has happened between us.

I turn to Alex, and she has a relieved look on her face, which makes me glad I did what I did. "Excuse me for a second," I say to Alex. "Gotta check on the grill before everything turns to charcoal." I leave Alex standing there as I rush into the kitchen.

Suddenly, Sarah materializes behind me, her face etched with worry.

"Bryan," she says, her voice low and urgent, "what's going on? Why is she here?"

Before I can answer, Sarah's gaze locks on Alex through the doorway. I'm sure Alex can hear every bit of this conversation. I feel a pang of sympathy for her, caught in the crossfire of a history she may not even understand.

"Sarah, I meant what I said in there." I place a hand on her shoulder. "I know things didn't end well last time, but Alex has been nothing but supportive lately and frankly, I trust her. And I would really appreciate it if everyone could just...lay off her today."

Rumors had swirled around Alex after our brief relationship, painting a picture that was far from the truth.

Sarah listens intently, her expression unreadable. When I finish, a long silence stretches between us. Finally, she sighs, the tension slowly leaving her shoulders.

"Alright." Her voice is softer now. "I trust your judgment, Bryan. But if anything...feels off, I expect you to tell me."

Due to Sarah's younger age, she sometimes feels more like a sister to me than an aunt.

I squeeze her hand in gratitude. "Of course. I wouldn't be caught dead keeping secrets from you."

"Well, that was rather unexpected," Alex says once I've rejoined her in the living room. "They must really not like me."

I wipe my damp palms on my jeans. "Yeah, well, my family can be a lot, but don't worry, you're my guest and so are they. True to my word, if anyone isn't comfortable being in the same space as you, they're welcome to leave."

A faint smile plays on Alex's lips. "You don't have to be so generous, you know."

"I absolutely have to be, even more. Why don't I give you a tour?" I suggest, hoping to pull her away from the judging stares and Sarah's lingering suspicion. "The living room's a bit of a war zone, but the rest of the house isn't so bad."

Alex smiles faintly. "I doubt anything much has changed since the last tour you gave me, but a tour sounds lovely."

I chuckle, the sound strained but genuine as I lead her away from the watchful eyes of my family.

As we walk down the hallway, she points to a framed photo on the wall. "Is that you?"

"Um, no. That's my cousin, Leo, when he was a toddler. He's the one who opened the door for you. Uncle Tom adopted him and his sister after we...well...broke up." The photo captures a chaotic living room scene, a younger Leo triumphantly holding aloft a plastic blaster, surrounded by the wreckage of fallen pillows and a toppled lamp.

Alex laughs, the sound breaking the tense silence. "Looks like he's a force to be reckoned with."

I grin. "He is. But he's got a good heart." We continue our tour, and I point out some new paintings I've acquired since Alex last toured the house, each one a story waiting to be told. I show her my reading nook, a cozy corner overflowing with books, and my small home office, where the remnants of my latest project are scattered across the desk.

"I can see you're still a voracious reader."

"You know me, always on the quest to expand my knowledge."

With each step, the awkwardness seems to lessen as I catch Alex up about what has happened with my family since she left. It's really nice, almost too nice. I'm a bit suspicious, just waiting for the other shoe to drop.

Chapter Seventeen

♥

Alex

Grace's worried grimace as I prepared to leave for the cookout at Bryan's didn't inspire any confidence.

She looked really worried, and no matter how many times I tried to reassure her that it was just a casual thing, she didn't seem to be buying it.

"I'm leaving now. Will you and Cooper be okay?"

"We will be, will you? Alex, you're walking right back to a place you weren't welcome before. And you've repeatedly told me that you and Bryan are just friends. So why are you putting yourself through all this again?"

I sighed deeply. "Friends invite each other to their family cookouts, don't they?"

"This is different, and you know it. I didn't want to bring this up before, but he is Cooper's father, Lex. Are you sure you're ready to continue keeping this a secret from him? Because it's going to get more difficult the closer you two get."

"I'll cross that bridge when I get to it."

"If there's any bridge left to cross after he finds out."

I knew Grace was right about Cooper, and about Bryan's family not really liking or accepting me. Now that I'm here, surrounded by their judgmental gazes, I'm starting to wish I'd listened to her.

I have been introduced to Bryan's family before, but that was years ago. I guess I thought they would've come around by now, but they obviously haven't. Since I got here, I've been trying to act all confident and tough, but deep down I've been a bucket of nerves, excited and terrified in equal measure.

Nevertheless, the fact that Bryan invited me for this special celebratory dinner brings a wide smile to my face. From the moment I arrived, he's been nothing short of a gentleman and a great host.

When he came to the door earlier to take over from his little cousin, he kissed me on the cheek. He smelled of sandalwood mixed with smoke, a very appealing combination and one that brought back a lot of pleasant and not-so-pleasant memories of the first time I attended one of his family's cookouts.

It was the first time the other members of his family besides his parents had met me, and they all immediately judged me by my appearance. Bryan had tried to get me to class it up with a makeover, but I believed his family wasn't so shallow as to judge a person based on their appearance. Safe to say I was sorely mistaken.

I could immediately tell from their expressions that they thought I wasn't good enough for Bryan. Unfortunately, those expressions are still the same on their faces today.

Ever since I walked in, it's like something in the atmosphere changed. I know that Bryan only offered to give me a tour because he wanted to get me away from their unfriendly gazes, but so far it's proven to be a great tour.

The way that Bryan went out of his way to defend me though, that caught my attention. I wasn't expecting it and it shows how much he's grown since we went our separate ways. The old Bryan would have never done that and him laying it all on the line to give his family an ultimatum, that was sexy as hell.

Right now, we're standing in one of the most exquisite rooms in the house. It's a mini-gallery, the walls adorned from floor to ceiling with a dazzling array of art. There are even some famous pieces, as well as some local and contemporary ones I can't identify, but all of which look quite tasteful. There are paintings in every style imaginable—bold abstracts, detailed landscapes, whimsical portraits. I feel myself drawn in, each piece vying for my attention with its own unique energy.

Bryan chuckles beside me. "I know, it's a bit much. But collecting art is kind of my thing now."

Without taking my eyes off the abstract piece in front of me, I scoff. "I thought art was just greedy people's way of getting rich people to part with their hard-earned money."

"Well, my opinion has changed, mostly thanks to you."

"I can see that. So many things have changed, except, of course, your family's feelings toward me." My gaze drifts to a photorealistic portrait of a little girl with golden flecks in her eyes and the warmth of the summer sun on her lovely face.

"Don't mind my family, they're idiots and they will definitely come around."

Time seems to melt away as I lose myself in the beauty before me, each brushstroke and each color palette a mystery that I can't seem to fathom. The attention to detail, the hues, the realistic nature of it all...it's quite overwhelming, to say the least.

My fingers tingle with the urge to reach out, to trace the lines and textures on the closest painting. A burst of crimson against a backdrop of swirling blues seems to pulse with an inner light. I can almost feel the artist's emotions bleeding through the canvas.

Suddenly, a deep breath tickles my ear. Bryan must have moved closer. Oh my God! I got so lost in this little world of art he's created for himself that I totally forgot he was standing just a few feet away from me.

"This one's my favorite," he murmurs, his voice tinged with reverence, an adoration I haven't heard in a long time.

My attention snaps to the piece he's pointing to—it's a seemingly simple charcoal sketch of a lone tree silhouetted against a fiery sunset. But as I look closer, I see the intricate details, the way the branches claw at the sky, the last embers of the sun casting long, desperate shadows, and the way the entire image is reflected in a pond. Simple, but bold enough to take one's breath away.

Just then, a loud laugh echoes from the other end of the hallway. I whip around, the spell broken, to see Bryan's mom standing there. Her gaze lands on me, and the smile on her face vanishes. I can tell immediately that Bryan didn't tell her I was coming.

Just then, a loud ruckus erupts, and I raise my head to confirm where the noise is coming from.

"That would be my uncle and Mark, they never seem to agree on anything," Bryan says. "Excuse me for a minute. Let me go see what all the noise is about this time around." He kisses my hand before walking away.

I find myself watching him, just for a little while until his figure disappears outside the door. Then I'm back to looking at the paintings, trying to ignore Mel's lurking presence in the other room.

My fingertips hover just above the charcoal sketch, the world around me fading into a blissful silence. Then, a voice dripping with a faux display of sweetness shatters the peace. A voice I dread.

"Whoa there, careful you don't get sucked in! Looks like they could use another set of eyes in those paintings."

I flinch, the spell broken in a split second. Look who it is. Mel is standing inches away from me, her smile sharp as a shard of glass. My stomach clenches, but not with fear—with disgust. Whatever she throws at me today, I am ready to give it back to her in equal measure, maybe even more. I won't be as nice as I was the last time she showed up at my doorstep.

"Oh. Hi, Mel." I look up, keeping my voice dry and unenthusiastic. I will not allow myself to be goaded by this woman, not today.

"How's the art therapy going? Bryan is ever so proud of his collection. He shows it to everyone, so don't think you're anything special."

"Actually," I counter, my voice cool and steady, "I would like to be left alone. Isn't there some other unsuspecting person you can bother until you make their life a living hell?"

Mel's smile falters for a second, but she recovers quickly. "My, my, aren't we feisty?" she purrs, her eyes narrowed. "I almost forgot how positively naive you can be, Alex. Trying to punch above your weight class and all."

The emphasis on my name is unmistakable, dripping with disdain she's harbored for years. She's such a sad woman.

"Why don't you go pick on someone your own age, Mel? I don't have the energy to indulge in your melodrama today. I'm here because

Bryan invited me, and I don't know about you, but I'd rather save my strength and use it to converse with someone who's worth it."

Mel's face flushes a shade of tomato red that clashes spectacularly with her lipstick. "Oh my, did I hurt your feelings, my dear? *Tsk, tsk, tsk.* See, that wasn't my intention. I never would have thought you were so weak. I'm just a mother looking out for her son. I'm hoping you can understand that."

I take a step closer, my voice barely a whisper. "And such a fine mother you make, Mel. An example to all of us here. In case you didn't quite catch that, that was me being sarcastic. A mother who truly cares wouldn't try to control his life," I say, my gaze fixed on a particularly gaudy ring on her finger. "Especially not with such unsubtle tactics."

Mel opens her mouth to retort, but the words die on her lips. Her carefully constructed facade is crumbling right in front of her eyes, and she has nothing to do or say about it. She just stands there trying to hold on to the pieces of it all, her controlled expression replaced by a mask of barely contained rage.

Then Mel plasters a smile back on her face, albeit a strained one. "I thought I told you to leave Bryan alone. What are you really trying to prove?"

"You have no idea."

A silent challenge passes between us, and I know this will not be the only clash we have. She's about to say something else, but Bryan walks in. "Mom, have you nothing better to do than to harass my guest?" He asks Mel with a glare.

" What? No? Why would you even think that? I would never."

" Sure, whatever you say." Bryan retorts humorlessly. "And by the way, Aunt Agnes is asking for you."

"Of course she is." Mel gives me one last glare before walking out of the room.

"Sorry I left you alone for her to find."

"It's fine. I can handle your mother."

"You shouldn't have to. I wonder what's her deal."

" Don't we all?" I mutter to myself and turn back to the art. "You have a really wonderful collection here. Now, shall we see the rest of the house?"

Bryan beams. "Absolutely! Come on, this way."

Chapter Eighteen

Bryan

Six Years Ago

The fluorescent lights seem to hum louder, their uncomfortably blinding glow amplifying the doomed atmosphere in the operating room and the blood spattering on the surgical drapes.

Jeez, that is a lot of blood.

The young girl on the table, barely eight with a smattering of freckles across her nose, has begun to bleed profusely. The calm symphony of the operating room dissolves into a frantic scramble.

"Someone turn off the damn music, I need to think," I bark out. I realize that's a bit over the top, but my head is starting to pound, and I need all the concentration I can muster.

I stand there frozen, unable to do anything as my mind goes back and forth, imagining the number of patients who go into surgery rooms and never make it out alive. The percentage is far too great and I don't want this patient, this little girl in my care, to be one of those people.

"Dr. Knight, we're losing her!" Dr. Ramirez, the anesthesiologist, calls out, her voice tight with barely suppressed panic.

I fight down the icy knot forming in my stomach. This isn't supposed to be happening. I glance at the team, their faces etched with worry, hoping that one of them has an idea, just one good idea that will help me save this poor child's life.

"Pressure's dropping," Dr. Chen reports, his voice grim. "We need to stop the bleeding, and fast, or else we'll lose her completely."

I know there's a rupture in the blood vessel somewhere—with this much blood that must be the case—but the source is elusive.

We have meticulously removed the tumor, but now it seems our young patient might not make it after all. We try everything by the book—packing the wound, applying pressure, administering clotting agents—but the blood just keeps flowing.

Desperation flickers in Dr. Lee's eyes. "Dr. Knight," she starts, her voice barely a whisper, "there's nothing more we can do."

I straighten, looking up at their faces for the first time in hours, my gaze locking with hers. "No," I say, my voice surprisingly firm despite the tremor in my hands. "I promised her mom, okay? I looked into that woman's eyes and I promised I would do everything to save her little girl." I slam the forceps down on the stainless steel tray with a metallic clang. "This isn't over. We need to think of every possible scenario."

The room hangs heavy with a tense silence. Dr. Lee gives me a look that speaks volumes—a mix of disbelief and a silent plea not to make things worse. But I ignore it. This isn't the time to wallow in my emotions. A patient needs me, a family is counting on me, and I will not fail them. My gut tells me that she'll make it, and I'll be damned if I give up just like that.

Thinking on my feet, I bark out orders, my voice regaining its command. "Dr. Lee, prep the vein scope. We need to visualize the source. Dr. Chen, ready the blood transfusions—type O negative, stat! Ramirez, keep her heart rate stable. We're going in again."

The next hour is a blur of focused intensity. Beads of sweat run down my brow, down my neck, and onto my back as my vision narrows to a small area within the girl's body. Finally, with a triumphant cry, I locate the site of the bleed—it's a nicked artery and I found it just in time. With a practiced hand, I stitch it closed, a silent prayer of thanks escaping my lips.

"Alright, team," I announce, my voice hoarse but steady, "let's close her up."

· ♥ · ♥ · ♥ · ♥ · ♥ ·

As I emerge from surgery, the tension in the room breaks. A wave of relieved applause washes over me, but I'm much too tired to do anything but offer a simple smile.

"She's stable for now," I announce, my voice hoarse. "Just have to wait for her to wake up."

Dr. Lee approaches me, a hesitant smile gracing her lips. "Great job in there, Doc. You should talk to the parents. They'll want to hear the good news from you."

I shake my head, a ghost of a smile playing on my lips. "Any of you can do that. Right now, I have something important to do."

I hurriedly shrug out of my bloody scrubs, a sense of quiet satisfaction warming me from the inside out. It's always a good feeling when a life is saved. The glory can wait. All that matters is that I fulfilled my promise. Right now, I have a very important phone call to make.

I step out of the hospital and into my car, exhaustion hitting me like a ton of bricks. It feels like I'm carrying the weight of the world on my shoulders. The cool night air feels amazing, a balm to my frayed nerves. I take out my phone, my thumb hovering over Alex's name. I need to talk to her, to tell her about this roller coaster of emotions I'm still on.

It seems to have become a habit, wanting Alex to be the first person I talk to when things like this happen. It happened when I separated those conjoined twins, and it's happening again.

At first, I chalked it up to adrenaline and just being excited, but if that was the case, there were other people I could've called. Truth is, it's only Alex I want to talk to.

Taking a deep breath, I dial her number before I can change my mind. The sound of her voice, warm and familiar, washes over me. "Hey, stranger," she greets, a playful lilt in her voice.

I chuckle, and the sound is rough. "Hey, Alex. You won't believe what just happened."

I launch into the story, adrenaline still coursing through me. I describe the surgery, the unexpected complications, the fear, and the way my hands were shaking during the entire procedure. I pour out my heart and Alex listens intently, her soft breathing a soothing presence on the other end of the line. When I finish, she pauses for a moment before speaking again.

"Bryan," she says, her voice thick with emotion, "I am so incredibly proud of you. You saved that little girl's life. That's...that's more than amazing. That's incredible. You're a hero."

"Calling me a hero might be taking it a little too far. It's my job."

"You should learn how to take a compliment, Bryan."

We talk for what feels like hours, about anything and everything. The more we talk, the more I realize that I'm falling for Alex, and I want her to know.

Since I can't just blurt it out over the phone, I quickly come up with a plan.

"So," I begin, "what do you say to a little celebratory drink at my place later? Are you interested?"

There's a beat of silence, then a teasing laugh echoes through the phone. "Is your mom gonna be there?"

I chuckle. "Actually, no. It's just me, you, and a few friends tonight."

"Hmm," she hums, drawing out the sound for dramatic effect. "Alright, I'm in."

A genuine smile breaks across my face as I say my goodbyes and pull away from the hospital's parking lot.

· ♥ · ♥ · ♥ · ♥ · ♥ ·

Later that evening, after I've had taken a pretty decent nap, my guests start arriving for our celebratory drinks. There's one guest I'm most excited to see, but she isn't here yet, so I engage in some light chatter with my friends.

Laughter fills the air, punctuated by the clinking of glasses raised in my honor. Colleagues commend my skills, praising my exceptional handling of the surgery. Each toast, each backslapping compliment, should feel gratifying. Yet, something doesn't feel right. It all feels incomplete.

Alex is late, which is quite unlike her. I've never known her to be this late, not even fashionably late, and if something came up she would have called and said so.

I keep glancing at my phone, but staring at it won't magically make her name appear on the screen. I've tried calling her several times, but it goes straight to voicemail. A knot of worry tightens in my stomach. Alex isn't one to flake on plans, especially when it's not something this important.

I don't even know when I begin to pace, my brow furrowed. I don't understand what the problem could be, and I can't bear to be this distracted. I need to know for certain that she's okay. Just as I'm about to grab my coat and head out to her place, a gentle hand touches my arm. I turn to see my mom, her gaze filled with concern.

"Is everything alright, honey?" Her voice cuts through the celebratory haze.

I force a smile. "Just...waiting for someone," I mumble, my eyes flitting toward the empty doorway.

My mom's knowing smile does little to ease my anxiety. "Why don't you step outside for some fresh air? I'll hold down the fort here."

Even though I didn't invite Mom to this little get-together, I nod gratefully. As I step out onto the balcony, the cool night air washes over me, momentarily clearing my head. I need to focus, to figure out what's going on. Pulling out my phone, I dial Alex's number one last time, hoping against hope that this time it will be different.

I don't realize that I've been outside for close to thirty minutes, dropping voice messages on Alex's answering machine, until my mom's voice drifts to me from the open apartment door. "Everything alright out here, honey? Your friend is still yet to show?"

"I don't know what the matter is, Mom. Alex would never bail on me like this. I'm so tired, but I can't even sleep because my mind keeps roaming."

Mom sighs, her gaze lingering on the cityscape before settling back on me. "You know, from all I've seen, Alex never did strike me as the type for commitment," she begins casually.

I stiffen, annoyance sparking in my gut. Our relationship has never been Mom's cup of tea, and I know where this conversation might be headed. "What do you mean?" I ask, my voice clipped.

Mom shrugs, a studied nonchalance in her posture. "Just an observation, dear. She's so young, you know. She just seems like she doesn't know what she wants, like she still has her whole life ahead of her and she hasn't figured out what to do with it yet. Girls like her just seem more interested in the finer things in life. I don't think she really loves you son, she's only grateful she's found a benefactor."

I bristle. "Alex is extremely hardworking. And so what if she's a little ambitious? What's wrong with that? A little ambition never hurt anyone. And you, of all people, should know that age is but a number."

"I'm just saying, you're ten years older than her. Surely, you know that this relationship is only headed for the rocks. And I don't begrudge her ambition. Dreams are lovely but they get expensive, don't they? Especially when they involve fancy dinners and weekend getaways." Her voice softens, taking on a conspiratorial tone. "Didn't you tell me you were thinking of taking her to Italy this summer?"

My jaw clenches. I'd mentioned Italy vaguely, a future aspiration, not a confirmed plan. Mom's words, however, plant a seed of doubt. Was Alex subtly pressuring me for a trip?

"Mom, I don't think you're looking at this whole situation objectively. Look, I'm sorry that my father left you for a much younger woman." The gasp that this earns me shows that I've hit closer to home than expected but I continue.

"I'm sorry, but it's the truth. I'm sorry that Dad did that to you, but your predicament is not my reality at all. You've allowed that part of your life to cloud your judgment about all younger women, but Alex is not like that at all. She's smart and even though she's young, we enjoy each other's company and we have a lot in common. Shouldn't that be all that matters? Isn't that enough?"

Mom leans in further, her voice barely a whisper. "Well, I suppose so. I just hope you're right, Bryan. I would hate to see you get hurt." She pauses for a while but just when I think the conversation has ended, it takes another turn. "Funny thing, I saw your ex-girlfriend earlier today. At the jeweler's on Elm Street. She looked ravishing as always."

"What are you talking about, Mom? What the hell are you trying to say?" I force out, the words hollow.

Mom raises an eyebrow, a flicker of triumph in her eyes. "Just putting the pieces together, dear. Maybe you should, too. Think about it. How did she manage to come into your life barely a week after you broke up with Rose? Her timing is convenient, wouldn't you say? I don't think she loves you at all, maybe you're simply her golden ticket to a comfortable life."

Mom's words, delivered with a practiced innocence, sink in. Could Alex truly be using me? I know that's how our deal started out, but I thought that things had changed, and I trusted that Alex felt the same way. My doubt seeps in and fills in the blanks on the page.

I desperately want to believe it's all a lie, a cruel twist of fate orchestrated by my eternally disapproving mother. But the seed of doubt has been sown, and a chilling possibility begins to take root in my heart.

I whirl on my mother, my voice laced with barely controlled fury. "Mom, don't do this! I know you and Alex have your differences, but I think I'm in love with her. You can't just—"

Mom holds up a hand, her gaze unwavering. "Son," she interrupts gently, "this isn't about me and Alex. It's about you. Look, I wouldn't say this if I didn't think it was true. You know I have no reason to lie to you. You're my son, and all I want is your happiness." She pauses, her voice softening further. "Think about it, Bryan. The timing...it's just too convenient."

"But, it was a fake relationship. We had an agreement. I'd help her through her final year of law school since she lost her scholarship."

She stills, her gaze capable of melting ice. "In exchange for what?"

I shrug. "What does it matter now?"

"Nothing, I suppose. Have you settled all her debts?"

"Yes, I gave her the final payment three days ago."

"Then I guess that answers your question. You're done putting her through law school, and she doesn't need you again, so she's gone. You could try calling her again, but you know deep down that I'm right."

I slump against the railing as the moments I've spent with Alex flash through my mind. I search for inconsistencies, for signs that Mom might be right. The truth is, Alex has always been particularly ambitious, and I knew this when I met her.

But lately, there have been subtle changes—an increased interest in expensive restaurants, and an insatiable desire to travel the world. Have I been so blinded by my feelings for her that I missed these red flags?

Chapter Nineteen

♥

Alex

Six Years Ago

After Bryan invites me his place to celebrate, and we end the call, I practically fling my phone onto the couch. Relieved laughter bubbles out of me and morphs into a giddy giggle. My heart thumps a happy rhythm against my ribs, a total change of pace from the dull ache that's sort of followed me for my entire life—an ache that I was starting to think was just a part of my existence.

Bryan. Just the sound of his name sends a jolt of electricity through me. He called, just like he promised, to tell me about his entire day and his surgery. My mind replays the call—his voice, warm and excited, overflowing with the weight of his accomplishment.

But then my excitement dwindles. I know I have feelings for Bryan, and I still don't know if he feels the same for me.

Suddenly, the bathroom door swings open, a cloud of steam revealing Cara wrapped in a fluffy towel, her hair still damp and dripping. Her eyebrows shoot up comically at the sight of me. "Whoa! What's wrong? You look like someone stole your puppy."

"I was just on a call with Bryan."

"Bryan, huh?" Cara's playful grin widens. "You mean the one you claim not to have feelings for. So what happened? Why do you look so sad?" She fastens her towel precariously around herself as she plops down next to me, sending her cascade of damp curls bouncing and a whiff of water my way.

I sigh and lean back on the couch. "You were right. You *are* right. I think I'm in love with him."

"And from the look on your face, I'm guessing you think he doesn't feel the same."

I shake my head. "Oh, Cara, he's amazing. Funny, kind, supportive...everything a girl could ever ask for," I gush, a gooey smile crossing my face. "What am I gonna do?"

She rubs my shoulder. "You have to tell him how you feel."

I bite my lip nervously. "And then what? He's a billionaire. Like, an actual billionaire, and who am I? A nobody who he's sponsoring through school. I don't fit into his life, his family hates me—especially his mom, and she doesn't hide it one bit. I always feel like second fiddle whenever I'm around his friends, and his ex, Rose, and all the other girls he's dated are all from rich backgrounds like him. I don't fit into his world, never have, probably never will. And what's worse? What if he doesn't feel the same way? I couldn't bear it."

"Look, Lex, I don't know what to say about all that other stuff, but I know it's better to tell Bryan how you feel instead of torturing yourself like this. Besides, if he doesn't like you like that then he deserves a swift kick in the balls."

I manage a chuckle. "Easy, tiger." I take a deep breath. "He invited me to his place later tonight. Maybe when we're alone I'll find the courage to let him know how I feel."

"Tonight is perfect. Just be honest with him. Trust me, it's better to know where you really stand with someone sooner rather than later." Pulling me into a bear hug, Cara whispers, "Seriously though, Alex, I'm happy for you. Not everyone is lucky enough to know what it means to love someone."

· ♥ · ♥ · ♥ · ♥ · ♥ ·

My hand is practically vibrating with nervous energy as I press the doorbell to Bryan's place.

My mind sways into deep thoughts again. Tonight is the night. I'm going to tell Bryan how I feel. My stomach fizzes with a combination of excitement and butterflies, anticipation building in my belly.

Before coming here, I used Cara to practice what I'd say to Bryan. And when she left for the grocery store, I practiced in front of the mirror. And yet, here I am still fidgeting.

The door swings open, revealing Mel, with a smile as sharp and as cutting as the diamonds dripping from her ears. Panic grips me—Mel isn't supposed to be here!

The last thing I need right now is her presence adding to my already charred nerves.

Her eyes roam over me, taking in my outfit with a disdainful sniff. "What are you doing here, Alex?"

"Mel, I know we've had our differences, and you've never really liked me, but please, not tonight."

"Not tonight you say, and what's so special about tonight, if I might ask?"

I know I shouldn't tell her anything, but I want to believe that in her twisted way, she really wants what's best for Bryan. "Tonight is different because I'm going to tell Bryan I'm in love with him."

I see a pitying look cross her icy-blue eyes before she bursts into hysterical laughter. "Oh, my dearest Alex, how delusional can you be? Just look at you, dressed like a pauper in hand-me-downs and all. I don't know what the hell he's getting out of this fling, but that's all this can ever be. Do you really think you can fit into Bryan's future? Into this family? Bryan needs someone he can be proud of, someone who acts and looks the part for the life he has ahead of him. You, my dear, are not that person. You know deep down that what I'm saying is true."

"But Bryan and I have a real connection. I'm not just after him for his money."

Mel scoffs, the sound harsh and dismissive. "This isn't some cheap romance novel, this is reality. We built an empire, and empires demand befitting queens. We can't let Bryan marry someone who has no worth whatsoever on our side of the social fence."

A prickle of anger rises in my chest. "Bryan's different, he doesn't care about all that."

"Don't be naive. He might not care, but I most certainly do. And let me tell you, sweetheart, I control everything. His dad and I have found a suitable woman for him, and she's in there right now. Do yourself a favor, Alex—leave and don't come back here. You really should be ashamed of yourself, pursuing an older gentleman like this. It's unbecoming, have a little dignity."

The weight of her words settles on me like a leaden shroud. A bead of sweat trickles down my forehead, and the bravado I've tried to maintain crumbles under Mel's icy stare.

Mel turns abruptly to head back in, but not before she tosses a wad of bills at me—enough to cover my transport back to the dorm.

Without another word, she turns and glides inside the house, leaving me alone with the wreckage of our conversation and the chilling certainty that what I have with Bryan is over.

I take one last long look at the house in front of me. Tears prick my eyes, blurring the vision of the manicured lawn and the mocking gargoyles adorning the roof. Bryan's mom's words echo in my head, each one a cruel blow, shattering the illusion of the night I had planned.

· ♥ · ♥ · ♥ · ♥ · ♥ ·

The slam of the apartment door echoes through the small living room, jolting Cara out of her reverie. She glances up from her well-worn paperback, concern furrowing her brow as I storm in, kicking the door shut with a resounding thud.

"Alex?" I hear Cara's voice, soft and concerned, as she sets her book down and pads over to the hallway. I slump against the wall, burying my face in my hands, shoulders shaking with silent sobs. My heart feels heavy as Cara kneels beside me.

"Hey," she murmurs softly, reaching out to pull me close. "What happened?"

I can't find the words to respond, so I just let out a choked sob, clinging to her as she holds me tighter, whispering reassurances. A long moment passes, punctuated only by my sniffles, before I finally pull back, my eyes red-rimmed and puffy.

"It's over, Cara. It's all over," I rasp, my voice thick with emotion. "Mel, she...she said these horrible things to me. She said I couldn't see Bryan ever again."

Cara gathers me into a bear hug. "Oh, Alex, it'll all be okay," she says, her words offering a glimmer of hope.

Exhaustion settles over my face as I lean against Cara's shoulder. "I don't even have the energy anymore," I mumble, my voice barely audible over the sound of my own heartbeat.

Over the next couple of days, what starts as a heartbreak becomes a full-blown fever, and Cara is there with me every step of the way. When vomiting follows the fever, she suggests I see a doctor.

At the doctor's office, the news hits like a physical blow.

Pregnant? With Bryan's child?

Panic grips me as I clutch the armrests of the chair, feeling utterly alone at this moment.

I stare blankly ahead, a chilling emptiness settling in my gut. But beneath the fear, a fierce protectiveness blooms. For this tiny spark of life flickering inside me, I will find a way. I have to.

As thoughts of navigating this uncharted territory flood my mind, one thing remains certain—I have to get through law school so I can finally be a lawyer. And a mom. This is my journey now, and I will face it with my head held high.

Chapter Twenty

♥

Bryan

Leaning against the railing of the balcony, I survey the sprawl of land below me. It's really a glorious view, one that most would pay an arm and a leg for. Having this view as my daily companion feels like a cruel joke, a reminder of all the fine things I possess which no longer seem enjoyable.

After the trial, and all the events of the last few months, it's like my head is on a swivel and I'm not thinking straight anymore. It's like the reality of it all, all of the beautiful things life has to offer, is lost on me.

Even though the hospital is open again, I can't go back to work quite yet. I'm still on probation, so technically, I'm on administrative leave until the state board gives their final verdict and I either return to work or never practice medicine again.

The initial thrill of the much-needed rest has faded, replaced by a suffocating sense of isolation. I'm buried under a mountain of thoughts that plague me every day. My mind is playing a dangerous game—the more I try to focus on something else, the louder the whispers of her name come calling.

Just being here, safely within the confines of my own home and not somewhere rotting in a prison cell, means that Alex took bold steps and fought for me, and I feel so grateful for the fact that she chose to take on my case.

The dust motes dance in the afternoon sunlight, slanting through my blinds. I'm sprawled on the couch, a half-eaten bowl of cereal perched precariously on my chest. My hair is all shaggy and floppy, it hasn't been cut in over three weeks, and my beard is unshaven.

There's a faint thrumming behind my eyes, probably due to staying up late last night to watch reruns of *Friends*.

With a groan, I reach for my phone, my finger hovering over Alex's name.

I hesitate, then hit the call button. You only live once, right?

"Hey, you." Alex's voice, bright and chipper, slices through my fog. "How's my favorite client doing?" she asks in what appears to be a sarcastic tone.

"Hi, Alex. I was wondering if you had a minute to talk."

"Um, sure. I hope nothing is the matter. What do you want to talk about?"

"Oh well, just random stuff, you know. Like, when can I go back to work? I'm dying of boredom in this house."

"Bryan, you know I'm busy and I'm at work. I can't take time off just to cuddle you. What's really going on?"

"This is something serious, I promise."

"Fine." Alex's voice is laced with concern. "How are you holding up, old man?"

I let out a humorless chuckle. "Feels like I'm under house arrest, Alex. The days are too long…the same four walls and the same questionable delivery menus. Has there really been no news from the board?"

A sigh crackles through the phone. "Ugh, I'm so sorry, Bryan. I really pushed for a quick decision, but they have their protocols."

A beat of silence hangs between us, punctuated only by the faint sounds of our breathing. Just when it threatens to get too heavy, I break the tension.

"Ugh, Alex," I whine, "is it socially acceptable to just stay silent when on a call? You're not saying anything. Have we known each other for so long that we've run out of things to say to each other?"

She laughs. "You do know that a phone works both ways, right? You aren't saying anything either, and it's a bit disconcerting. Was there a particular reason you called, or did you just want to annoy me?"

"You know me too well. How are you doing?"

"Living the life," Alex replies. "Just got back from court about an hour ago, and already I've had to attend to two very opinionated clients."

"I assume you have no problem with that. Those clients of yours are probably so stunned by your beauty they have no choice but to tell you the truth and nothing but the utmost truth."

"Actually, you would think that would be the case, but it's far from it. These people, it's like they don't care that I'll find the truth later. They lie through their teeth, and it gets me in trouble sometimes, but I've learned to stop trusting clients."

"Except me, of course. I have no reason to embellish the truth or keep secrets from you."

"You're a special case." We lapse into a comfortable silence for a moment, the kind that only comes from a long, shared history.

"So, what have you been up to recently? What's been keeping you busy?" Alex asks in an attempt to continue our conversation.

"Oh, just discovering the many amazing shows available for streaming these days. It's crazy the amount of hours one can spend staring at a TV screen."

"That's not so bad, is it? Remind me to make you a list of my favorite shows so you can catch up."

"Actually, Alex," I say, a hint of intrigue in my voice, "there's this new art exhibit downtown. Supposedly, it's wildly interactive and...well, a little out there."

"Don't even think about it, Bryan."

"Come on, I'm depressed. Hanging with a friend could really cheer me up."

"You're a big boy, I'm sure you can handle yourself. Goodbye, Bryan."

I hang up with a smile, a spark of life returning to my eyes.

· ♥ · ♥ · ♥ · ♥ · ♥ ·

The steam from the shower stings my eyes, but it can't quite clear the blurry image of Alex from my mind. I know it's a terrible idea, showing up unannounced at my ex's workplace. But the thought of spending another night staring at the same four walls is unbearable. Even more unbearable would be going another day without seeing Alex.

I carefully shave, throw on a pair of jeans, and pick out a clean T-shirt from the closet. Minutes later, I'm in my car, headed toward Alex's law firm.

The imposing building looms in front of me. Taking a deep breath, I run my fingers through my deeply conditioned hair and march toward the reception desk. A young woman with a bright smile and a name tag that reads "Tiffany" greets me.

"Hi there, sunshine," I greet her with a wink, hoping to disarm her with a little charm. "Name's Bryan. Here to see Alex. That is, Ms. Collins."

Tiffany, clearly not used to such a forward approach, blushes slightly. "Uh, hello, Bryan. I, uh...I don't think we have an appointment scheduled..."

"Appointment?" I feign surprise. "No, no appointment. This is a matter of utmost importance, you see. I'm her childhood friend and I haven't been in town for a while. I'm leaving again tomorrow, and I just thought to pop in and surprise her. Alex isn't expecting me, but she would be so happy that I'm here."

Tiffany's smile falters for a moment. "Childhood friend, you say? That's great. But I'm afraid without an appointment, I can't just let you waltz right up. There are protocols that must be observed."

"You don't strike me as a woman who cares about proprietary rules, Tiffany. In fact, you seem like a rebel to me."

"Well, I try my best," she says quietly. "But I could get fired for this."

I lean in conspiratorially. "Look—" I lower my voice. "I know Alex can be a bit...intense sometimes. Especially when it comes to her work. Trust me, a happy Alex is a good thing for everyone. Think of it as a public service. And I promise, I'll put in a good word for you so you can keep your job."

Tiffany bites her lip, torn between amusement and following protocol. "Well, when you put it like that. I wouldn't want to be responsible for her missing the chance to see you before you get on a flight bound for...well...wherever you've come in from." She hesitates, and then a playful glint enters her eyes. "But if Ms. Collins throws you out, don't come crying to me."

I flash a triumphant grin. "You won't regret this, trust me."

Tiffany giggles, completely won over by my playful charm. "Just take the elevator up one floor, and then right. Ms. Collins is at the end of the hall. But be warned, she's in a bit of a foul mood today."

"Challenge accepted." I wink, stepping into the elevator, a newfound spring in my step.

I swagger off the elevator, the ghost of a grin still playing on my lips from my victory with Tiffany. Spotting Alex's nameplate on a sleek office door, I push it open with a flourish.

Behind the desk sits a woman with a stern expression and a bun so tight I wonder if she can breathe properly "Can I help you?" she inquires, her voice clipped and professional.

"Indeed you can," I reply, deploying my charm once more. "I'm here to see the lovely Alex Collins. Tell her it's Bryan, her favorite..." I pause dramatically, searching for the right word. "...friend in the whole world. She'll know who you're referring to."

The woman's expression remains impassive. "Ms. Collins is in a meeting, and people who aren't scheduled for an appointment are not permitted to see her."

"But it's an emergency!" I plead, my voice mock-desperate. "I could be dying, you know. This seems highly unfair."

The woman raises an eyebrow, unmoved. "Sir, I suggest you make an appointment."

Just as I'm about to unleash another round of playful persuasion, the office door swings open, revealing Alex herself. She stops short, surprise flickering across her face as she takes in the scene.

"Bryan?" she exclaims. "What are you doing here?"

I whip around, relief washing over me. "Thank goodness, Alex! This nice lady here almost threw me out. Apparently, I am not on the VIP guest list, can you imagine that?"

Alex casts an apologetic smile toward her secretary. "It's alright, Sarah. He's an old friend." Turning back to me, her smile fades as she ushers me into the office and shuts the door firmly behind us. The playful glint in her eyes vanishes, replaced by a steely glint that mirrors Sarah's.

"Care to explain why you decided to show up at my workplace unannounced?"

A sheepish grin creeps onto my face. "Actually," I start, scratching the back of my neck, "I came here with only one intention today." Alex raises an eyebrow, arms crossed. "Look, I know this is crazy," I blurt out, finally meeting her eyes, "but I was cooped up all day, going stir crazy, and…well…" I take a deep breath. "I came here to ask you out."

The air crackles with tension. Alex's expression hardens. "Like on a date?"

"I know, I know," I concede, my voice dropping. "But things can be different this time. We're not the same people we were back then."

"Exactly!" Alex counters, her voice sharp. "And that's why this can't happen. It's too redundant. It's too expensive, this love thing."

I counter quickly. "Come on, Alex, we're not talking about some grand romance here. Just lunch. Two old friends catching up. Surely there's no harm in that, is there?"

"Lunch can lead to more," Alex points out, her voice softer now. "And I can't risk jeopardizing our professional relationship."

I press on, sensing a slight shift in her resolve. "We can handle it. Besides, wouldn't it be easier to discuss these things with someone you actually enjoy talking to? What harm could it possibly do, really?"

A ghost of a smile plays on Alex's lips for a fleeting moment. "This is a really tempting offer, but still…"

I take a calculated risk, a playful jab, knowing it might work on her. "Don't be scared, Alex. It's just lunch. I won't bite…well, not unless you ask me nicely." I wink at her, and I'm sure I've broken down her defenses.

Chapter Twenty-One

♥

Alex

We still haven't talked about everything that happened between us all those years ago. I think it's easier for both of us to just pretend like nothing ever happened.

After lunch, Bryan takes me to an art gallery he mentioned during lunch. True to his word, these pieces are divine. I'm guessing it's either a private art viewing, or he paid for some privacy, because there's no one else around.

We turn a corner and come across one of the most beautiful pieces I've ever seen. It's a painting made from shards of glass and some thread.

"My God, to be able to capture something so...so divine. I envy artists a lot," I say out loud, obviously entranced by the beauty of it all.

"You can be whatever you want to be if you set your mind to it."

I shake my head. "No, those are the lies they tell us in elementary school to make us feel special. It didn't take me long to realize there are many things I can't do. I think it would be a travesty to believe otherwise."

He cocks his head. "You're good at what you do, though. That's all that matters. I've watched you work these past few weeks. You're smart and dedicated enough to quit being a lawyer and find success in any field you want."

"Yeah, but I could never do something like this. This piece of art...I mean, stuff like this and others exactly like it, they're what makes life the beauty that it is."

"No, you're what makes life the beauty that it is."

I can't stop the pink from coloring my cheeks. "Bryan?"

"Alex? It's just a compliment."

I scoff. "It's never just a compliment with us, Bryan."

He comes to stand in front of me, blocking my view of the artwork. "It's not? What exactly are you afraid will happen between us?"

A lump forms in my throat. "You know what."

He comes closer until I'm forced to turn to him. "If you don't want it to happen, why are you so nervous?"

"I'm not nervous." I barely get the words out in a whisper.

He's so close now that I can smell the scotch he had with lunch on his breath. "Really? Your heavy breathing suggests otherwise." His eyes drop to my lips.

"Bry—" His lips cut me off as they crash down onto mine, and he takes my lower lip into his mouth and sucks on it.

His hands go around my waist and pull me closer to him until we're pressed together.

He smells like citrus and sandalwood, a familiar scent that intoxicates me and breaks down my defenses as Bryan's kisses, soft but firm, prods me to give in to my desires. I want this kiss, maybe more than Bryan does. Otherwise, why have I been going to lunches with him, going to his house for barbecues, meeting him at parks, and agreeing to go out with him today when I could've easily said no?

Throwing my hands around his neck, I deepen the kiss, letting my tongue into his mouth to explore the depths of his kisses.

He grabs my ass and squeezes it through my pantsuit, sending shivers throughout my body. He breaks our kiss and my eyes flutter open. "I know a hotel close by…" His words trail off as I give him a nod of agreement, too stunned to speak.

Thank God for Ferraris. We're at the hotel in less than five minutes, tearing the clothes off each other's bodies the moment we enter our suite, like lovers in a long-distance relationship who haven't seen each other in a while.

As Bryan takes off my suit jacket and throws it to the side, he pops open the first three buttons of my shirt and impatiently sucks on the flesh above my breasts while he undoes the rest of the buttons.

Once the last button is undone, he pulls the shirt off, and without missing a beat, he unhooks my bra and gasps when my breasts come into view.

"God, Alex. They're even more beautiful than I remember."

Lowering his head to my breasts, he licks and sucks each mound of flesh, avoiding my nipples until I'm begging him to take them into his mouth.

He obliges, and as soon as his warm mouth covers one of my nipples, a moan escapes my lips. I hold his head in place as he sucks and tugs on the stiff bud.

Still sucking on my nipples, he unhooks my fly and lowers the zipper, and I tug on my pants until they pool at my feet before stepping out of them.

He pulls on my panties too, and I slip out of them as his hand trails down my belly and finds my exposed flesh. He slips two fingers into my soaking wet pussy. Using the wetness, he finds my clit and rubs it slowly, teasing me by moving his fingers back and forth and side to side and around in circles, driving me closer to an intense orgasm with every move.

Soon, I feel the pressure in my belly. Holding onto his neck for support, I buck my hips as I come all over his fingers. The moment I stop shaking, he puts his fingers back inside me, removes them, and licks my juices off his fingers. Then he kisses me so I can taste myself on his lips.

And fuck! That's the hottest thing I've ever seen.

As we kiss, I pull up his shirt and he raises it over his head, giving me an eyeful of his broad chest, rock-solid abs, and lean torso. There's not one ounce of fat on his body—unlike a few years ago, he's absolutely ripped now.

I instinctively run my hands over his chest, tracing over every curve like he's a living, breathing piece of art. Stepping back, he buries his gaze into mine as he takes off his jeans.

When he takes them off, my eyes can't help but drop to the bulge in his briefs. And as the briefs follow the jeans to the ground, revealing his dick, hard and erect, I can't help but swallow. I remember Bryan being endowed down there, but I guess my memory played a quick one on me because he's hung and heavy and larger than I remember.

Our lips meet again, and as we kiss, he picks me up to wrap my legs around his waist as he drops me onto the bed.

Picking up his jeans from the floor, he removes a condom from the pocket and tears it open with his teeth. I watch him roll the rubber onto his throbbing member, my body tingling as I imagine the pleasure I'm about to experience.

In seconds, he's done and he positions himself at my entrance. "Are you ready for me, Lex?"

I nod and he pushes into me, slowly but steadily, until his dick is buried inside me to the hilt. I impatiently arch my hips, desperate for more of the sweet sensations I got when he drove into me.

He starts moving, pulling out and driving back in again, each movement flooding me with sensations too delicious to describe.

"Oh, Alex, I've wanted this for the longest time, ever since the second you walked into that courtroom." He moans deeply, looking at me with eyes so dark they may as well be black.

"Me too," I say, grabbing his ass and pulling him deeper into me.

"Fuck, you're so tight, Lex." He finds my lips again.

As his thrusts become faster, he hits my sweet spot and I dig my nails into his back, my eyes fluttering closed as another intense orgasm starts brewing in my belly.

"Oh, Bryan—faster, harder!" I scream and he drives in and out of me like we're in a race against time.

It doesn't take long before my climax hits me, taking over my whole being as I lose myself in its intensity.

Bryan lets out a guttural groan and I know that sound—it means he's coming too.

"Lex, you made me come so hard," he says, grunting as spurts of cum shoot into the condom.

When he's done, he gives me one last kiss and rolls off me, our heavy breathing lacing the otherwise quiet suite.

We stay quiet for a while, but the silence is not uncomfortable—it's relaxed. It's like our souls are communicating what our mouths can't say. It always feels this way when we're together. Everything seems right with the world.

It's the same feeling that made me almost tell him I loved him six years ago.

We rest for a few minutes and then get up to freshen up. When we're done, I put on his shirt and lie down beside him. My back is to him, my ass pressing against his crotch, and he wraps his big arms around me.

"That was beautiful, Lex."

I chuckle. "It was something, alright."

"Any notes?"

I laugh and shake my head. "I'm not telling you anything that's going to add to your ego." We both laugh and he sucks on my earlobe.

"What happened to us, Lex?"

I stay quiet, contemplating the weight of his question. "I really don't know, Bry. I guess we just drifted apart."

He takes his arm off me and I spin around to face him. "No, we didn't. Alex, we were good. Things were better than ever between us. Our relationship was—"

"You mean the fake relationship where I helped you secure your inheritance and made your ex jealous while you paid for me to finish law school?"

He runs his hands through his hair. "We were more than that and you know it."

"No, actually, I didn't know it. You never told me we were anything more than our arrangement."

A beat of silence follows. "Tell me what happened that day. Why didn't you come to my party?

I hesitate, then take a deep breath. "I was there, Bry."

Chapter Twenty-Two

♥

Bryan

I look at Alex, hardly believing what she's saying. "What do you mean you were there? I stood outside for over an hour that night waiting for you."

She meets my eyes. "That's probably because your mom had already sent me away by then. From the cars packed in front of your house when I got there, I guess I was one of the first people to arrive, but I met your mom at the entrance and she wouldn't let me in, no matter how much I pleaded with her."

Somewhere deep down, I'm just praying that Alex is mistaken and all this is some sort of misunderstanding, because if it's true, my heart will be shattered.

"This is absurd, you're being absurd. I know my mom has her faults, but she would never do something so awful. If you wanted to call things off, you should've just told me instead of pinning it on my mom."

Alex is shooting lasers at me now. "Bryan, you know your mom, and deep down you know I'm telling the truth. Why would I lie? I've got nothing to gain. Do you really believe I would leave you hanging like that without so much as a second thought, after all we shared? Believe me when I tell you all of the many ways your mother humiliated me that night. She said that I ought to feel sorry for myself for trying to trap you into marrying me when you were so much older than me. She told me I had nothing to offer you or your family, being a nobody on the other end of your social ladder. She said I wasn't fit for all the wealth and affluence of your family, and that she and your dad would never accept me since they'd already chosen a better woman for you."

My jaw clenches tight. Disbelief colors my voice. "My mom?" The question comes out strained as if the very idea is absurd. "She never told me that. She wouldn't..." My voice trails off, the anger simmering in my chest replaced by a slow, dawning realization.

I don't want to believe it, but what Alex is saying sounds exactly like something Mom would say.

I shake my head with a flicker of defiance. "No, you don't understand. My mom was there for me after...after we..." I falter, the memory still raw. "I was devastated. I could barely function, and she was there with me every step of the way, helping me recover."

"Convenient, isn't it?" Alex counters, her voice laced with a sharp edge. "That she was there at the right moment, picking up the pieces of your broken heart and finding ways to piece it back together again."

My stomach clenches. "What are you talking about? You're just being dramatic," I force myself to say, even though a part of me already knows the truth.

"No, Bryan. I'm not being dramatic, I'm being honest." She takes a shaky breath, her voice thick with emotion. "I wrote letters, Bryan. I called. I tried everything in my power to reach you after..." Her voice trails off, the unspoken words hanging heavy in the air.

A jolt shoots through me. Letters? Calls? My mind races back six years, back to the raw, suffocating grief that followed our breakup. A memory surfaces, faint, of the phone ringing incessantly during those dark weeks. My mom would always be the one to answer, her voice strained and clipped as she spoke to whoever was on the other end, warning them sternly never to call this line again.

"Wrong number," she'd say dismissively when I'd ask who it was. "Just a telemarketer." Or, "The phone company, something about a service upgrade."

Suspicious. It had seemed suspicious then, but I'd been too lost in my own pain to question it. Now, with Alex's words echoing in my head, the pieces begin to fall into place.

"I wrote you letters, Bryan. I poured my whole heart into them." Her eyes search mine. "I sent you letters after everything fell apart. You never saw them?"

The memory slams into me with terrifying clarity. A few weeks after it happened, after I started getting my wits back, my mom had rushed into the kitchen and grabbed up a particular piece of mail from the pile I'd thrown on the table. She ripped open the envelope, and then dismissed it as her own mail from her doctor.

"Wow, Mom. You're having them deliver your mail to my house? It's almost like you live here now," I said, causing her to laugh out loud and shove it into the recycling bin before I could even glance at it.

An unimaginable pain burns through me, hot and acidic so that I think I might explode.

"No," I rasp, the word a bitter pill on my tongue. "I never saw any letters."

The truth hangs between us, heavy and suffocating. My mom, a woman who I loved despite her many faults, had actively kept me from Alex. The implications are staggering, shattering the carefully constructed image I held of her.

Shame washes over me, bitter and cold. I can't meet Alex's gaze, the shattered pieces of my reality swirling before me. My silence speaks volumes, the fight draining out of me. My stance softens, my shoulders slumping as the weight of the truth settles in.

Just when I think the revelation can't get any worse, Alex speaks again, her voice barely a whisper. "And if even now you don't believe me, ask her why she came to my house a few days ago." I raise my head, inquiring if this is a joke. "Yes, Bryan, your mom came to see me."

"What?" The word escapes in a strangled gasp.

"She offered me money, Bryan," Alex says, her eyes filled with a mixture of hurt and anger. "Money to stay away from you. To not represent you in court anymore."

The blood drains from my face. This can't be happening. It's unthinkable. A wave of nausea washes over me, threatening to spill over.

"She...she said what?" I manage to croak, my voice barely above a whisper.

"She said you were better off without me," Alex continues, her voice trembling slightly. "That I was with you for the money, and that you were starting to see through the act."

"She said that?" I choke out, the betrayal thick on my tongue.

Shame burns in my gut, hotter and more insistent than before. All those years, all those insecurities about Alex's motives...it was all a lie. A lie my mother had spun, so intricately that I hadn't even noticed the strings.

"She planted the seeds long before," I confess, my voice rough with the effort to speak. "Little comments here and there, about how you were just using me, how it was all about the money." My voice drops to a whisper. "I...I believed her."

The raw pain in Alex's eyes mirrors the storm raging inside me. "You believed her over me?"

I want to deny it, to somehow erase the colossal mistake I've made. "I'm so sorry, Alex. I'm so, so sorry for what I did, and what my mom did, but I promise I'll fix this." I get up and start putting on my clothes, fury tearing through me like a sledgehammer.

"Where are you going, Bry? What are you going to do?"

"I'm going to look for my mom—she needs to explain herself."

Alex blocks my path. "Can you just calm down for a second? This isn't entirely your mom's fault."

"What are you talking about? She lied to the two of us to keep us apart."

"Yes, your mom took advantage of the situation, but truth be told, most of the things she said were things I was already insecure about, which was why I left that night. Bryan, I really felt like I wasn't good enough for you, and that I would never fit in with your friends or family, and Mel saw through it."

I sigh and slump into the bed. "You're right. I was beginning to wonder if you were just with me for the money and perks that come with being with a rich guy, and of course, to get through law school, and Mom fed my insecurities and made them so big that they blinded me from seeing what was right in front of me. Doesn't mean my mother won't answer for this, though."

· ♥ · ♥ · ♥ · ♥ · ♥ ·

As soon as I step through the front door, the scent of freshly brewed coffee, a familiar comfort, does nothing to soothe the storm raging within.

"Mom?" I call out, my voice clipped.

A moment later, she appears in the kitchen doorway, a surprised look flitting across her face. It's quickly replaced with a strained smile. "Bryan? Dear, you look a bit flustered, what's going on?"

"There's something we need to talk about," I state, my voice tight.

Her smile falters. "Is everything alright?"

"No," I say, stepping into the kitchen. "It's not."

I launch straight into it, the words tumbling out in a furious torrent. Alex's accusations, the phone calls, the letters, the money—I lay it all bare, watching the color drain from her face with each revelation.

"It's not true," she finally manages, her voice weak. "I would never—"

"Don't try to play games with me anymore, Mom!" I roar, the hurt and anger boiling over. "You kept me from Alex! You poisoned my mind against her!"

She flinches at my outburst, but her jaw firms. "She wasn't good for you, Bryan," she insists, her voice tight. "You were so infatuated with her that you couldn't see, you were blind to all her faults. She was so much younger than you and she was just here for the money. I was just trying to save you from the potential heartache of when she would realize her mistake and leave you for someone more age-appropriate."

"That wasn't your decision to make!" I shout back. "You had no right to interfere in my life like that! I loved her and I'm pretty sure she felt the same way but you kept us away from each other all this while. I'm ashamed to call you my mother because how can a true mother act like this? How can she put her own selfish interest above her child's happiness?"

The room spins, anger threatening to consume me. Mom opens her mouth to speak again, but I cut her off.

"Mom, we're done! I'll tolerate you at family functions, and when we see each other around town. Other than that, we're through."

Without waiting for a response, I storm out of the kitchen, the echo of my mother's bewildered voice trailing behind me. I slam the front door shut with the sudden realization that everything I thought I knew about my life, about my mother, has been a lie.

Chapter Twenty-Three

♥

Alex

Six Years Ago

My stomach lurches, and it's not from morning sickness. Thankfully, that shitty phase of the pregnancy has passed. My present lurching stomach is from a knot of worry tightening in my gut.

Grace—my rock, my confidante, my older sister who loves me more than anything and anyone, and has been there for me since I called to tell her about my predicament—is finally leaving.

She put her life on hold to come out to Bright Sands to look after me and help mend my broken heart. Four months pregnant and recently dumped—I'm not exactly a picture of self-sufficiency.

"Are you absolutely sure you don't want me to stay longer?" She hovers near the door as I gingerly step around her massive suitcase. It's overflowing, threatening to burst, like she's stuffed a whole country into it.

"No, Grace. You've done more than enough for me. Honestly. I can handle myself from here. I'm not fragile anymore. Besides, you can't just pack up your whole life and move to this town just because your baby sister needs you. I'll never forgive myself."

Grace straightens up, a wry smile on her face. "Alex, darling, you're the one with a tiny human growing inside you. That trumps every other thing. Just say the word and I'll run back inside and unpack now. I'd be all too happy to stay here and take care of you until further notice."

I force a laugh. "I can handle myself, you know? Independent woman and all that. Besides, I think I deserve a little peace and quiet without my overprotective big sis fussing over me and the baby, all day, every day. I'm a big girl, Gracie. I can take care of myself.

"I'm not so sure about that. I mean, the last time I left you to your own devices, you somehow managed to get into a fake relationship with a billionaire–still don't know how you managed that by the way, get knocked up, and now you're on the outs with him and his entire family," Grace counters, her voice laced with mock seriousness.

I wince, a prick of heat rising in my cheeks. "Ha, ha. You're very funny. In fact, you're hilarious."

"Of course, I'm the best," she says, then softens, her hand reaching out to rest on my still-flat belly. "Hey, you'll be okay. You're strong, Lex. Stronger than you know."

I lean into her touch, the familiar warmth, a comforting feeling that I've come to take for granted. "But what if—"

"No what-ifs," she cuts me off gently. "You've got this. Besides, I'm just a phone call away. And who knows, maybe this whole experience will turn out to be the best thing that ever happened to you."

I can't help but smile at her optimism. Grace always sees the silver lining, even in the darkest clouds. "You think?"

"I know," she declares, her eyes twinkling. "Now, go back inside and put your feet up before I change my mind about kidnapping you and taking you with me."

I was okay with her leaving, but now that the prospect is right in my face, I feel so sad. A wave of conflicting emotions washes over me—relief that we spent these past few months together after being apart for quite a while, sadness at seeing her go, and a prickle of fear about facing the next few months alone and heavily pregnant.

"You sure you don't want me to book you a flight?" I ask again, just to be sure.

Grace shakes her head, a mischievous glint in her eyes. "Half the fun of traveling is in the journey, don't you think? Besides, I've always loved driving through the desert. It's like an adventure. And you know me—never could say no to anything fun."

A pang of envy shoots through me as I watch my sister wrestle her overflowing suitcase into the car. "Ugh, I wish the doctor hadn't stuck me on this bedrest nonsense," I grumble. "We could have gone on this crazy road trip together. It's been ages since we've done something spontaneous." But I shouldn't complain. I should be thankful for every kind of blessing—and that's what this baby is.

Grace pauses, a knowing smile playing on her lips. "Hey, don't worry about me. You focus on having that little miracle safely. There'll be plenty of time for adventures later, for both of us."

"I wish," I sigh. "Everyone keeps saying motherhood consumes you, and I'm terrified. What if I can't do this alone? This baby might be the death of my social life, and I'm just not ready for that."

Grace squeezes my hand, her eyes filled with reassurance. "You won't be alone, Alex. I promise. I'll always be a call away, and let me tell you, I'm chomping at the bit to be the coolest aunt ever. This kid's gonna adore me."

I chuckle, a flicker of warmth chasing away the worry. "Well, you are his only aunt."

Grace raises an eyebrow. "Wait, Bryan doesn't have any siblings?"

"Nope," I confirm. "Only child, heir to the Knight fortune, the whole shebang."

"Damn." Grace whistles. "So, your little one's set for life then, huh?"

A shadow crosses my face. "That's only if he ever finds out about the baby, and if he even accepts him. If Mel lets him."

Grace nudges me playfully. "Let's not jump to conclusions, okay? It's still early days."

We share a few jokes, the familiar ease washing over me for a moment. Grace finally wrestles her suitcase into the trunk, and we cling to each other in a fierce hug. Our arms are tight around each other, unspoken words hanging thick in the air. As she pulls away, I wave, a lump forming in my throat. It won't be easy, but Grace is right. I can do this. For myself and the tiny miracle growing inside of me.

"Take care of yourself, Alex," she murmurs. "And call me anytime, no matter the hour."

My voice thickens with emotion. "Okay."

"Are you sure you don't want to come crash with me in the city?" she asks, her brow furrowed.

"Don't worry." I manage a weak smile. "I'll take you up on that offer when the baby comes. Right now, I just need to figure things out."

We hug again, a wordless goodbye hanging heavy between us. "I love you, Alex."

With a final blow of kisses, she climbs into the driver's seat. I watch the car shrink in the distance, a wave of loneliness and disquiet crashing over me already. Tears well up in my eyes, but I quickly blink them back, blaming it all on the pregnancy hormones. It's easier that way.

· ♥ · ♥ · ♥ · ♥ · ♥ ·

The weeks have rolled by so quickly, melding into each other, that even the dizzy spells I was having so frequently have taken a back seat.

I wake up one morning with the energy of a thousand horses, and I decide to take advantage of it and deep clean the whole house. I don't know when I'll feel this great again.

I connect my phone to the Bluetooth speakers and play my music at the highest volume, my dance steps coinciding squarely with the rhythmic swish of the mop and the satisfying whir of the laundry machine.

When I'm done and the place is looking the best it's been in weeks, I light some scented candles and soon the entire house smells refreshing and divine. Exhausted but strangely exhilarated, I sink into a steaming shower, the hot water sighing against my overheated skin. My sore muscles loosen, along with the dull ache in my lower back.

I diligently do my skincare routine and settle in front of the TV to watch a few reruns of *The Bachelor* with a bag of chips. But then I start to crave some ice cream. I try to ignore the craving at first, but it doesn't go away. In fact, it gets worse.

Heaving myself off the couch, I waddle to the car and head to the supermarket around the corner. I'll use this opportunity to get some much needed groceries.

Of course, what I end up getting is a ton of junk food because, apparently, that's the only thing my body allows me to keep down during this part of my pregnancy.

While I'm checking out my items, something catches my attention. It's a giggling toddler tugging on his father's hand. A bittersweet pang shoots through me. A vision, fleeting and vivid, of what could have been—Bryan and our little one. But we don't always get what we want, do we?

Back at home, I settle on the couch with a magazine I picked up from the checkout counter and a tub of mint chocolate chip ice cream settled on my ever-growing tummy. Flipping through the glossy pages, I land on the dreaded gossip section. My breath hitches as a familiar face leaps from the page—Bryan, his arm possessively wrapped around a svelte blonde, both plastered with practiced smiles for the ravenous paparazzi.

The accompanying article is a scathing indictment. Apparently, Bryan has been quite the social butterfly, flitting from model to model, dashing any hopes of him reforming his playboy ways. So this is why he stopped taking my calls. Who would have thought?

I never took Bryan to be such a coward. If he really didn't want anything to do with me anymore, he could have just said so instead of sending his mom to do his dirty work and then reverting to his nonchalant ways.

I have tried to reach Bryan in every way possible, but he doesn't take my calls, he never calls me back, and he doesn't respond to my texts. So I decide that maybe I ought to go the traditional route and send him a handwritten letter.

The blank page mocks me, and even though I have a million things I want to say, I settle for only telling Bryan that the result of our last night of lovemaking is growing in my belly. In a shaky hand, I address the envelope—*Bryan Knight* scrawled across the front, along with his address.

With a silent prayer, I slip the letter into the mailbox and hope for the best.

Several days pass by, and I don't get an acknowledgment or a response, only suffocating silence. As the days tick by, I begin to lose all hope of ever hearing from Bryan again.

Instead, images of him with one girl or another keep popping up all over social media. The straw that finally breaks the camel's back is when I see Bryan frolicking with a woman while at the farmer's market.

I make sure he doesn't see me, and when I get home, I bawl my eyes out. After wiping my tears, I reach for my phone and dial Grace's number.

"Hello? Alex, are you okay?" My sister's voice sounds worried. "What's going on, have you been crying?"

"Grace? Is your offer to come live with you in the city still on the table?"

"Of course. You can come whenever you want. You're always welcome here. But first, tell me what's happened."

"My whole world has ended." My voice echoes as I begin to narrate everything that's happened to my sister.

Chapter Twenty-Four

♥

Bryan

I pick up my phone from the nightstand. *12:17 a.m.*

How could I have been lying in bed awake for over three hours and it's still not even close to daybreak? The night air whispers gently through the window, mocking the sleep I'm not getting. Restless, I scroll through my apps, not social media, because Alex has warned me to stay away from social media.

Besides, I don't need to see some dimwit who knows absolutely nothing about me or my family analyzing this entire situation and giving their opinion about what today will hold for me and my career.

I try to play some word games, but I'm a little off, so I scroll through my contacts, stopping as I land on Alex's name, which I have saved as Lex.

A hesitant smile plays on my lips. What the hell am I doing? She won't be happy about this, but if I know anything about her, it's that she's not someone who goes to bed early. She's probably up late reading, and it would be fun to catch her before she goes to bed, especially after everything that happened between us a couple days ago.

With a deep breath, I hit the dial button. The familiar ring echoes in the quiet room, my anxiety growing with each unanswered beat. Finally, her voice, laced with a hint of sleep, fills my ear.

"Hey, why are you still awake?"

"Hey, yourself," I chuckle, forcing a lightness I don't quite feel. "I'm sorry, did I catch you at a bad time?"

"No, I was just lying in bed, almost drifting to sleep, but I'm awake now."

"It's nothing. I just wanted to hear your voice."

"You miss me?"

"Haha, you wish. I don't miss people. I'm superior to other people in that department."

"Oh, wow. A real live twenty-first-century demigod walking among us mere mortals? Who would have thought?" Alex says, her attempt at dry humor making me laugh so hard that my belly starts to ache.

Talking to her has always been my favorite thing to do. It just feels so easy, so natural. There's no need to try too hard.

"Where are you at the moment?" she asks.

"My bed, where else? Why? Do you want to come and join me?"

I can practically hear the blush in her voice. "As much as that sounds very enticing, I'm sorry, but I'll have to decline your generous and obviously selfless offer."

"Are you scared you won't be able to keep your hands off me?"

The silence stretches between us, thick with unspoken desire. Finally, I take the plunge. "Do you want to come over? Or, you could send me your address and I'll come to your place. It's weird that I've never seen the inside of your house before."

The line goes quiet. I wince, picturing her rolling her eyes at me. Then, a nervous laugh escapes her. "Oh please, Bryan. I wouldn't want to give your mother any more reasons to dislike me."

I notice that she completely avoids the part about me never having been to her house, but I decide not to push any further.

"Don't worry about Mel. She's not an issue anymore."

"Did you just call her Mel? That's strange."

"Yep, strange is appropriate, because she feels like a stranger to me right now."

"She's your mother, Bryan," Alex finally says, her voice soft. "She'll never be a stranger."

Disappointment gnaws at me. "She won't be a problem. We had a long nice talk last night after I returned home. We agreed that it would be best for us both if we took some time away from each other."

There's a long silence, and then a sigh. "Oh, Bryan, I'm so sorry. I hope you know I never meant to come between you and your mom. I know how close you two are."

"The only thing that came between me and my mom's relationship is her misguided ego, not you. And I'm the one who is sorry, for everything. For not seeing through her bullshit back then and letting her manipulate me, for never defending you all those times she laid into you even from the very first day you met her. You deserve so much better than that, Alex and I should have believed you the moment you told me." I pause, gathering my courage. "I won't make those mistakes again and I can't go back and change them so please give me a chance to start trying to make it up to you. Please, come over?"

The hope in my voice hangs heavy in the air. I can practically hear her internal battle. A tiny part of me worries she'll say no, but another bolder part knows she feels it too. This connection, this spark.

"Wow, you're relentless, aren't you? I'll give you an A for your effort. I want to come over, Bryan, believe me. I want to, more than anything in the world, but I can't." There's a tinge of regret in her voice. "Besides, isn't today the day the medical board gets to decide if you're still allowed to practice medicine or not?"

"Yes, it is."

"Then you need to get some sleep."

Disappointment washes over me, but there's also a grudging respect. "Alright," I concede, a small smile playing on my lips. "But this isn't over. You're coming over soon, no arguments."

"We'll see, old man," she teases, the playful edge back in her voice.

"Taking a dig at my age? You're a monster, Alexandra Collins."

She lets out a throaty laugh. "Bye Bryan."

"Bye."

The line goes dead, leaving me staring at the phone with a mixture of frustration and a flicker of excitement.

·♥·♥·♥·♥·♥·

Sunlight, the color of weak tea, sneaks in through the blinds, striping the walls with pale bars. I hear the familiar jingle of keys outside before a muffled curse echoes through the door. I know it's Mom, but I'm not feeling very motivated to go help her or prepared to listen to more of her attempts to justify her actions. I sigh, getting up from the table.

"Mom?" I call out, pushing open the door cautiously. Steam from my coffee mug swirls around my face as I see her fumbling with the doorknob, her brow furrowed in confusion.

"The funniest thing just happened," she begins, a nervous edge to her voice. "This key wouldn't open the door, and I swear I have the right one."

The truth is a bitter pill on my tongue, but I swallow it whole. "Actually, you do, Mom," I say, taking a long sip of coffee to buy myself some time. "I just, uh, changed the lock again yesterday. I know you made yourself another key somehow after the first time I did it."

Her smile falters for a moment, a flicker of something unreadable crossing her face. "Now, why would you go and do that again when you know I come to visit you all the time?" Trust my mother to act like we're the best of friends even though she knows I'm still pissed at her. "Well, aren't you going to offer me a spare key? For emergencies and all," she says, a touch of forced playfulness in her voice.

I pretend to ponder for a second, tapping my chin with a finger. "Nah, I think I'm good with the way things are. At least I'll get a break from seeing you here at odd hours of the day."

Mom chuckles, a brittle sound that doesn't quite reach her eyes. "Fine, suit yourself. Speaking of which," she starts, launching into what I knew was coming, "that's why I'm here. To drive you to your hearing. I want to be there for you."

The unspoken weight of her words hangs in the air. *There for you.* Like she always has been. A pang shoots through me, but I force it down. "Mark's picking me up," I say, my voice flat.

"But, dear, I woke up so early and drove all this way to get here. I'm here already. Don't you think you should just call Mark and cancel? Tell him I'm taking you instead."

"I really don't think so. Mark and I already had plans, and I can't just rearrange my life to accommodate you whenever you show up unannounced."

Disappointment clouds her eyes, but it's fleeting. "But I want to be there, Bryan," she insists, her voice losing its forced cheer. "What's wrong with that?"

The question hangs heavy in the air. "The fact that you don't understand the gravity of what it is you did," I mutter, my voice laced with bitterness. "That's another problem entirely."

Silence presses in on us, thick and suffocating. Mom clenches her hands, her gaze falling to the ground. I can't bear to look at her anymore, not today. Before I'm tempted to say something that I might regret later or listen to her try to make a comeback, I hear Mark's car honking outside. I rush out to meet him, but not before dropping my cup of coffee on a side table and making Mom step back so I can lock my door.

It pains me to be this forceful with her, but Mom doesn't understand any other language. If I falter now, she'll think what she did was okay, and I can't have that.

· ♥ · ♥ · ♥ · ♥ · ♥ ·

An hour later, Mark and I arrive in Phoenix, where the meeting with the medical board will be held to determine the future of my career.

We walk into the building, and as soon as we introduce ourselves to the receptionist, she takes us down a hallway and tells us to wait there until they call for me.

Mark tries his best to get me to calm down, but I'm way too worked up for that. The board has been following the case via the court, so they have all the facts, and I'll be getting the final verdict from them today.

As I tap my finger on my knee, like I do when I'm anxious, the door of the room opens and a man in a gray suit ushers me in. Mark wishes me good luck as I walk into the room, which feels like I'm walking into the lion's den.

Court was tough, but at least I had Mark, Alex, Jim, and even my mom to support me. Now, seeing the twelve members of the board all seated, watching me as I walk toward them—it feels ball-breaking.

"Please have a seat, Dr. Knight. Let's begin right away." I sit down on a chair and lean forward on the desk where a microphone has been placed for me. "So, we have all the facts of your case, including Judge Denver's *not guilty* verdict, but we have a few questions of our own."

For the next hour, they fire off questions about the incident and the hospital's administration. After what feels like an eternity, I'm told to come back in two hours after they confer.

It's the slowest two hours in the history of time, but it finally elapses and I go back into the room to hear my fate.

"We have reached a verdict," the chair of the board declares after I sit, her voice ringing through the room. My heart hammers against my ribs as I hold my breath.

"Dr. Bryan Knight, after a thorough review of all the evidence presented and the deliberations between us, we have decided that you have the full right and freedom to continue practicing medicine here in Arizona and anywhere else in the United States of America. This is because the investigation revealed that the accusations of negligence stemmed primarily from understaffing and excessive workload placed on the medical team. While the hospital made a fatal error in judgment, it was a result of fatigue, not malice."

I almost leap out of my seat in excitement, but I stop myself as she continues. "We doctors are the guardians of the thin line between life and death, so when patients are placed in our care, we should do everything we can to make sure they don't die when it can be prevented. You can return to your duties at Knight Memorial Hospital."

I thank everyone and leave the room.

Mark, who's pacing back and forth in the hall, stops and tries to read my expression. "So what happened?" he asks impatiently.

"I'm free. I'm free to be a doctor again."

He sighs with relief and hugs me tightly. "I'm glad to hear that, brother. I can't wait to start kicking your ass again."

"You wish. Let's get out of here, man."

Immediately when we get into the car, I call Alex and tell her the good news. She says she'll come see me as soon as I get back.

An hour after we get back to Woodvale, my doorbell rings. As I open the door, relief and joy battle on Alex's face and she throws her arms around me.

"They cleared you," she whispers, her voice thick with emotion.

"Yes, they did." I bury my face in her hair. The scent of lavender and honey, familiar and comforting, washes over me.

After hugging for a long moment, we head inside and I open a celebratory bottle of champagne.

"Here's to going back to doing what I love after a brutal wait."

Our glasses meet and so do our eyes, Alex's bright with genuine excitement for me. That's one thing that hasn't changed about her, the genuineness of her feelings. If Alex was happy for you, you'd know. If she was angry, you'd know, which is why I know right now that she wants me to kiss her. Her eyes have dropped a shade darker and there's this far away lust in them.

Dropping my glass on the table, I pry hers from her fingers and move over to her on the couch.

"Waiting to hear the board's verdict today was hell, more hell than I thought was possible but there wasn't a second when I wasn't thinking about you, about capturing your lips with mine and kissing it till there's no color left in them."

She pushes her face towards mine and licks her lips. "I'm here now, so what are you waiting for?"

I kiss her, long and hard, and passionately, till we're both out of breath. We remain fully dressed, making out for what seems like ages, kissing, nibbling, and stroking. There's no rush to go further, we're just savoring each other and enjoying being close, up until Alex begins to rub her pant-clad core against my leg.

I push back on my arms and gaze down at her, nodding toward the stairs. "You want to move this to the bedroom?"

"No, I'm okay here if you are."

I take off her polo and unhook her bra, and her nipples pebble as I graze my teeth over them in turn, alternating with soft taps to her swollen nubs and pressing them between my fingers. Her body undulates below mine as she becomes more turned on.

"Bryan, what are you doing to me?" she sighs, her body and mind absorbed with desire. I take a moment to stare at the woman below me, at the faraway look in her eyes.

Alex's cheeks are flushed, and her breathing is short and ragged, her breasts rising and falling in time with her breathing. I can't get enough of looking at her glorious body. The one that's all mine and waiting for me to claim her.

After removing her pants, I slowly take off her cream lace panties and see her pussy lips glistening with her juices.

Pressing my mouth on her clit, I flick my tongue against the swollen nub, alternating between slow and fast strokes while she writhes, moans, and grinds her pussy against my face.

As I continue sucking on her clit, she cries out, "Bryan, I'm coming!" Her thighs grab my head tighter as her orgasm washes over her.

"Bryan, I want you inside me," she says, her eyes so clouded with desire that I practically run up to my bedroom and come back in a flash with a condom.

Taking off my clothes at the speed of lightning, I put on the condom and enter her oh so slowly, just the tip of my cock at first. I feel her trying to raise her hips to get me to sink further inside her, but I pull my hips back so she can't do it.

"Bryan," she mewls.

I inch gently into her, keeping my leisurely pace until she's full of me, and then I rock in and out of her. She clings to me, her hands gripping my ass as I thrust inside her. I catch a pert nipple between my teeth and nip at it while I move, and Alex sighs happily.

"Oh my God, oh my God," she cries as I encircle her clit with my finger and bring her to the brink. I feel her body begin to tense under me, and then she explodes, wave after wave of her climax shuddering around my cock.

The way her pussy grips my dick tightly as she comes pushes me over the edge, and I let myself go, grunting as I pour spurts of cum into the condom.

Chapter Twenty-Five

♥

Alex

I've just dropped Cooper off at school and returned home to start on a few chores. I'm taking a personal day off from the office today because I'm quite sore after the night Bryan and I had.

After the couch encounter, we took things to the bedroom, where he gave me two more earth-shattering orgasms in quick succession. He wanted me to spend the night, but of course I couldn't, and I couldn't tell him why.

He's growing suspicious of the fact that he's never been to my house, and I never agree to spend the night or come over at night, but I've told him I just have a lot on my plate at the moment.

I know I have to tell him about Cooper sooner or later, and even just thinking about it has my stomach in knots. My phone rings. It's my boss.

"Hello, Mr. Patel?"

"Hi, Alex. I heard you won't be coming in to work today."

"That's right, sir. I'm coming down with something, and I wouldn't want to give what I have to anyone." I feel bad for lying, but I'm really exhausted and need a break today.

"That's okay. We heard about Bryan Knight's complete exoneration by the medical board. That's really great, Alex, well done."

"Thank you, Mr. Patel."

"After how well you handled Knight's case, you need a break anyway. When do you think you'll be getting back to the office?"

"I should be there bright and early tomorrow, depending on how I feel."

"Alright, come see me as soon as you get in."

"Yes!" I scream when I end the call. A call from Mr. Patel only means one thing—I'm getting promoted to partner.

I fucking did it!

I immediately want to call Bryan and share the good news with him, but I stop myself before grabbing my phone. But then it rings anyway and when I look at the screen, it's Bryan calling.

"How weird is it that you called me when I was just about to call you? That's spooky."

"Oh, really? Is this your way of trying to say that you miss me or something?"

"Only you would interpret a sentence like that into something of your own choosing."

"A man can hope, can't he?"

"I thought you'd be really busy at the hospital today, how do you have time to be talking to me right now?"

"No matter how busy I am, Lex, you know I'll always make time for you."

"Aw. Now tell me the truth, what's really going on?"

"No patient wants to see me."

"What? Didn't they hear you were exonerated? Besides, why are they acting like you're the one who caused the deaths of those patients? You just own the hospital where the incident happened."

"Unfortunately, they don't care about that. They just know what they saw on the news, and what they saw in gossip columns, so they don't trust me. I'll have to find a way to regain their confidence in me."

I sigh heavily. "I'm so sorry, Bryan. I'm sure if anyone can handle this, it's you."

"And this is precisely why I called you. I was sure you'd give me some uplifting words. I've truly missed our heart-to-heart sessions."

My doorbell rings and I look through the peephole, opening the door when I see it's Grace. "I missed them too." She walks past me and I close the door.

"Alright, we'll talk later. Mark just entered my office to give me what I'm sure is a pity case, or to ask me something he already knows so I don't feel too useless."

I laugh. "Thank God for friends like him. Bye."

"Bye."

I end the call and turn to Grace. "Hey, sis. Didn't know you were coming."

"I wasn't, just passing by on my way back from the grocery store and thought to stop by and drop a few things off for you. Was that Bryan?" she asks as she casually unpacks some of the milk and cereal she got for us.

"Yes, that was him."

"You two seem to be getting quite close these days."

I shove my hands into my pockets. "Yes, we've been getting closer."

She suddenly stops unpacking the groceries and turns to me. "Alex, are you really sure you know what you're doing?"

"What do you mean?"

She runs her hands through her hair, her round face masked in worry. "When are you going to tell him about Cooper?"

I start putting the milk cartons in the refrigerator. "I thought we already talked about this. I'll tell him soon."

"But have you ever stopped to wonder how he doesn't know about Cooper yet? Lex, you wrote him a letter telling him you were pregnant, and he never wrote back or came to see you. Haven't you stopped to wonder why?"

"As a matter of fact, I have." I lean against the refrigerator. "I've thought about it since we reconnected, but I haven't been able to bring myself to ask. Maybe because I'm afraid of his answer."

"You need to ask him. If he knew about Cooper and deliberately abandoned the two of you, you wouldn't want a man like that in your life, would you?"

I shake my head. "No. You're right, Grace. I'll talk to him."

"Sooner rather than later, okay?"

"Alright. So, that aside, guess who called me a few minutes ago?"

"Who?"

"My boss."

"Mr. Patel himself?"

"Duh!"

"This maybe means you're finally getting the partner position you've wanted for so long?"

"Exactly. I'm so happy."

"I'm happy for you. You deserve it. In fact, I'm going to go pick Cooper up from school today and take him to the park. You can come with us if you like?"

"Nah, I have a lot of cleaning to do and a new case to catch up on, so I'll catch you guys later."

"Alright, bye. Love you."

"Love you too, sis."

After Grace leaves, I get into everything I've planned to do today and before I know it, four hours have flown by. I whip up some lunch of reheated pizza. Just as I bite into it, my phone rings.

"Hey, Grace. Are you guys at the park yet? Is Cooper having fun?"

Grace's voice, usually dripping with sarcastic humor and wit, is all but a frantic rasp. "Alex, it's Cooper. I went to pick him up, and there's been an accident at his school. He's...he's in critical condition. We're heading to Knight Memorial."

"Oh my God, why didn't anybody call me?" I gasp, the words a ragged whisper. Panic claws at my throat.

"They did, but they couldn't get through to you."

Clutching the phone tighter, I listen as Grace explains, her voice choked with tears. Cooper was riding the merry-go-round at school and had fallen off of it, landing terribly against the pavement. All of the details start to blur. All I know is that my son, my bright, mischievous five-year-old boy, the only light in this dark world, is fighting for his life.

"I'm with him en route to the hospital now," Grace continues, a sob breaking through. "Nobody is telling me anything yet, Lex. I have to get back, hurry up and get here."

Without waiting for the rest, I'm already scrambling to my feet. "I'm on my way."

In a blur, I gather myself and pick up my bag, stuffing essentials into it with trembling hands.

I race to the driveway, get into my car, and zoom away. At this point, I don't even care if I get a ticket for driving past the speed limit. This is a life-and-death situation and if anything happens to my son, I'll never forgive myself.

In less than ten minutes, I pull into the parking lot of Knight Memorial Hospital and run straight to reception.

Finally, I get the information from the clerk at Knight Memorial who confirms that there's a patient named Cooper, a little boy suffering from multiple trauma.

I scan the hospital waiting room, my eyes landing on Grace huddled in a corner chair. Worry is etched across her usually vibrant face, tears clinging to her lashes. It pains me to see her like this. She loves my son as if he were her own, and this is equally as heartbreaking for her.

"They put him on a tube to assist his breathing," Grace rasps, her voice thick with emotion. "But he is still in the CT scan room for them to check the extent of his injuries."

I sink into the chair beside her, our hands instinctively clasping. A silent prayer forms on my lips, a desperate plea for Cooper's well-being. It takes a moment for the adrenaline coursing through my veins to subside, and the tremors in my hands to lessen. Just then, a nurse with gentle eyes and a sympathetic smile approaches.

"Ms. Collins?" the nurse inquires, holding out a clipboard with a form attached. "We need you to sign this, confirming you're Cooper's mother, and we'll need to see some ID."

I take the offered pen, my gaze falling on the hospital's logo emblazoned on the top of the form. In a split second, the world seems to tilt again.

Knight Memorial. This is Knight Memorial.

My heart lurches, a cold dread replacing the fading panic. This is Bryan's hospital. The realization hits me like a physical blow. How would I even begin to explain to him that our son is the one lying in that hospital bed?

A son he doesn't know about.

My grip tightens on the pen, the paper suddenly creasing under my trembling fingers. A thousand questions swirl in my mind, tangled with gnawing fear for Cooper. But for now, I have to put them aside.

My focus, my only focus, is on my son.

I guess I'll cross that bridge when I get to it.

Chapter Twenty-Six

Bryan

"Hey, man, if you're here to ask me the correct dosage of some painkiller, information which I'm certain you already know, then I really am not interested. As you can see, I have a hospital to run," I say, half-jokingly.

Mark gives me an accusatory look. "From where I'm sitting, this hospital seems to be running itself, and according to your secretary, you've been in here since this morning folding paper airplanes. Am I right, or am I right?"

I chuckle. "Asshole. Yes, I've been in here since this morning, but I'm pretty sure Gina didn't tell you about the paper airplanes because she promised me she would never. Am I right, Gina?" I ask, pressing the intercom button.

Gina's voice crackles through the intercom. "Yes, you're right, Dr. Knight."

Mark shrugs. "Fine, I came up with that part by myself, because I know you like I know the back of my hand. I know what you do when you're nervous."

"True. How are you here right now? I thought your hands would be full with all the patients that are refusing to come see me."

"Actually, most of us aren't doing anything out there either, it's a slow day."

I scoff. "A slow day at one of the two hospitals in town? St. Agnes must be having a ball." I toss my phone onto the table. "It's because of the case, isn't it? Are we ever going to live this down? I thought people were supposed to stick together in small towns, but it seems they don't trust me anymore. They've ganged up on me."

"I'm sorry, man. I know how much that can suck," Mark says sympathetically.

I shake my head. "You have no idea."

"I agree, and that's why I'm here to cheer you up, and we can spend the next few hours thinking of strategies to get your patients to trust you again," Mark suggests.

"Thanks, man. I knew there was a reason I liked you," I say. I've never had a friend like Mark, and I'm so grateful that he's in my life. Not only is he with me when things are good, but he's also right there riding with me when I'm down in the dumps and things get shitty. He's more than a friend to me, he's like a brother.

"Alright, let's do this. " I pull out a notepad. "The responsibility of coming up with some solid PR strategies to regain the trust of our patients lies in our hands."

Mark nods, leaning forward. "Agreed. What do you think of organizing a community health fair? You could offer free checkups, consultations, maybe even some health workshops."

I tap my chin thoughtfully. "That's not a bad idea. It would show that we're committed to the well-being of the community and willing to go the extra mile to ensure they stay in good health."

"Exactly. Plus, it's a great opportunity to engage with the community directly, and address any concerns they might have."

I jot down some notes. "We could also leverage social media to spread the word about the event and showcase the positive impact we're making in the community."

Mark nods in agreement. "And how about reaching out to local schools and offering educational sessions on health and wellness? It could help build trust with both parents and children."

"That sounds like a pretty solid plan to me," I say, impressed.

Mark smiles. "Glad you think so. I'll start reaching out to my contacts so they can spread the word and get the ball rolling on these ideas."

I nod, feeling more optimistic. "Let's show the townsfolk that we're still committed to serving them with integrity and dedication."

"You do know that there's a fat chance all of this might not work, right?

"I just knew this was coming. Why do you have to be such a downer?"

"No, man, that's not it. I'm just saying you should manage your expectations is all. Small-town folks are surprisingly good at ostracizing people with their self-righteous attitudes."

"I understand. I'm just happy that we get to work on this together."

As we continue brainstorming the pros and cons of our PR strategies, Mark's phone keeps pinging constantly. I finally interrupt, "Damn, man, did you go missing or something? Don't let me stop you from responding to those texts."

Mark takes a look at his phone and smiles.

I narrow my eyes. "Who is she?"

"How do you know it's a she?"

I chuckle. "Because I know that look. It's the same stupid one I have whenever I read any of Alex's texts."

"I don't know what you're talking about," Mark protests, but in one swift move, I grab the phone from him.

"Hand it over," Mark threatens, but I manage to glance at the screen before handing it back.

"And who is Natalia?"

Mark tries to play it cool. "I know you read the text."

"Come on, tell me," I insist.

Mark finally relents. "She's this girl I met at the airport lounge."

I grin. "Is she hot?"

Mark's eyes light up. "Unbelievably."

We high-five, and I say, "Nice, man."

Just as we're about to resume our earlier conversation on PR strategy, my pager goes off, signaling my first patient since the court case. It's a code red, and I'm being called to the OR.

· ♥ · ♥ · ♥ · ♥ · ♥ ·

I tear through the hospital at lightning speed, the fluorescent lights a harsh contrast to the natural lighting in my office.

I don't bother with pleasantries, just a curt "Where?" to the confused receptionist. Dr. Lee, a wisp of a young doctor with worry etched on his face, is waiting by the elevators.

"OR three," Lee blurts, already leading that way at a breakneck pace. "It's a five-year-old boy, an accident at the playground. Severe internal injuries and a possible hematoma."

I nod, a grim determination settling into my bones. As we reach the OR doors, the familiar scent of disinfectant and nervous energy fills my nostrils. Scrubs, masks, gloves—the motions are practiced and professional.

"Brief me, Dr. Lee," I demand, my voice tight as I pull on my gloves. Lee launches into a rapid explanation—the extent of the injuries, the failed attempts at stabilization. By the time I stand at the sterile operating table, scalpel glinting in the overhead lights, I have a mental map of the situation.

My gloved fingers dance across the exposed abdomen, the harsh overhead lights reflecting off the glistening instruments. Blood wells in the cavity while Dr. Lee hovers beside me with suction to keep the field clear as I assess the damage.

A wide laceration snakes across the boy's small intestine, a result of the brutal impact of the accident. "Intestinal resection," I bark, my voice calm amidst the storm. Lee reacts instantly, handing me the scalpel. With practiced ease, I excise the damaged portion, the metallic tang of blood filling the air.

I focus on the task at hand, expertly repairing the severed intestine, my movements a blur of practiced efficiency. Sweat beads on my brow, but my hands remain steady, guided by years of experience and an unwavering focus.

Finally, with a flourish, I get the bleeding to stop. Relief flickers in Dr. Lee's eyes. We've stemmed the tide, for now. The battle isn't over, but we've given him a fighting chance, which is all that matters right now.

The hours tick by, marked only by the rhythmic beep of the heart monitor and the hushed exchanges between me and Dr. Lee as I assess and stabilize the patient. It takes all of three hours, but with a satisfied grunt, I suture the last incision and allow myself a single moment of relief, my shoulders slumping slightly.

"Surgery complete," I announce, my voice hoarse.

The tension in the room bleeds away, replaced by a palpable sense of accomplishment. Dr. Lee lets out a shaky breath, a relieved smile breaking through his exhaustion.

"Great work, Dr. Knight," he says, his voice filled with awe. "You saved his life."

I nod curtly, the adrenaline slowly draining from my system. I know the boy isn't out of the woods yet, and recovery will be a long road. But for now, we've bought him a chance. As I peel off my gloves, a pang of concern flickers across my mind.

"Dr. Lee," I begin, "is there a family member waiting?" Lee's eyes betray an affirmative expression.

"Yes, Dr. Knight. His mother and aunt have been here since he was brought in. Do you want me to go and tell them, or will you do the honors?"

"Go tell them. I plan to slip out of the hospital unannounced, enjoy a meal, and head to bed. Make sure you keep our young patient stable. I'll be back to check on him tomorrow."

As I head out of the OR, my mind already halfway home, I catch a glimpse of someone who looks like Alex. But I don't give it much thought until her voice stops me dead in my tracks.

There she is, disheveled and bawling her eyes out, screaming at the receptionist. My heart sinks as I realize it is indeed Alex. I've seen this play out before, a family member concerned about their loved one and taking it out on one of the staff, so I decide to step in.

"Alex? Are you okay?" I ask, and when she turns to me, her tear-streaked face is contorted with emotion.

"Thank God, you're here. Maybe you can help me. My son, Cooper Collins, was taken into the OR about three hours ago and I still haven't gotten any updates."

"Cooper Collins is your son?" I ask, confusion masking my features.

Her eyes light up. "Yes. You heard about him?"

"I didn't just hear about him. I operated on him just now. He pulled through the surgery, but they're taking him to the ICU as we speak. Lex, I didn't know you had a son...and he's five years old?" I guess she sees through the question I'm afraid to ask.

She hesitates for a moment, then nods. "He's your son too."

Chapter Twenty-Seven

♥

Alex

I'm still reeling from the shock of seeing Bryan in the hospital, and I desperately try to avoid his eyes after the heavy revelation I just dropped on him.

From the look on his face, I can tell he had no clue of Cooper's existence. I want to talk to him, but right now, I need to see Cooper. "I need to see him, where did they take him?"

"I'll show you." His voice sounds hollow as he leads me down the hallway.

I signal to Grace and she quickly follows me as we make our way to Cooper.

As we walk into his room, I almost break down in tears. My son is lying on one of the beds, all kinds of wires and tubes connected to his tiny body.

I swallow hard as we walk closer to him, my hand holding Grace's so hard that I'm afraid I'll break one of her bones.

"Oh, baby," I say, kissing Cooper's bandaged head. "What have they done to you, my boy?" I can't hold back the tears now, so I allow them to flow as I fall into Grace's comforting embrace.

I know her heart is breaking too, but she's trying really hard to keep it together for my sake.

Pulling myself together, I look over at Bryan, who still hasn't recovered from the shock of finding out he's a father. He's standing in the doorway as if he doesn't want to intrude upon our private moment. But Cooper is his son too, so I motion for him to join us.

He stands beside us and looks down at Cooper, and I see a slight smile form on his lips. "He's a fighter, just like his mom. I'm sure he'll pull through. He has a concussion, and some broken bones in his ribs and shoulder which I repaired during the surgery, but I believe he'll be awake soon enough."

I look up at him in appreciation. "I'm really glad he was treated by the best doctor in Woodvale, and I know you have a lot of questions. I promise to tell you everything, but for now, I just want to sit with him."

"Of course. I'll be in my office whenever you're ready to talk."

"Thanks for taking care of our boy," Grace tells him before he leaves.

As the door clicks shut, I take Cooper's hand—the one that isn't connected to an IV drip—and bring it up to my lips. "Hey, baby. Mama is here, and Aunty Grace too. Dr. Knight says you're a fighter just like me, and I agree. You have to be okay for Mommy, because I can't lose you. You're my life. You keep fighting until you come back to me, okay?" I let out a sob and Grace squeezes my shoulder.

I sit with Cooper for hours, watching his chest rise and fall as he breathes. A nurse comes in at some point to tell us that there can't be more than one person in the room with Cooper at a time, so Grace went back to the waiting room. I decide to go check in on her, just for a moment before coming back to Cooper.

Just like I imagined, she's sitting in the waiting room, her hands buried in her dark curls as her knee jerks like it always does when she's nervous.

She stands up as soon as she sees me. "Is something wrong?"

"No, of course not. I just wanted to check in on you."

She heaves a sigh of relief. "Oh, alright. How's Coop?"

"He's still the same, but the last time a nurse checked on him, she told me that his vitals are improving."

"That's really great news."

"It is. Have you had anything to eat?"

She turns her head from side to side. "Not since lunch, no appetite. Besides, I should be asking you that question. Did you have lunch before I called?"

"Was about to, but it's fine. I'll just go back in there and drive myself crazy with worry until Cooper wakes up."

"You know who else is probably going crazy right now? Bryan. I could tell he never knew about Cooper, so he deserves some answers."

"I don't want to leave Cooper."

"I understand, but I asked, and he's staying in some other doctor's office for the night so he can be close to the ICU in case of any emergency." She points to a room just down the hallway. "I'll stay with Cooper until you get back, and if there's any development, you'll be the first to know."

"Thank you," I mutter before heading to the office to see Bryan.

When I get to the door, I take a deep breath, steady my shaky hands, and knock lightly.

"Come on in," a voice calls from inside, and I open the door and walk in.

Immediately, Bryan gets up and pulls me into a hug. I'm amazed he's being this gentle with me after I ambushed him with the news about his son. He releases me and I sit in the chair opposite him.

"How are you holding up?" he asks.

"I've been better."

"I'm so sorry about Cooper."

"It's okay. If anything I should be thanking you for being here to save his life."

He gives me a tender look. "Can I get you anything to drink, maybe some coffee?"

I nod, eager for anything that will help me get through the difficult conversation we're about to have. Bryan leaves, and a few minutes later he's back with a steaming cup of coffee in each hand.

He hands me one, his eyes lingering on me for a fraction of a second too long. I can practically feel the questions brewing beneath the surface, unspoken yet burning in his gaze. But he holds back.

Taking a fortifying sip of the coffee, I meet his gaze head-on. "Ask me anything you want to know."

He remains silent for a few seconds that drag on for eternity, and then he blurts out, "Is he really my son?"

"Yes, he is. I found out I was pregnant with him days after your mom turned me away from your house."

"Alex, why didn't you tell me? I know things seemed bad between us at the time, but this is a whole human being—my son. Knowing about him would've changed everything."

"After I tried to reach you several times and you never picked up or called me back, I figured you wanted nothing to do with me or the baby."

Regret is evident in Bryan's eyes. "Like I already told you, that wasn't intentional. My mom deleted every evidence that you had called as she handled my phone for weeks after we broke up. But what about all this time we've been reconnected, especially after you found out what my mom did? Did you really think I would know I have a son and keep quiet about it?"

"I guess I kept putting it off, and then we got so close. As time passed, I became afraid to tell you because I didn't know how you'd react. I'm so sorry, Bry."

"No, I'm the one who should be sorry about what my mom and I put you through, sorry that I wasn't there for you when you needed me the most, sorry that I wasn't there for the first five years of Cooper's life. I can't imagine how hard it must've been going through all that alone." He reaches out, his thumb gently brushing away a stray tear running down my cheek.

"Thankfully, I wasn't alone. I had my roommate Cara, and my wonderful big sister Grace to help me through it."

He smiles, but I can see how much he hates that he wasn't there, how much pain it causes him. "I'm glad to hear that."

Our gazes linger on each other for three heartbeats before I get up. "I need to go back to Cooper, but feel free to come by and see him anytime."

"I'll take you up on that offer."

Chapter Twenty-Eight

♥

Bryan

I swivel back and forth in my office chair, its familiar groan mimicking the churn in my gut. Leaning forward, I click open the email from Alex. The subject line is simple: *Memories*. A wave of familiarity washes over me as a photo fills the screen—a five-year-old boy, covered head to toe in mud and grinning like a maniac.

The memory of last night's conversation with Alex overwhelms me. The one where those words I wasn't expecting at all came tumbling out of her mouth. The one where she told me about my son, *our* son, Cooper.

My gaze drifts back to the photo, a lump forming in my throat. This little guy with the mischievous grin on his face—he's mine. *My child*. The weight of that truth settles onto me, a terrifying and exhilarating mix. A few days ago, I didn't even know he existed, and now I suddenly can't do anything without craving to be a part of his life.

My heart thumps in my chest. The resemblance is uncanny. That mop of messy brown hair, the way his brow furrows in concentration as he builds his Lego spaceship—it's like staring into a reflective surface and seeing a younger, more carefree version of myself. I grab my phone, dial a number on speed dial.

"Mark, pick up, pick up," I mutter under my breath.

"Bryan? Everything alright, man?" Mark's voice booms through the speaker. "You are about to make me late for a date with a very beautiful woman."

"What woman?"

"Natalie, the girl I told you about two days ago. The one I met at the airport. Have you forgotten?"

"Oh, her. I figured, knowing you, you would have moved on by now."

"I've tried, man. Believe me. Anyway, tell me why you called so I can get back to preparing for the date."

"Mark..." I take a shaky breath. "You won't believe what I'm about to tell you, and you're gonna think I'm crazy, but here goes—I have a son."

There's a beat of surprised silence at the end of the line, then a snort of laughter. "Yeah right, buddy. They don't just sell kids at the market, you know."

I clench my jaw, a wry smile pulling at my lips. "Hilarious, Mark. Really. But listen to me for a second. I'm not kidding, okay? This is serious shit."

"Woah," Mark chuckles, "I just saw you a few hours ago. Did you, in the spirit of celebration, go out and adopt or perhaps steal a child?"

"Come on, Mark." I roll my eyes as if he can even see me. "Which option sounds more likely? Kidnapping a random kid or finding out I have a son I never knew about?"

Mark hesitates, stalling for a beat. "The latter, definitely the latter," he concedes. "But hey, in my defense, the first one doesn't sound quite as scandalous, does it?"

"You're an asshole, you know." I laugh, a touch of relief washing over me.

"You really have a child from a past relationship? How old is he?"

"Five," I blurt out too enthusiastically. "He's five years old, and he looks exactly like me at that age."

Mark does a quick calculation on the other end. "Oh," he gasps in realization. "That puts it right around the time you were dating Alex. Is she the mother?"

"It's a long story," I sigh, pinching the bridge of my nose. "She just told me last night."

"Hold on," Mark says, a hint of skepticism in his voice. "Are you sure he's yours?"

I glance back at the photos of the boy on my laptop screen, completely engrossed in constructing his Lego masterpiece. "God, Mark, you should see him. This kid looks so much like a younger me, there's no denying it. He really is my son."

The words hang heavy in the air, even in my own head. *I can't believe I just said that out loud*. A strange mix of excitement and apprehension bubbles in my gut. *My son*. It sounds so foreign, yet strangely familiar.

"Hey, I'm happy for you," Mark says, sincerity lacing his voice. "I always knew you'd make a fantastic dad to some poor kid someday, and even though it's happening a lot sooner than I expected, I'm just glad you finally get to live those dreams."

A warm feeling spreads through me. Maybe Mark's right. Maybe this crazy turn of events is actually a good thing.

"So when am I gonna meet the little rascal?"

"You already did. It's Cooper, the boy I operated on two days ago."

He pauses, stunned. "You operated on your own son? That's intense."

"Yeah, I didn't know he was mine at the time. Imagine if things had gone sideways or I wasn't able to save him—I wouldn't be able to live with myself."

"Hey, man, don't spiral. Nothing went wrong, you saved him because you're fantastic at your job, end of story."

Before I can dwell on it any longer, my pager lets out a shrill beep, pulling me back to reality.

"Let's talk later, duty calls," I sigh, a hint of a smile still playing on my lips. "Talk to you later, buddy." I hang up, the weight of the revelation settling in. My life just took a sharp turn, and I have a feeling this is just the beginning.

Glancing at the display on my pager, I see it's a message from one of the nurses. She's the one in charge of the children's ward, and I told her to keep me informed of any developments. I call down to her nurse's station immediately and she picks up. "The little boy you asked me to keep an eye on, Cooper, he's awake."

My heart leaps as relief floods through me, so intense it almost knocks the wind out of my sails. "Great," I manage, a genuine smile tugging at my lips. "Thanks for letting me know. I'll be right there."

A strange mix of excitement and apprehension churns in my stomach as I make the journey to the pediatrics section of the hospital. I instruct the nurse to inform Alex that Cooper has woken up.

When I enter the room, Cooper looks up, his eyes widening in surprise. A wave of emotion washes over me. This is really my son. My gut clenches with a pang of regret. Years, precious years, stolen by a secret I had no control over.

"Hey there, champ," I say cheerfully before proceeding to check his vitals. Everything seems great. Except for his broken bones, which will heal with time, he seems perfectly alright. "How are you feeling, buddy?"

"My head hurts, and I want my mommy," he mumbles, his bright eyes looking up at me.

"She'll be here soon, big guy. She just went home to pick up a few things for you. The nurse already told her that you're awake, so she'll be here to see you soon."

A smile tugs at the corner of Cooper's lips, and I want so badly to tell him I'm his father, but of course, I don't.

He needs time to heal, both physically and emotionally. Besides, a part of me hesitates. How do you explain to a five-year-old that the friendly doctor is actually his father, a father who's been absent for his entire life?

Just as we're beginning to find our groove, the door creaks open and Alex walks in looking every bit as beautiful as always.

When she sees Cooper awake, she rushes to his side and hugs him.

"Mom...Mommy," Cooper babbles between squeezes from his emotional mother.

"Oh, baby, you're awake. Mommy missed you so much, sweetie. How are you feeling?"

"My head hurts. What happened, Mommy? Why are we not at home?"

"You fell at the playground and hurt yourself a whole lot, so we're here at the hospital so Dr. Knight can fix you all up, okay?"

"Okay..." He seems satisfied with her explanation.

"How about I read you a story?"

"Okay," he says weakly.

Alex pulls me to the side. "Thank you for being here when he woke up. I'll tell him about you, but not yet. I need to ease him into it."

I nod. "I completely understand. Take your time."

"You can come see him later, spend some time with him."
"I'd like that."

A few hours later, I get a text from Alex telling me that I could come see Cooper now, as he's awake and much stronger.

When I walk into the room, my smile falters for a second, but I force it back on, clutching the bright red fire truck I snagged from the gift shop. "Look what I found for you! This fire truck looks like it needs a brave captain to drive it, don't you think?"

He doesn't seem excited, and my heart sinks a little. Maybe starting with fire trucks wasn't the best idea. I clear my throat. "Right, of course. I'm sorry, I should have figured you would be too tired to play with toys today. My bad. Let's start over. I'm your doctor. Everyone calls me Dr. Knight, but because you're so cool and we're friends now, you can call me Bryan."

Another long pause. God, I'm extremely awful at this. I'm sure he's not usually this unresponsive—he probably hates me. Just as I start to think my attempt at conversation has failed, Cooper's head snaps toward me. His hazel eyes, so like my own, hold a flicker of interest. "Are we really friends?"

"Sure" I grin. "We can be whatever you want. I could even let you borrow my stethoscope so you can listen to my heartbeat. That sound good?"

He nods with as much gusto as he can muster, and a small giggle escapes his lips as he stretches out his hands to collect the toy truck from me while I settle down in a chair beside him.

Alex turns towards me with an encouraging smile that does strange things to my stomach, and then Cooper and I play with the stethoscope for a little while.

"Do you want me to read you another story?" I ask, and my stomach flutters with excitement when he nods yes.

For the next few minutes, I read him the story of the brave little squirrel who saved other animals from impending doom, and he seems to really enjoy it.

Soon, Copper is giggling as I do some silly animal voices and read each character in a different voice. I can tell he's enjoying this as much as I am. It's a glimpse into a life I could have been a part of. My heart, a tangled mess of emotions, threatens to burst at the seams. Love, longing, and a fierce protectiveness for this little boy I barely know bloom within me.

I read him two more stories while Alex feeds him. Soon after eating, he's fast asleep again—which is normal because his body needs a lot of rest to recuperate.

"Thanks for letting me do this, Lex. It was great."

"You're welcome."

I linger for another moment, watching as Alex tucks Cooper back into bed. The scene burns itself into my memory.

As I turn the corner to leave, I almost bump into Grace, who gives me the warmest smile I've ever gotten from her.

"Hi, Grace."

"Hey, Bryan. Thanks for taking care of our little boy."

"My absolute pleasure."

· ♥ · ♥ · ♥ · ♥ · ♥ ·

Later that evening, I walk briskly toward Cooper's room, carrying with me a basket full of food. Cooper is asleep and Alex is sitting in a corner, looking through her phone and nursing a cup of coffee.

"Hey, I figured you'd be sick of hospital food," I say, offering the bag. "Grabbed you something real from a real restaurant."

Alex's eyes widen in surprise. "Oh wow, Bryan, you shouldn't have," she says, a smile warming her features as she takes the bag.

As we unwrap our food, a comfortable silence falls between us.

"He's such an adorable kid," I finally say, taking a bite of my burger.

Alex chuckles. "You both have that going for you," she replies, a playful glint in her eyes.

My smile falters for a moment. "He looks so much like me, it's almost frightening. This whole thing…being a father…I don't know if I can do it, Alex. I'm scared. Scared of making a mistake, of screwing it all up, of hurting him or letting him down somehow."

Alex smiles softly in response to my vulnerable confession. Reaching across the table, she squeezes my hand gently. "It wasn't your fault, Bryan," she says softly. "You didn't know. And besides, his best years are still ahead of him. There's still so much time left for you to get to know him and make an impression."

"That part's true," I sigh. "But I shouldn't have let you go all those years ago. I should have fought for us."

A flicker of sadness crosses Alex's face. "I should have tried harder too. I should never have given up on us, or let your mother get in my head."

My gaze meets hers, a silent apology hanging in the air. "I was a fool to even doubt your intentions. My fears got the better of me, and I lost you for six years. It was the stupidest thing I've ever done."

I pause for a moment and look into her eyes.

"Forgive me, Alex," I plead. "Give me a chance to make it up to you and Cooper."

Tears well up in Alex's eyes, and she leans forward, pulling me into a warm embrace. "Don't worry about Cooper," she whispers. "He loves you already. He wouldn't shut up about the 'nice doctor' who played games with him. He'll love you even more when he discovers the truth."

I pull back, feeling a glimmer of hope. "What if I mess things up, Alex?"

She cups my face, wiping away a stray tear. "You won't," she says with conviction. "You won't because you're amazing. And because I'll be right here on this journey with you. You'll never be alone. I got you."

Chapter Twenty-Nine

♥

Alex

The steam from the hot bath dances around me, clinging to my tired limbs. I haven't felt this exhausted in such a long time, and it's really not a comfortable place to be.

Relief washes over me as the tension of the past few days begins to melt away. I dry my hands with a towel and reach for my phone on the floor next to the tub. A new text from Bryan sends a smile creeping across my face, and I sink deeper into the hot water as I read it.

Bryan: *I went up to Cooper's room and Grace said you went home for a while. Is everything alright?*

I quickly type out a response: *I'm fine, everything is good. Just came to freshen up and get some things. Haven't been home in days. So exhausted.*

The phone buzzes again, this time with an incoming call from Bryan. I grin widely before answering.

"That's rough," he says, his voice laced with concern. "I'm sorry."

"Why are you apologizing?" I chuckle. "It's not your fault."

"Still, I'm sorry you're going through this," he persists. "I know how much you love Cooper, and this accident...him being in the hospital like this where you don't have any power over what happens to him...it's putting such a strain on you."

"I'll be fine," I assure him, a touch of weariness in my voice. "Honestly, I just need our son to get better soon so I can return to my boring life."

A laugh escapes his lips. "Your life has been anything but boring, Alex. You should give yourself more credit."

I feel a playful jab coming on. "Are you the custodian of my life now, Bryan?"

"Even better," he teases. "I'm your baby daddy."

"That much is true."

The playful mood of the conversation has me giggling. "What are you even doing? Don't you have someone's life to save?"

"Not right now. I'm in my office, just going through some patient files. What are you doing?" A hint of a smirk creeps into his voice,

"Just having a bath, I need this hot water to kill the tension in all my joints and muscles."

"I know something else that could help with all of that. It's even more effective."

My laughter dies down, replaced by a blush that could rival the now lukewarm rose- and jasmine-scented water I'm submerged in. "You have a dirty mind, Bryan," I chide playfully.

"Hey, I thought you liked me because of my dirty mind," he protests. "Or was it something else that fascinated you?" His amusement is clear.

Suddenly, there's a sharp knock on Bryan's door on the other end of the phone.

"Shoot," he mutters. "As much as I'd like to continue this conversation with you and explore how far you're willing to test me, I have to go. There's someone at my door."

"Okay," I say, a hint of longing in my voice. "Talk to you later."

Ending the call, I lean back against the cool tile. I need to stop thinking about all of that when my son is lying in a hospital bed. First things first. Cooper needs to be healthy, and I need rest and respite from it all.

A soft sigh escapes my lips as I scroll through my phone, a kaleidoscope of memories flooding back. It's been a whirlwind month since Cooper's accident. Everything has been a blur—the constant visits to the hospital, nights I've stayed up late worrying if my baby boy will ever be okay again, and those rare, stolen moments I've shared with Bryan.

I remember one particular stormy night, the hospital was very quiet because it was past midnight and everyone was tucked away in their rooms for the night. Except for Bryan and me. It was deadly quiet, and the silence was broken only by the low hum of the refrigerator and the occasional rumble of thunder.

We were huddled in the patients' cafeteria, each of us nursing a mug of lukewarm coffee that offered little comfort against the chill that seemed to cling to the air. The storm raging outside mirrored the turmoil within me. Cooper was finally asleep after a particularly trying day, but I couldn't stop worrying. It was hard seeing him like this…so painful.

Suddenly, a deafening crack of thunder split the night, making me jump. A shiver ran down my spine, and I instinctively wrapped my arms tighter around myself, a childhood fear clawing its way to the surface. My fear of thunderstorms was a secret I had never shared with anyone, not even Bryan, but somehow he must have sensed it. Before I knew what was happening, there he was.

A warmth brushed against my shoulder, and I glanced sideways to see Bryan, his presence a silent reassurance. He didn't say a word, but the unspoken understanding in his gaze was all the comfort I needed. A sheepish smile tugged at my lips.

"Thanks," I mumbled, turning to face him.

He leaned closer, his voice barely a whisper. "Always." His eyes, the same hazel eyes as Cooper's, held a tenderness that made my breath hitch.

He knew. Somehow, he just knew...

I didn't even realize I'd fallen asleep in the bathtub. The steam has turned the bathroom into a hazy sauna by the time I finally jerk awake. Disoriented, I reach for the faucet, the cold water a shock to my sleep-addled system. I peer down at my wrinkled, prune-like fingers.

Groaning, I clamber out of the tub and get dressed. When my stomach begins to rumble, I remember that I haven't eaten since this morning. I quickly whip up a sandwich, plating another for Grace who's supposed to be watching Cooper. After grabbing a few essentials, I hurry back to the hospital, guilt gnawing at me for leaving them alone for three hours.

At the front desk, a cheery nurse intercepts me. "Good afternoon, Ms. Collins. Dr. Knight requested you see him in his office."

My heart skips a beat. "Do you know what it's about...?" I stammer, trailing off.

"No idea, ma'am," the nurse replies with a smile.

"Thank you," I say, offering a smile of my own.

I head to Cooper's room—which is no longer in the ICU because he's doing so much better—to check on him and Grace. After I give

Grace her food and see that they're not missing me too much, I head over to Bryan's office.

"Come in," a familiar voice calls out when I knock on Bryan's door.

Pushing open the door, I find Bryan leaning back in his chair, a playful glint in his eyes. The sterile office suddenly feels...comfortable.

"Hey," he says, gesturing to the empty chair in front of him. "Just wanted to see you."

"Oh," I say, surprised. A blush creeps up my neck as I sink into the chair.

Bryan leans forward, his voice dropping to a conversational whisper. "Dropped by earlier to see how our little champion's doing. He's a lot better."

A smile blooms on my face. "Yes he is, thanks to you and your wonderful staff. I helped him build a spaceship out of blankets this morning, and he convinced me to join his crew on a mission to Mars." I launch into a detailed account of Cooper's latest adventures, a warmth filling my voice as I speak.

Bryan listens intently, a genuine smile playing on his lips. He interjects with questions here and there, his interest in Cooper evident. As we talk, an unspoken ease settles between us, a comfortable space where we can simply be ourselves—parents united by our love for our son.

Maybe, I think as I steal a glance at Bryan's warm hazel eyes, *this unexpected turn of events isn't so bad after all*. There's a chance, however slim, to rebuild something beautiful. And even if things don't work out the way I secretly hope, at least we can find a way to co-parent Cooper together.

I'm on a roll, recounting Cooper's elaborate jokes. A comfortable silence settles as I finish the story, a smile lingering on my lips.

Then, I feel it. A warmth radiates from across the desk. Bryan's gaze holds mine, his eyes a golden hazel that seems to see right through me. A blush creeps up my neck, a self-conscious giggle escaping my lips.

"Why are you staring at me like that?" I blurt out, suddenly aware of the close proximity and the shift in the atmosphere.

"I'm staring at you like I would stare at anyone else," he replies, a hint of amusement in his voice.

"Oh, come on," I counter, playfully rolling my eyes. "We both know you're not."

He leans back in his chair, a wry smile playing on his lips. "Well, how would you know? Unless..." He trails off, his voice dropping to a low murmur. "...you have the same thing in mind that I do."

A heat wave floods my cheeks, and I look away from Bryan, over to the stack of books on his shelf. Bryan's gaze feels like a tangible presence, drawing my attention back to him like a moth to a flame.

"Here you go again with that look," I accuse, unable to keep the smile from my face.

"What look?" He feigns innocence, but a flicker of desire dances in his gaze.

"Like you haven't eaten in days and I'm a cheeseburger," I tease, my heart hammering against my ribs.

He leans forward, his voice a husky whisper. "Would that be such a bad thing?"

The air crackles with tension. Our eyes lock, a silent conversation passing between us. Time seems to slow, the office fading away. Before I can form a reply, Bryan gets up and stands next to me.

He pulls me out of my seat and stares into my eyes with such intensity that it feels like my skin is on fire. "You look absolutely ravishing today."

Leaning against the edge of his desk, I can't help teasing him a little. "Is that a problem, Doctor?"

His hands find their places on my waist, pulling me closer. "Oh, it's a problem, all right. A deliciously distracting problem."

He momentarily leaves me and walks over to the door, and when I hear the lock click, my whole body vibrates with anticipation of his next move.

When he comes back to me, his lips meet mine in a searing kiss. I surrender to the magnetic pull that draws us together, embracing the delicious consequences of our shared naughtiness.

When he finally pulls his lips from mine, his eyes have darkened and his lips are flushed from the intensity of our kiss.

"I want to taste you, baby."

"Now?" I ask, my breath still heavy. "What if someone knocks?"

"They won't."

Without another word, he tugs at my jeans and my panties follow, dropping to my feet. He lifts me up and seats me on his desk, then falls to his knees and puts my legs over his shoulders before lowering his mouth to my pussy.

Instinctively, I lie back on the table and sharply inhale when his tongue finds my clit. Without holding back, he holds my ass in place and goes to work, flicking his tongue back and forth on my clit while I bite my lips to keep from moaning.

He's slowly but consistently flicking his tongue over my clit now, and I feel my orgasm racing toward me like a flood. When it hits, it hits hard, and my entire body vibrates in its wake.

"Let me make love to you, Alex," he says when he comes up for air from between my legs. Then he kisses me, unconcerned with where his mouth had been just seconds earlier.

"I'm yours to take," I say. He reaches for his drawer, pulls out a condom, and pulls it over his rock-hard dick.

I'm way too turned on to wonder if he always has a condom in his drawer at work, or if he planned ahead for this. I can still feel his heart pounding rapidly against my chest as he aligns himself to me and nudges the head against my opening, easing into me slowly. Every inch sets fire to my skin.

He groans into my neck. His entire body is vibrating with tension as he thrusts into me and pulls out, again and again.

My entire body feels flooded—flooded by how good he feels, how stupefying the pleasure, how smoothly he slides in and out. How right this feels.

"Oh, Alex, baby, your pussy feels so fucking good," he grunts, driving into me with so much force that I tip over the edge. My pussy tightens as another orgasm hits me, gripping him harder, sucking him deeper.

At that same moment, he loses it—he lets out a grunt and shudders, pumping hard and muttering nonsense into my skin about how perfect I am, how beautiful, how long he's wanted this, how he'll never let go of me. I feel his orgasm soar, the blinding, scalding pleasure as he trembles on top of me.

I smile. And when new shivers begin to roll down my spine, I bite Bryan's shoulder and let myself go under.

Chapter Thirty

♥

Bryan

The fluorescent lights hum overhead, their monotonous buzz blending with Dr. Thompson's droning presentation on laparoscopic cholecystectomy. Finally, the last slide flashes on the screen, declaring his recent discovery in the modern medical revolution.

I force my gaze back to the screen, but the image of Alex's worried face refuses to fade. We argued last night—not a full-blown fight, but enough to hang a cloud over us. She's frustrated with my absence, and I can't blame her. Cooper, our little boy, is in the hospital, and it's really putting a strain on Alex's professional life.

Guilt gnaws at me. I care so much about Alex and Cooper...they're my world. And I really want to be there for them, but my job won't let me. I hate it.

My phone buzzes with a text from Alex: *Cooper finally napped. Just missing you.*

The guilt intensifies. How can I be here when they need me?

I glance at the screen again—Dr. Thompson's words blur into background noise as I zone out completely and begin to look at photos that Alex sent to me earlier.

Moments later, polite applause fills the room. People begin to move out of their seats and make polite conversation, indicating the end of today's workshop.

I know what's expected of all of us. The post-presentation discussions—networking, they call it—the eager question and answer sessions from colleagues. But today, the thought of going through the motions feels suffocating. All I want is the quiet of my hotel room, a sanctuary away from the buzzing energy of the conference.

Dr. Nakamura and Dr. Chen approach me with smiles on their faces. They're keen to discuss my research on pediatric cardiac surgeries, but I can't bear the thought. Just as panic grips me, Dr. Patel, my conference buddy, appears with a coffee in hand.

"Great presentation earlier, Bryan," he says, oblivious to my inner turmoil. "Fascinating stuff about reduced recovery time. I quite enjoyed your speech, and you know I don't really like speeches."

Relief floods me as Dr. Nakamura and Dr. Chen turn their attention to Patel. Seizing the chance, I mumble a hasty excuse and make my escape.

"Thanks, Patel," I say, my voice strained. "Urgent family matter. You know how it is."

With a quick goodbye, I gather my things and scribble a quick note. Then, I discreetly slip out of the conference hall. I practically flee, drawing curious glances from those who recognize me. Shame flickers within me, but the urge to escape overwhelms it. In the elevator, each second feels like an eternity.

The fresh air from the lobby hits me like a wake-up call as I walk to my room, take a shower, and have room service sent up. When I'm done with my meal, I take a light nap, but the shrill ringing of the landline wakes me. It's the receptionist calling to ask me if I want dinner sent up.

Dinner? *Shit.* I must've overslept. I quickly grab my phone and there are four missed calls from Alex.

I call her back. "Oh my God, I'm so sorry I missed your calls, I fell asleep," I ramble when she picks up. "Are you okay? Is Cooper okay?"

"Yes, he's fantastic actually. I have great news for you. Mark just came in, and he says Cooper's making a fantastic recovery! He's talking about letting us go home by the weekend."

My heart soars. Relief courses through me, erasing the anxieties of the conference. "That's amazing! I'm so happy to hear that. Is there anything I need to do? Should I come back early?"

"Hold on, Dr. Knight," Alex chuckles, the sound warming me from the inside out. "Don't worry about rushing back. Finish your conference commitments first. We're just fine here. Cooper and I aren't going anywhere."

I sigh, feeling a knot loosen in my stomach. "Are you sure? I just...Alex," I say, my voice trembling slightly. "I...I've decided I can't stay in Alaska any longer. It's so cold here, and I miss you guys. I'm getting my ticket and coming back tomorrow."

There's a stunned silence, and then she speaks, hesitant. "What? But the conference...didn't you say it was going to end on Saturday?"

"Some things are more important," I say firmly, my resolve strengthening. "You are. Our son is. I miss you. I miss Cooper. I'm coming home."

"We miss you, of course," she says gently, "but we also know how important your work is to you. Besides, won't you feel worse leaving things unfinished?"

I concede the point. "Yeah, you're right," I admit. "Still, I can't wait to get back and hold you both."

"Don't worry," she assures me. "We'll be here waiting with open arms—well, maybe not Cooper. He's still stuck in bed, so there won't be many hugs coming from him. He can shake your hands, though."

We both laugh, the sound a balm to my frayed nerves. The tension of the day dissipates, replaced by the warmth of our connection.

I find myself talking about the conference, the irony not lost on me. "Honestly," I say, a touch of disbelief in my voice, "there's normally nothing I enjoy more than this stuff. New research, exchanging ideas with colleagues...it's like a professional playground. But now I'm just fed up, and I've only been here for three days."

"Wow." Alex feigns surprise. "Even a nerd like you is finding medical conferences boring?"

I chuckle. "The truth is, Alex," I say, my voice softening, "I've always poured myself into my work. Locked everything else out. But now, with you and Cooper, it feels like my life is so much bigger. And suddenly all the things that used to take precedence, they've just...melted away."

A contented sigh escapes her on the other end. "I know exactly what you mean," she says. "Before Cooper, my job was everything. But then, you know...you get to experience a love that's just greater."

We talk for hours until finally, with a yawn, Alex announces it's time for her to go to bed. "I can't wait to see you, Bryan," she says, her voice thick with sleep.

"Me too, Alex," I reply, my heart full. "More than you know." Even just talking to her has made me feel so much better.

Relief washes over me as I step out of the airport terminal, greeted by the familiar small-town air. It's invigorating, a stark contrast to that hotel room that felt like a cage. I clutch the brightly colored paper bags in my hands, gifts for my two favorite people in the whole world.

I don't even bother going home to drop my bags. Instead, I head straight to the hospital, leave my things in my office, and head upstairs to the pediatric ward. Reaching Cooper's room, I see Grace walking out.

"Hey, Grace!" I greet.

"They've been waiting for you." She jerks her head toward the room and a smile takes over my face.

Taking a deep breath, I walk in to see not only Alex, but a little whirlwind of energy—still in his hospital gown but looking very handsome and with more color in his cheeks than I've ever seen.

"Dr. Knight!" Cooper shouts, his eyes lighting up like Christmas lights. "Where have you been? I've made Mom look all over for you."

I look over at Alex, pleasantly surprised. This isn't the listless child I saw here four days ago before I left. Somehow he's become more enthusiastic, and more open, and that makes me so excited. This is a sparky, energetic little boy—and undeniably, I see a reflection of myself in those bright, curious eyes.

"Hey, champ. I'm sorry, but I just had to go out of town for a while. You know, doctor stuff, but I'm back now."

I show him the toy stethoscope I bought for him and a book filled with colorful pictures of animals.

Alex, who looks radiant as always, flashes me a smile and I have to get a hold of myself to keep from swallowing my tongue. How can one person have so much effect on me?

Alex and I have discussed it, and we've decided it's time we tell Cooper the truth about who I really am. I couldn't be more excited, and in truth that's why I was so eager to come back home.

Taking Cooper's hand, she sits beside him, her eyes filled with a mixture of love and apprehension. "Hey, sweetie, remember how you've always asked about your dad, and I keep telling you that maybe you two might meet one day?" He nods. "Well, this man...he isn't just your doctor, he's your dad."

Cooper stares at me, his brow furrowed in confusion. "No, he's not. He's Dr. Knight, he told me so."

"Coop, you know I would never lie to you. He's your father."

"So why hasn't he been with us?"

A knot tightens in my chest. This is the moment I've dreaded, the explanation I haven't prepared for. Alex, sensing my struggle, squeezes my hand reassuringly.

"Sometimes, adults fight," she explains gently. "Your dad and I were angry with each other and chose not to be friends anymore. That's why he didn't even know about you. But we're friends again, and now your dad knows about you, and he's back in our lives."

Cooper remains silent for a long moment, his tiny face a mask of contemplation. My heart pounds, every second an agonizing wait. Finally, Cooper turns to me, his eyes searching.

"Will you leave us again?" he asks, his voice barely above a whisper.

Tears sting my eyes. "Never," I promise, my voice thick with emotion. "I'll always be here, Cooper. I promise."

A smile, hesitant at first, then widening, spreads across Cooper's face. "Okay then, I'm happy you're back," he declares, and before I can react, he stretches out his good arm for a hug.

Alex, tears shimmering in her eyes, wraps her arms around both of us. And in this moment, enveloped by warmth and love, I know I'm exactly where I belong. With these two people, I've never felt better in my life.

The following days are a whirlwind of magical moments. I spend every available moment with Alex and Cooper. I marvel at how quickly Cooper warms up to me, the way his face lights up when we play together. I see echoes of myself in Cooper's curiosity and boundless energy.

One afternoon, while playing catch in the hospital park, I watch as Cooper chases after a bouncing ball. A lump forms in my throat. Here, amidst the whiteness of the hospital grounds, a strange sense of belonging washes over me.

I'm not just Dr. Knight anymore, the respected surgeon with a reputation for complex procedures. Here, I'm simply a dad, throwing a ball with his son, the simple act holding a weight of significance that no surgery ever could.

"You're a natural, Cooper," I call out as the little boy catches the ball with a triumphant yell.

He beams, his chest puffed out with pride. "Just like you, Dad!"

It's the first time he's ever said that out loud, instead of calling me Dr. Knight. It's such a significant moment for me I wish I could record it for posterity.

My heart swells. The past few weeks, with their arguments and missed moments, seem to melt away in the warmth of Cooper's innocent admiration.

There are challenges, of course. Learning to navigate the delicate balance of co-parenting with Alex and figuring out how to be a present father while juggling a demanding career. But for the first time, I feel a sense of purpose that transcends my work.

One evening, as Alex tucks Cooper into bed, I sit beside them, reading a story about a brave little bear. Nestled between his parents, his eyes heavy with sleep, Cooper reaches out a tiny hand, his fingers brushing against both Alex's and mine.

"You know what I've learned?" Alex whispers, a soft smile gracing her lips. "We are a family. Just like the story."

I squeeze Alex's hand, a silent promise hanging between us. We might not have had the picture-perfect beginning, but we're building something special, a family stitched together with love, forgiveness, and a whole lot of laughter.

Chapter Thirty-One

♥

Alex

Relief washes over me as the hospital staff wheel Cooper, still a little groggy but grinning from ear to ear, in a wheelchair toward the exit. Grace has already gone downstairs to make sure the car seat is properly fixed and the transition from hospital back to home life is going to go smoothly.

In the confines of the hospital room, Bryan is helping me gather our belongings. The task seems mundane, but the fact that he's here, doing this with me, means a lot. I can't explain why.

"You know, Alex," Bryan begins, his voice tentative, "we could always go to my place." I snap my head up to meet his eyes. "It's bigger and has more space for Cooper to run around, and he'll have both of us under one roof."

"What are you doing, Bryan? I was wondering when this was going to come up. You do know that I have a house of my own, right? Please don't spoil a good thing."

I see a flicker of disappointment cross his features. "Of course," he says, quickly backtracking. "I didn't mean it that way. Just...it would be easier, wouldn't it? Cooper wouldn't have to adjust to two different environments. He could see you all the time, and..."

I study him for a moment, feeling a tenderness fill my gaze. "It's a great idea, Bryan," I admit. "Really, it is."

He breathes a sigh of relief, a smile blooming on his face. "So, you agree?"

I laugh with a little amusement. "Yes, but not right now. It's too much change, too soon. We have to remember Cooper has only just begun to adjust to the idea of having a father, so throwing a whole new world into the mix might be a bit overwhelming."

His disappointment is evident, but he masks it with a forced smile. "Okay," he agrees, a touch of defeat in his voice. "We can take things slowly. But eventually..."

"Eventually," I echo, squeezing his hand softly. "But for now, let's get settled back home."

"You do know that Grace needs a break too, right? I'm sure she'd like her privacy sometimes, so...what I'm suggesting isn't all that crazy."

"I understand. Let's revisit this in two months or so."

He nods, understanding my logic. We finish packing, and a comfortable silence settles between us. I feel my phone vibrate with a text notification, a gentle reminder that it's time to go.

Bryan helps Cooper into the car seat, buckling him in with a practiced ease. He kneels before our son, his gaze meeting Cooper's bright and curious eyes. "You're going home today, champ," he says, ruffling our boy's hair gently.

Cooper grins, his eyes sparkling with a mischievous glint. "Can we play hide-and-seek?" he asks, his voice barely above a whisper.

Bryan chuckles, and a warmth spreads through me. "We sure can," he says, glancing at me where I stand watch with a soft smile gracing my lips.

· ♥ · ♥ · ♥ · ♥ · ♥ ·

The afternoon sun casts long shadows across my backyard as Bryan and Cooper engage in a spirited game of hide-and-seek.

Grace and I sit on the porch swing, sipping lemonade and watching with soft chuckles as Bryan crouches behind the towering oak tree, his concentration evident. Cooper, barely visible among the tall blades of grass, inches toward the back door, a mischievous grin on his face.

Bryan springs from his hiding spot just as Cooper reaches for the doorknob, his theatrical roar filling the air. Cooper shrieks with laughter, tumbling onto the grass. Tears of joy well up in my eyes at the sight of them, so carefree and full of life.

"Not fair, Dad!" Cooper protests, wiping away imaginary tears. They play a bunch of different games, running around the yard with so much gusto and laughing so much. God, I wish I had their energy. As soon as the sun starts to come down, Bryan says he has to leave to get back to the hospital and make his rounds.

But before he leaves, Cooper tugs on his shirt. "Don't go, Dad!" he whines, a tiny frown marring his features.

Bryan kneels before him, and I can tell his heart is melting at the sound of those words. "I have to go do something important at the hospital, champ. I have to go take care of all those sick people so they can get better and go home like you," he explains gently. "But I'll be back soon, okay?"

"Promise?" Cooper insists, his lower lip trembling slightly.

Bryan can't resist. He pulls Cooper into a tight hug, burying his face in the soft curls of his hair. "Promise," he whispers, the word a vow that he makes to me as well, meeting my eyes over Cooper's shoulder.

With a final goodbye, he leaves. Outside, as he rounds the corner, his gaze drifts back to the house where he sees us both peeking through the window, Cooper's small hand waving frantically at him.

· ♥ · ♥ · ♥ · ♥ · ♥ ·

It's been three weeks since Cooper got back from the hospital, and he's back in school too. Grace isn't available today, so I had to cut off my lunch break to go pick him up from school.

When we get home, Cooper dashes inside first, and I follow him up to the door. As I reach for the handle, I hear someone call my name from behind me. I turn around to see a figure coming up the steps of the porch who I instantly recognize as Mel. My blood begins to boil.

"Mel," I force out, my voice tight and dry. "What the hell are you doing here?"

Mel, usually impeccably put together, seems a touch flushed, her designer sunglasses failing to hide the weariness in her eyes. This person standing before me is a stark contrast to the smug, know-it-all woman who made my life a living hell.

"Alex," Mel begins, her voice surprisingly devoid of its usual condescension, "listen to me. I'm not here to fight."

I scoff. "No? Oh, God. Who would've thought? Every single time we've been in contact, you've gone out of your way to humiliate me.

Well, no more, Mel. I'm not obligated to stand here listening to you talk anymore."

I step inside my house and close the door, the satisfying bang causing me to feel just a tiny bit triumphant.

I plan to just leave her stewing there on the porch when a thought stops me. Cooper. He wouldn't understand the situation, and witnessing a shouting match wouldn't do him any good.

With a sigh, I push the door open again. "Alright, Mel," I say, my voice laced with forced calm as I usher her in. "What do you want? Why are you here? I thought we were done with each other, never to see each other again."

Mel steps inside, her eyes flitting nervously around the room. Gone is the usual aura of superiority, replaced by a vulnerability I wouldn't have believed possible, at least not in this woman.

"Alex," Mel begins, her voice softer than I've ever heard it, "you and Bryan are involved again, so we can try to stay out of each other's way, but what good will that do? Eventually, we'll be forced to be in the same space, no matter how painful. It's only right that we try to repair the rift between us."

I raise an eyebrow. "You mean the rift that you caused?"

Mel flinches, a flicker of shame crossing her features. "Don't act all innocent in this, Alex. You're as guilty of goading me as I am."

I throw my hands up in exasperation. "Wow, Mel," I say, my voice dripping with sarcasm. "If this is your version of an apology, it really sucks. And you should leave my house."

I start toward the door again, intent on ushering Mel out, when her next words stop me cold.

"Wait, Alex," Mel pleads. "What I wanted to say is…I'm sorry for how I treated you all those years ago, and even recently when you came back into Bryan's life. I was horrible to you, and you didn't deserve it, especially since you were carrying my grandson. I went to the hospital to see Bryan, and ran into Mark. He told me about what happened—Cooper's accident. I'm so sorry. Do you think you can ever forgive me?"

I stare at her, momentarily speechless. I didn't expect to get an apology from her, ever, so I'm at a loss for words.

Mel's shoulders slump, her carefully constructed facade crumbling. I watch her for a moment, a surge of conflicting emotions warring within me. Maybe, just maybe, there's a chance for a fragile truce, a sliver of civility for the sake of Cooper and Bryan, but I need answers first. "I wrote a letter to Bryan telling him I was pregnant. What did you do with it?"

"I'm really so sorry, but I threw away every letter coming in for Bryan at that time, because I didn't want you to contact him under another name. I didn't even read most of them. I didn't know you were pregnant." My eyes widen in shock. "Yes, I know, I'm a horrible person. In my own twisted way, I thought I was protecting my son, but I know better now. I won't get between you two ever again."

I sigh heavily. "Mel, I forgive you. I've never been one to hold a grudge for too long anyway."

"Thank you, you don't know what this means to me."

"You're welcome."

"I know it may be too soon to ask, but can I see my grandson?" she asks, a hint of vulnerability peeking through her usual bravado.

My jaw clenches. "It's nothing against you, but Cooper doesn't know about you yet. He just found out about his father a few days ago, I want to let it sink in first before bombarding him with more people."

Mel's face flushes a faint pink, a flicker of shame battling with her usual arrogance. "Don't you think he should meet everyone at once?" she argues. "He'll get used to it all at the same time."

"This is my system, Mel," I counter, my voice laced with steel. "I let you into my home, please don't make me regret it. You may be his grandma, but I'm not ready for him to meet you yet."

Mel opens her mouth to retort, then thinks better of it. "Okay, fine," she mutters.

"She's my grandma?" a soft voice coos from behind me. I spin around to see Cooper standing there, bright-eyed.

"Oh my God! Is this him? He looks just like Bryan at this age. Oh my! He has Bryan's eyes, hair, and lips." I watch as Mel looks over Cooper adoringly. "He's perfect."

I hold Cooper close, his tiny face peeking over my shoulder with wide, curious eyes. Taking a deep breath, I realize this is a moment that can't be avoided.

"Cooper, this is your Grandma Mel, she's your daddy's mommy," I say gently.

Cooper tilts his head, processing the new information. "Cool," Cooper declares, a smile spreading across his face. Then, a new question pops into his head. "Why don't you have a mom or dad, Mom?"

My heart aches. "Because, honey," I say, my voice thick with emotion, "they've gone away to heaven."

I steal a glance at Mel, surprised to see a genuine look of contrition on her face. Maybe, beneath the layers of arrogance and selfishness, there's a flicker of maternal instinct after all.

"Come here, sweetie, I want to give you a hug." She turns to me. "If it's okay with you?" I nod my consent, and Mel hugs Cooper so affectionately that I wonder what's come over her.

As the afternoon wears on, an unexpected truce settles between Mel and me. I watch her closely, and to my surprise, she seems genuinely interested in Cooper. She listens intently as he babbles about his toys, even offering a bar of chocolate—which I confiscate after a stern look.

We even find ourselves bonding over a particularly impressive finger painting Cooper created.

Who would have thought Mel and I would ever find common ground? It's our love for Cooper, a fierce and unconditional love, that bridges the chasm between us. Even our mutual love for Bryan couldn't achieve this. I'm grateful it's Cooper who's bringing us together—I'm exhausted from all the fighting. I know there's still much to mend, but I'm hopeful.

This feels like the beginning of something better. The years of animosity, fueled by past hurts, seem to melt away in the warmth of his innocent smile. The fire of our old hatred hasn't burned out entirely, but for now, it dims in the face of something far more powerful.

As Mel rises to leave, a tentative smile playing on her lips, I surprise even myself by extending an olive branch. "Maybe," I say hesitantly, "we can do this again sometime. As long as you understand it's on my terms."

Mel grins, a genuine one this time. "Wouldn't have it any other way, Alex," she replies.

I watch her leave, a sliver of hope flickering within me. The path ahead won't be easy, but for Cooper's sake, I'm willing to try. And as for Bryan...well, he's yet to find out about this latest antic of hers. But when he does, I'll be ready.

Chapter Thirty-Two

♥

Bryan

The phone is pressed against my ear, and the Friday afternoon sun pours through the hospital window, casting a warm glow on the linoleum floor. "Hey," I say, unable to suppress the grin as I imagine Alex's smile on the other end of the line.

"Hey, you." Her voice instantly calms the stress of the day with its familiar warmth.

"So," I begin, stretching my legs under the desk cluttered with charts, momentarily forgetting the weight of responsibility. "How's our little champion doing?"

There's a playful lilt in her voice as she replies, "If I didn't know any better, I'd think you're just in this for the endless cuddles with Cooper. No single regard at all for the woman who birthed him."

I let out a laugh, the sound filling the otherwise quiet nurses' station. "Come on, Alex," I tease, picturing her rolling her eyes with a playful smile. "You know I'm not just after our son's affections—having you around isn't too shabby either."

"Haha," she says, lacking genuine amusement. "You're hilarious. Very funny. Nice one, Dr. Knight."

"Cut me some slack," I chuckle, feeling the tension of the past weeks easing with each word. "You know I'm kidding, you both mean the world to me."

"Of course I know that," she says, her tone softening, warmth seeping through the phone.

I'm momentarily lost in thoughts of her.

"What are you up to?" she asks. "Doesn't the fate of the human population rest on your shoulders or something?"

I sigh. "The fate of humanity can wait."

She laughs, a throaty and full laugh, the sound like music to my ears. "Are you taking a break?"

"Even better, I just finished my shift," I confirm. "Thanks to the new staff that the court mandated the hospital to hire, I've managed to cut back on my hours a little bit. Can I come over?"

"Good news," she says genuinely. "Cooper will be thrilled to see you."

"Hey," I say, playfulness creeping back into my voice. "Just Cooper, what about you?"

"I have other things to do besides missing you all day."

"I think you'll change your tune once I get my hands on you, Ms. Collins," I counter confidently.

"Bring it on, Dr. Knight," she chuckles, a playful challenge in her voice that ignites excitement in me. The weight of the week melts away completely as I anticipate the joy of being with my family, my two favorite people in the world.

The gravel crunches under my tires as I pull out of the hospital, feeling a sense of satisfaction wash over me.

It's Friday, and with the new staffing in place, I finally have some real free time on my hands. Grace is out of town for the weekend, and Alex mentioned that Cooper has been a handful lately. Putting two and two together, I figure she could probably use a break from grocery shopping and meal prep.

With a grin, I pull into the mall parking lot. The next hour is a whirlwind of activity—navigating the supermarket aisles, grabbing Cooper's favorite cookie brands, and even venturing into a nearby store for a pint of Alex's preferred ice cream. I don't stop there. I pick up a pineapple pizza, frozen yogurt and fruit drinks for dessert, and Kung Pao chicken from her favorite Chinese takeout place to round out my shopping spree.

By the time I reach Alex's place, the back of my car looks like a shopping cart. I can't believe how quickly I've been domesticated. It feels truly refreshing. A quick honk from the driveway has Alex peeking out the window, a surprised smile blooming on her face.

"Damn, Bryan," she exclaims when she comes to hug me and peers into the back seat of my car. "When you said you were bringing food, you really meant it."

Her jaw drops a little further when she sees the grocery bags stacked neatly inside the trunk of the car. The surprised giggle that escapes her lips is pure music to my ears. This is what I live for—making this woman happy.

In a flash, she's by my side, throwing her arms around me in a tight hug. "You're incredible," she whispers, planting a grateful kiss on my cheek. "Honestly, I don't know what I'd do without you. You're so thoughtful and so generous. How did you even know I was running low on supplies?"

I wink, a playful smile on my face. "Because I pay attention, Alex."

Her eyebrows shoot up playfully. "Really? 'Cause for a minute there, I thought you were just trying to find a way into my pants."

A laugh rumbles in my chest. "Well, there's that too," I admit, leaning in conspiratorially. "But mostly, it's because I like you, a lot. I don't go around doing grand gestures for just anyone, you know. I have a reputation to maintain on these streets. Don't tell anyone."

She throws her head back and laughs, a clear, joyous sound that warms my heart. "Indeed, Dr. Knight. Your secret is safe with me."

I double-check that my car is locked before heading in after Alex. I call out her name and she answers from somewhere inside, presumably in the kitchen. I'm about to ask her if Cooper is asleep, but the question dies on my lips before it can escape. I know the answer the moment I step through the doorway.

There, in the living room, bathed in the warm glow of the setting sun, sits a sight that both shocks and infuriates me. My mother is on the floor, her silver hair cascading down her shoulders as she laughs, her hand gently ruffling Cooper's unruly curls. Cooper, his face alight with joy, is building a precarious tower of wooden blocks, his infectious giggles filling the air.

My first instinct is to turn to Alex, a bitter question clawing its way up my throat. "What is she doing here?"

Mel, sensing my arrival, finally looks up. A practiced smile, the one that always masks her true intentions, stretches across her face. "Hey, Bryan," she chirps, her voice overly chipper. "How are you?"

Cooper, momentarily distracted from his masterpiece, squeals, "Hey, Dad! You should come and join us! Grams and I are building a duplex!"

I force a smile, the effort almost painful. "I can see that, son," I rasp, my gaze flickering back to my mother. I don't want her here. Her presence in Alex's home feels like a violation. She's like an octopus, getting her tentacles into everything, and it's so annoying. But creating a scene, especially in front of Cooper, isn't the answer.

I grit my teeth, anger simmering just beneath the surface. Mom, oblivious to the storm brewing within me, seems perfectly at ease. From the way she interacts with Cooper and the ease with which she's settled onto the floor—it's clear this isn't her first visit.

My simmering anger reaches a boiling point. I can't take it anymore. Taking a deep breath, I excuse myself from Alex and Cooper, a steely glint entering my eyes as I signal for my mother to follow me toward the porch.

"What are you doing here, Mom?" I demand, my voice low and dangerous. "I thought I made myself clear—we need a break from each other."

Her smile falters slightly, and she feigns innocence. "And I respected your wishes, son," she says, her voice dripping with honeyed sweetness. "But you didn't really think you could keep me away from my grandson, did you?"

"Don't play games with me, Mom," I spit back, my patience wearing thin. "You're the reason we didn't know about him in the first place. And now you dare to walk back in here like nothing happened?"

"Bryan, don't be overly dramatic," Mom scoffs. "I'm just getting to know my grandson. There's no agenda here."

"There always is with you," I counter, my voice laced with bitterness.

She hesitates, her eyes flickering away. "If you think that, that's on you then, isn't it?" she finally mumbles. "Besides, you didn't tell me about him either. I had to hear it from Mark of all people."

"Mark?" My voice rises a notch. "I'll deal with him later. But right now, I'm afraid your visits are over. I won't allow you around my son. I won't allow you back into my life. Go home, Mom."

Her facade falters completely. Disbelief flickers across her face, then morphs into something that looks suspiciously like hurt. "You can't be serious, Bryan," she sputters. "I'm your mother!"

"And you betrayed me," I shoot back, my voice cold.

"Everything I did, I believed I was doing for your own good!" she pleads, her voice cracking. "I love you, Bryan. Don't you see that? And now, out of spite, you're going to keep your own child away from his only reliable grandparent?"

I stare at her, my jaw tense. A million emotions swirl within me—anger, hurt, and a flicker of something that might be sympathy. But mostly, there's a fierce protectiveness for my son, a burning need to shield Cooper from the machinations of the past.

"Tough luck, Mom," I finally say, my voice firm as I stand my ground.

Her shoulders slump, the fight seeming to drain out of her. She opens her mouth to retort, then closes it again, a defeated sigh escaping her lips. For a long moment, we stand there on the porch, the tension thick enough to cut with a knife.

Suddenly, the front door creaks open, and Alex steps out, her brow furrowed in concern. "Hey, guys, what's going on?" she asks, her gaze flitting between the two of us.

I turn to her, my anger momentarily forgotten in the face of her questioning eyes. "I don't even know what to say to you," I confess, my voice raw with emotion. "How could you let her..." I trail off, unable to complete the sentence. Alex holds up a hand, silencing me.

"Because it's not about me or you, Bryan," she says calmly, her voice surprisingly steady. "I was listening to the whole argument from inside. And I have to say, I agree with what Mel said last."

My jaw clenches. "You agree with her?" I cry in disbelief.

"Hear me out," Alex continues, her voice firm. "This is exactly what she did—go behind your back. And now you want to do the same to our son? I'm pretty sure Cooper overheard part of your argument too, before I sent him to his room. That's not exactly a healthy environment for him."

"But what about everything she's done?" I plead, frustration creeping into my voice. "What about the past?"

"The past is the past," Alex says, her gaze unwavering. "What if Mel stops showing up? What will you tell Cooper then? He adores her already, and he knows about her. You can't just shove her back into a closet and pretend she doesn't exist. Are you going to lie to him, Bryan? Start your relationship with your son off the same way your mother kept things from you and manipulated you?"

I flinch at her words, the weight of her accusation hitting me hard. I hadn't considered that, hadn't thought about how my actions would affect Cooper.

"I...I don't understand how you can be so calm about this," I stammer, feeling increasingly lost.

"I'm not," Alex admits. "Mel and I get on each other's nerves plenty. But we both love Cooper more than anything. That means putting him first, and that means finding ways to let go of the past and look toward the future. Please, Bryan, get on board. She's your mother. You can't run from her forever."

I stare at Alex, my gaze flickering between her resolute face and my mother's defeated posture. I know she's right. I can't keep hiding from my past, can't shield Cooper from his family forever.

I finally turn back to my mother, a deep breath escaping my lips. "I never expected that Alex would be the one mediating on your behalf."

"Well, she did apologize for all her wrongdoings, promised no more stunts, and she's very good with Cooper," Alex admits. "And I suppose that's what really matters."

I look at Alex, a silent question hanging in the air. She meets my gaze with a small, understanding smile.

"Alright," I concede, the word heavy on my tongue. "But, Mom," I continue, my voice firm, "I swear to God, if you ever create problems in my life again, that will be the end of our relationship."

Mom's shoulders straighten, a flicker of defiance returning to her eyes. "I promise no more meddling," she says, her voice surprisingly sincere. "I'm getting too old for this. I just want to get to know my grandson."

Taking a deep breath, I offer my mother a tentative smile. "Whatever you say, Mom." I guess I'll have to take her word for it.

Chapter Thirty-Three

Alex

I grip the armrests of my chair, knuckles white. The air in the conference room crackles with tension as Mr. Rusk, co-founder and senior partner of this firm and the most versatile legal mind I have ever come across, dissects a particularly brutal assault case. Each gruesome detail feels like a punch to the gut, my stomach churning with a mix of nausea and righteous anger.

But as the discussion shifts to a potential class action lawsuit against a discount shoe manufacturer, I feel a familiar tug—the insistent pull of daydreams and stolen glances. Ten hours, ten glorious hours until my date with Bryan.

Mr. Rusk's voice drones on about the merits of the case, but I can't focus. Visions of a candlelit dinner with Bryan, his hand warm in mine, take center stage. My pen taps a maddening rhythm against the polished mahogany table, a counterpoint to the dry legalese washing over me.

Suddenly, a sharp rap on the table shatters the internal world I've constructed. Mr. Rusk, his steely gaze fixed on me, booms, "Ms. Collins, any thoughts on the potential witness tampering in this assault case?"

I jolt back to reality, cheeks burning with the heat of a thousand suns. My mind is a blank canvas, the legal jargon a foreign language. Have I zoned out for the entire discussion? Panic claws at my throat. How long have I been AWOL? Worse, what bombshell revelation have I missed?

"I, uh..." I stammer, my gaze flickering to the open file in front of me. It should hold case notes, but per my luck, it doesn't.

Taking a deep breath, I decide to take a gamble. "Witness tampering in assault cases," I begin, my voice surprisingly steady, "is often a calculated move to silence a victim's voice. But the psychological impact can be equally damaging..."

I launch into an impromptu analysis, weaving together the legal aspects of witness intimidation with my own thoughts on the emotional trauma such actions could inflict on victims. I speak of the chilling effect it could have on future victims coming forward, the power dynamics at play, and the need for swift and decisive action.

The room, initially stunned by my near-miss, falls silent. Mr. Rusk, his initial scowl replaced by a flicker of intrigue, strokes his chin thoughtfully. "Intriguing perspective, Ms. Collins," he rumbles. "Fresh take on a well-trodden path."

More than half the partners in the room nod in agreement. Relief washes over me, a cool counterpoint to the earlier heat of shame. Even lost in a daydream, my legal mind still buzzes like a well-oiled machine.

That's why it's a surprise to me that despite Mr. Patel's call to me the other day, I still haven't been offered a promotion. "Thank you, Ms. Collins," Mr. Rusk says, gesturing for me to sit. "Now, back to the matter at hand. My partner, Mr. Patel, would like to say something important."

Having been to these meetings many times, I know this is the time when Mr. Patel launches into talks about how the legal system is flawed, blah blah blah, so I zone out, thinking instead of my first official comeback date with Bryan.

He asked me out officially after weeks of stolen glances, playful banter, and a late-night heart-to-heart at the hospital. The anticipation thrums through my veins like a live wire.

Suddenly, a sharp rap on the table jolts me back to reality. Mr. Patel's face looms before me, his bushy eyebrows arched in question.

"I'm sorry, what?"

"I asked how you felt about giving up your next month's salary to one of our pro bono cases. It's a divorce case—a father who has been absent all through his children's lives suddenly wants full custody of them to spite their mother, because she met someone and is remarrying. Father is a multi-millionaire, mother is a waitress, so she can't afford to fight his lawyers. We want to help but we need funds."

"Um," I stutter, trying to collect my thoughts. "I guess I can part with one month's salary for the greater good."

The room is silent for a second, and then everyone bursts into laughter. "I was just testing you, Ms. Collins, and you passed. Congratulations on becoming a partner."

"I'm sorry, what?" I sit up in my seat and gaze around the room in shock. "Are you serious?"

"As a heart attack."

"Oh wow, I don't know what to say. Thank you for this amazing opportunity, Mr. Patel, Mr. Rusk, I promise you won't regret it."

"I know we won't." Mr. Rusk smiles at me. "You're brilliant."

More than half the partners in the room nod in agreement. I feel a surge of heat bloom in my chest, this time from pride, not embarrassment.

At the end of the meeting, the conference room door clicks shut behind me, and I practically skip down the hallway toward my office.

My secretary, Sarah, glances up with a knowing smile. "Dr. Knight called, Ms. Collins. Seemed quite eager to speak with you."

My cheeks flush a rosy pink. "Thanks, Sarah."

She squints at me. "You look awfully chirpy, and no, it's not just because Bryan is calling."

"You're right. I was just promoted to partner."

"What? Shut the front door! This is amazing, Alex! And well deserved. You're the most hardworking person at this firm."

"Thanks, Sarah, and you're a wonderful secretary. Unfortunately, I'll need to hire another secretary who's more suited to my new role."

Her face turns white. "Wait, what?"

"Oh God, I'm kidding. That was a joke."

Her hand flies to her chest. "Too far, Alex. Too far."

I wince. "Sorry."

After my horrible attempt to joke around with Sarah, I practically bound into my office and sink into the chair before dialing Bryan's number.

"Hey, stranger," he answers, his voice bubbling with amusement. "Bad time?"

"Perfect timing, actually."

"What's going on? I can tell you're about to burst open from excitement."

"I was just promoted to partner."

"Oh my God! That's amazing, Lex. It's about time they got off their asses."

I chuckle. "Thanks for the vote of confidence. It almost ended in a disaster, though," I admit, a playful tone to my voice.

"Uh-oh. What happened?"

"*Almost*," I stress. "Thankfully, my beautiful legal mind decided to show up at the last minute, saving me from looking like a complete idiot in front of the entire board moments before my promotion. Turns out daydreaming about our date while in a meeting was a very bad idea."

Bryan's laughter booms through the phone. "I wonder what your partners would say if they knew you were having...uh...sex fantasies about me while discussing million-dollar lawsuits at the quarterly review?"

Heat crawls up my neck. "First of all, shhh! Don't say that out loud! Second of all, they weren't sex fantasies Just...regular dreams."

"The lady doth protest too much," Bryan teases.

"Oh, stop it! It was a simple daydream, alright?"

A comfortable silence settles between us, filled only with the soft sound of each other's breathing. It's a new kind of intimacy, this quiet understanding that transcends words.

"So, are you ready for our date tonight?" Bryan finally blurts out.

My heart skips a beat. "Ready?" I whisper, a breathless laugh escaping my lips. "I've never been more ready for anything in my life. I'm more excited for this than senior prom, and that's saying something considering that's when I had my first kiss. Although, the boy in question did bite my tongue rather severely that night."

Bryan's laughter fills the phone again. "Ouch. Well, I can assure you, my kissing skills are a tad more refined than Mr. Bitey-Tongue. Hopefully, tonight will be a much more pleasant memory for you."

"I have a feeling it will be," I say, a thrill coursing through me. We continue to banter for a while longer, the conversation flowing easily as we share stories and steal moments of laughter. Finally, with a lingering reluctance, we say our goodbyes.

· ♥ · ♥ · ♥ · ♥ · ♥ ·

The weight of the day finally crashes down on me as I step through my door. My earlier giddiness has evaporated, replaced by a bone-deep weariness and a dull ache in my head. Grace, seated on the couch with a book, looks up in surprise.

"Alex? You're home early. Everything alright? You look horrible."

I manage a weak smile. "Yeah, just…tired. Maybe coming down with something. The stress of work is finally catching up to me, I guess."

Grace raises an eyebrow. "Stress? You're the one who wanted to make partner, remember? Living the dream, aren't you?"

"Touché," I concede with a sigh. "Doesn't mean I don't get to complain about it once in a while, though."

The thought of my date with Bryan, just a few hours away, flickers in my mind. Briefly, a spark of excitement flares, but it's quickly extinguished by the growing nausea in my stomach.

Ignoring the warning signs, I decide to push through. The shower feels tepid against my chilled skin, and my reflection in the mirror confirms Grace's earlier observation—I look pale, almost sickly.

"Alex," Grace says, concern etched on her face as she helps me towel dry my hair, "you really don't look good. Maybe we should call Bryan and..."

"No!" I interject, the protest coming out a little too forcefully. "I can't cancel. He'll think I'm flaking out. Besides, if I'm truly sick, it's a good thing he's a doctor, right?"

Grace's lips purse. "And what if you get him sick too?"

I consider this for a moment, a mischievous glint returning to my eyes. "Then we can lie in bed together, miserable and contagious. Can't think of a more romantic gesture than being forced to convalesce together."

Just as I reach for my dress, a wave of nausea crashes over me. Rushing to the bathroom, I barely make it to the toilet before my stomach empties its contents.

As I surrender to my sister's ministrations, guilt gnaws at me. I can hear Grace on the phone with Bryan, her calm yet firm voice explaining the situation.

By the time Grace returns, I'm drifting off to sleep. A comforting hand smooths my hair, and a warm mug is pressed against my lips. The chicken broth is bland, but it settles my stomach and warms me from the inside.

"Sleep, Alex," Grace murmurs. "You'll feel better in the morning. And we'll figure something out with Bryan."

· ♥ · ♥ · ♥ · ♥ · ♥ ·

The aroma of freshly brewed tea fills the air as I shuffle into the kitchen the next morning, my face weary with the lingering effects of the previous night's ordeal.

"Morning, sunshine," Grace greets, her voice laced with concern. "How do you feel?"

I offer a weak smile. "Like I spent the entire night throwing up."

Grace chuckles, a hint of relief in her eyes. "I know, I was unable to sleep too. I was super worried about you."

"Sorry, Gracie," I mumble, sinking into a chair at the table.

"Hey, you're the sick one, no apologies needed," Grace says, bustling around the kitchen. "Now, how about some breakfast to settle your stomach?"

The sizzling bacon on the pan, however, has the opposite effect. A wave of nausea washes over me, and I bolt for the bathroom, the scent of bacon clinging to the air like a taunt.

I emerge from the bathroom, wiping my forehead, only to see Grace grinning at me with a knowing glint in her eyes. "What are you smiling about?" I ask, suspicion lacing my voice. "What could possibly be funny about my current predicament?"

"I think I might know what's going on here," Grace declares.

"Enlighten me, oh wise one." A flicker of hope battles with skepticism in my voice.

"When did you last have your period?" Grace asks, her voice gentle but firm.

I scoff. "That's impossible. You can't be serious. Bryan and I use protection, always, and I'm on the pill."

"Alex—" Grace's tone takes a serious turn. "You know condoms aren't a hundred percent efficient in preventing pregnancy, right? And you were so stressed at the hospital you may have forgotten to take it."

A jolt of realization shoots through me. The frantic afternoon in Bryan's office, the stolen moments of passion—it all comes flooding back. I gasp, a knot forming in my stomach. Grace is right. Grace is always right about these things.

Needing confirmation, I grab a pregnancy test from the drawer. The seconds tick by as I wait in the bathroom, a nervous energy thrumming through my veins.

Grace paces outside the door, her ear pressed against it. Finally, the bathroom door creaks open, and I emerge, a small plastic tube clenched tightly in my hand.

"Well?" Grace asks, her eyes searching my face. "Am I going to be an aunt to another adorable little munchkin or not?"

I hesitate, a thousand emotions warring within me. Finally, I meet Grace's gaze, a single tear tracing a path down my cheek. I nod slowly.

Before Grace can react, I crumple to the floor, overcome with a wave of uncertainty. Grace rushes to my side, her smile fading into a look of concern.

"Hey, hey," Grace soothes, pulling me into a hug. "What's wrong? I thought you'd be happy."

My voice trembles as I speak. "I don't know, Gracie. I don't know how Bryan will react. What if..." My voice trails off, lost in a maze of worry.

Chapter Thirty-Four

♥

Bryan

The silence in the living room stretches out, thick and heavy like a cloudy night. The pregnancy test Alex handed me when I came in is lying on the coffee table, the two blue lines burning into my retinas.

Beside me, Alex remains uncharacteristically quiet and stoic, her hand hovering tentatively over mine. The air crackles with unspoken anxieties, a million questions swirling in the space between us.

Taking a deep breath, Alex finally breaks the silence. "Well," she starts, her voice barely a whisper, "there you have it. Do you have anything to say about it?" I can tell she's nervous and honestly, I am too.

Not that I never thought about the possibility of having more children with her, but I'm still getting used to the idea of being a father to one boisterous almost six-year-old and now I have another child on the way.

My hand tightens around hers, just to show support and let her know that I'm here with her while I figure out the words to say. I meet her gaze. A flicker of fear is evident in her eyes, but it's quickly replaced by a surge of determination.

Any other woman would have minced words, but not my woman—my Alex got straight to the point and handed me the test so I could see for myself. I'm so proud of her because I know that took strength.

"Alex," I begin, my voice thick with emotion, "this is…this is incredible. We're going to have a baby!"

Relief, a sweet wave of it, washes over Alex, evident as she releases a sigh she's been holding in. I'm quite certain that after everything that's happened between us in the past, she didn't anticipate such an immediate, positive reaction. A hesitant smile crosses her face.

"Are you sure you're okay with this?" she asks, the question laced with a tremor of doubt. "With everything going on—"

I cut her off, my expression resolute. "Are you kidding? I am absolutely sure. This changes everything, Alex. In the best way possible. The only thing better than one kid is two little children to love and dote on."

I cup her face in my hands, my gaze burning with an intensity that makes her tremble beneath my touch. It's a look she hasn't seen before, a look that speaks of a love that is fierce, unwavering, and utterly consuming.

"Alex, I love you," I confess, my voice husky with emotion. "More than words can say. And this new baby is a chance for us to build a future together, and do it right this time around."

Much later, when we're lying in bed, Alex tells me that my words struck a chord deep within her because it's all she's ever wanted. A future with me, a family—it's a dream she's secretly harbored for years, a dream she relegated to the realm of fantasy. But now, with my declaration echoing in her ears, it feels possible, tangible, within reach.

"Oh, baby, you don't know how relieved I am to hear that. I love you too, always have, always will."

Just then, the living room door bursts open. Grace has brought Cooper home from school. Our son, oblivious to the charged atmosphere, barrels in. "Guess what happened at school today?"

I chuckle as Cooper bounces around with his infectious energy. I ruffle his hair, preparing to share the news.

"Whoa, slow down there, champ," I say with a grin. "Guess what? There's a little surprise coming our way in a few months."

Cooper tilts his head, curiosity etched on his face. Alex takes a deep breath, squeezing my hand for support.

"Are you finally getting me a pet hamster like you promised?"

"Not exactly, honey," she says softly. "This surprise is something even more special."

"More special than a new pet to play with?" Cooper gasps, his eyes wide with wonder.

I laugh. "Way more special! You see, your mom and I are going to have a new baby very soon. That means we'll have a new member of our family."

For a moment, the world seems to stand still as the news sinks in. Then, a slow grin spreads across Cooper's face, replaced by a moment of thought.

"A baby? Like a real one that cries and stuff?"

"Yep, a brand new little brother or sister to play with!"

Cooper's grin returns, wider than ever. He jumps on the couch, bouncing with excitement.

"A baby! We're gonna have a baby? That's awesome! I can read the baby all my favorite dinosaur books? And maybe we can build a giant pillow fort together? Can we name it Rex, like my T-Rex toy?"

Alex and I exchange a glance, full of amusement and affection. Grace steps into the room, her knowing smile adding to the warmth of the moment.

"Hold on there, champ," she says, ruffling Cooper's hair with a playful smile. "There's a lot to think about before you name the baby and build forts. But yes, having a little brother or sister is pretty amazing, isn't it?"

As the afternoon unfolds, the initial shock of the news subsides, replaced by a joyous commotion. Cooper bombards us with a million questions about the baby.

Through it all, our hearts swell with warmth and excitement. This chaotic, funny, and utterly endearing scene is a glimpse into our future.

For Alex and me, the whirlwind of emotions continues unabated. We spend hours talking about the future, our dreams and aspirations for our growing family.

After a few more weeks, we make the move to live together as a family in my house, and we get Cooper settled into his new bedroom. Late nights are spent curled up together, poring over baby names and meticulously decorating the nursery in a delightful shade of sunshine yellow. Alex finds herself succumbing to strange cravings, devouring pickles with the same gusto as one would ice cream. It's a whirlwind of chaos, but a beautiful, exhilarating chaos nonetheless.

I realize that as often as Alex has woken up beside me in bed, I'll never stop being in awe of how beautiful she looks right when she wakes up in the morning.

Alex groans in her sleep, shifting against my solid frame behind her, my arm thrown over her chest like a roller coaster safety bar.

I want to sleep in—it's the weekend, after all, and we should really enjoy this time, especially since Cooper is spending time at my mom's. I look over at Alex. She's shivering from the morning cold. Using what strength I can muster, I roll over, taking Alex with me, and wrap her in the duvet.

Satisfied, I cradle her head and drop sweet little kisses over her face and across every part of her body that's open to me. I decide that I very much like the sensation of her body, the entirety of her weight sprawled over mine.

Sunlight, playful yet insistent, stripes across the sheets where Alex and I lie entangled. The remnants of sleep are soft tendrils, echoing the warmth of the morning light.

Alex stretches beside me like a cat, sunlight glinting off her black curls. I watch, propped up on an elbow, as adoration paints her eyes a deeper brown.

The silence stretches between us, comfortable and familiar. It hasn't always been this way. There were storms before, misunderstandings that crackled like lightning, leaving the air thick with tension. But those storms have brought us closer—we've weathered them together, and now, peace has settled into our lives like a tranquil ocean after a turbulent tide.

When you stay with someone for a long time, you tend to mirror their personality, and you tend to become more comfortable in their presence and more understanding of their actions. God, I love Alex so much that it's difficult to imagine we were ever at odds.

"We've come a long way, haven't we?" I whisper to her.

Alex nods, smiling. A lump forms in my throat at the thought that we almost lost each other in a maze of miscommunication, and now we're building a life brick by brick, stronger with each shared sunrise.

I reach out, tucking a strand of hair behind her ear, the feel of her skin sending a familiar current through me. "And I wouldn't trade this journey for anything. I wouldn't want to walk this mile, not with anyone else," I say, my gaze holding hers captive.

Heat rushes to Alex's cheeks, turning them a soft pink. The butterflies in my stomach are taking flight, not with nervous anticipation, but with a certainty that warms me from within.

"I love you so much, Bryan. I don't think I can ever get tired of saying it, and I think I've loved you for as long as I can remember," Alex says to me, kissing my forehead. "But I need to get to work, okay? I wish I could stay here all day with you in this bed, but I can't, or I'll get fired." She moves as if to get up, but I reach for her, stilling her with a touch.

I chuckle. "Just hold on a sec, sunshine," I say, my voice husky with something more profound than amusement.

I rise from the bed, my movements imbued with purpose, and cross the room to my dresser. From inside one of my folded shirts, I retrieve a small velvet box and whisper a silent prayer before slipping it inside my pocket.

Turning back to the bed, I take a deep breath—a mix of nervousness and unwavering determination in my gut.

Alex, sensing the shift in the air, looks up at me slowly, moving to sit on the edge of the bed. Anticipation blooms into certainty as she sees me kneeling before her. Her eyes reflect the sunrise and a wealth of unspoken emotions.

"Alex—" My voice trembles slightly. "You are the laughter in my mornings, the warmth in my nights, and the anchor in my storms. You've seen me at my best and my worst and loved me through it all. So, here, at this moment, I want to ask you…God, the way you're looking at me…you're putting me off my game and I rehearsed this so well."

Her smile, which could turn my world upside down, is even more radiant than I remember. As our eyes meet, a spark ignites within me, brighter than the summer sun filtering through the leaves.

"Alex," I say, my voice carrying a soft tremor. I can't help but marvel at the depth of emotion reflected in those beautiful brown eyes that I've become so familiar with. "I've longed for people before," I begin, my words deliberate. "I've loved people before, but not like this, never like this. Yours is a passion that sweeps me off my feet completely."

Alex's gaze softens, her attention fully captured by my words.

I move closer, still kneeling, and taking her hands in mine, the familiar touch sending a wave of warmth through me.

"Alex," I say, my voice filled with sincerity that echoes through the serene surroundings. "I can't rewind time, erase the mistakes, or change the past. But what I can do, what I want to do, is spend the rest of my life making up for all those moments when I wasn't with you, when we weren't together, and all the times we've argued, and I said things I'm not proud of…"

I reach into my pocket and pull out the small box, opening it to reveal a delicate ring that sparkles in the dappled sunlight. "Will you…" I pause, my eyes locking onto hers. "…spend the rest of your life with me? Will you be my partner, my confidante, my love? Will you marry me?"

Alex's eyes well up with tears, and her lips curl into a radiant smile. She nods, words catching in her throat. "Yes, Bryan. A thousand times, yes."

A mixture of relief and joy floods me as I rise to my feet, gently pulling her up with me. I slip the ring onto her finger, and we hold each other, the magnitude of this moment washing over us. We're not just committing to each other, but to building a family together.

My mind drifts to how our family has evolved. I think of my own parents—how my once-strained relationship with my father has gradually improved. He's made efforts to be present for Cooper, and I can only imagine how he'll react when he learns about the new baby. Even my parents have found a way to set aside their differences for the sake of their only grandchild. It's not perfect, but it's progress. This journey with Alex has shown me the power of second chances—in love and family.

I hold her close, our unborn child nestled between us, and I'm filled with hope for the future we're creating together—a future where past wounds can heal and new bonds can flourish. Needing to feel her even closer, I tighten my embrace, and we stay like that for so long that I lose all sense of time.

Epilogue

♥

Alex

Sunlight streams through the kitchen window, painting golden stripes across the heavily polished wooden floor. The aroma of sizzling bacon hangs heavy in the air, competing with the sleepy murmur of Cooper's cartoons blasting from the living room. I'm propped up on cushions on the plush corner bench, cradling a mug of hot cocoa in my hands, my gaze fixed on the gorgeous man flipping bacon in the kitchen.

Bryan, his hair a mess from sleep and a flour-dusted apron tied around his waist, hums along to the off-key singing emanating from the television. Every few seconds, Cooper, perched precariously on a stool beside him, reaches out with a tiny spatula, mimicking Bryan's motions with exaggerated concentration.

"Careful there, bud," Bryan cautions with a smile, dexterously dodging Cooper's errant spatula. "We don't want any burns on the most handsome member of this house."

Cooper puffs out his chest, mimicking a superhero pose with his plastic spatula held high. "But I'm a chef!" he declares in a voice that cracks slightly on the last word.

I can't help but chuckle. The sight of Bryan, ever patient and playful, teaching Cooper the finer points of pancake-flipping, is a scene straight out of a domestic dream. The way Bryan's eyes soften as he interacts with our son, the playful banter that flows between them—it fills my heart with a warmth that rivals the glow of a thousand rising suns put together.

Bryan glances over his shoulder, catching my gaze. A slow smile spreads across his face, crinkling the corners of his eyes. He winks, then gestures toward the stove with a playful flourish. "Care to join us, Chef Alex?"

"No, it's your duty to feed me today. I object to leaving this chair," I say.

Cooper, his face smeared with pancake batter, giggles as he attempts to stack his creation, a tower that defies all laws of physics. Bryan, with a playful groan, salvages the situation by adding a generous dollop of whipped cream, transforming the lopsided stack into a culinary masterpiece in Cooper's eyes.

As I sit down at the table, my plate piled high with fluffy pancakes and crispy bacon, I take a moment to appreciate the simple beauty of the scene. It isn't a magazine-perfect breakfast, with perfectly arranged food and spotless surfaces. It's a breakfast filled with love, laughter, and the messy joy of family. And at this moment, with my heart full and my loved ones around me, I know this is exactly where I'm meant to be.

After breakfast, I stretch languidly on the plush living room couch, the morning sun painting warm stripes across my face. The rhythmic thump of small feet and the rise and fall of playful voices drift in from the kitchen, a comforting melody that fills the air.

My hand instinctively rests on the little swell of my belly, a silent connection to the tiny life growing within me. It's a constant reminder of the beautiful chaos that's about to erupt in our lives, and a wellspring of both excitement and trepidation.

"Well, I want a baby brother so we can play with my trains and play catch," Cooper declares from the kitchen, his voice thick with enthusiasm.

Bryan's laughter, warm and rich, fills the air. "That sounds like a great plan, buddy. But wouldn't it be fun to have a baby sister? Someone to play dress-up with and share all your secrets?"

I can practically picture Cooper's face scrunching up in mock disgust. "Oh no, girls are gross. They play with dolls and they cry all the time."

A teasing smile plays on my lips. I can't resist chiming in. "Hey, now," I say, my voice laced with amusement. "Girls aren't gross. Remember, Mommy is a girl."

"Wrong!" Cooper counters with a triumphant giggle. "Mommy's a woman, and so is Grandma."

"Girls grow up to be women, duh," Bryan says. Jesus, when he's with Cooper, you never know who the older person is because they argue like little kids. It's so adorable that my son has a best friend in his father.

"Maybe they stop being annoying when they get big like Mommy and Grandma."

I chuckle at his flawless, albeit simplified, logic. Bryan chuckles too, then says placatingly, "Alright, alright, point taken. But girls can be pretty awesome, just like your mom."

"Yeah, but they're still..." Cooper trails off, searching for the right word to express his disdain.

"Different?" I supply with a smile.

"Yeah, different!" Cooper agrees, nodding vigorously. "I still say a baby brother would be way cooler. Dad, will you let me name the baby, no matter what it is?"

Bryan, ever the indulgent father, readily agrees. "Sure, son. You can name the baby."

Cooper's face lights up like a Christmas tree. "Awesome!"

I'm immediately nervous about whatever name Cooper might come up with, but I can't help smiling. The way Bryan includes him in the decision-making process truly matters. This little one, boy or girl, is going to be so loved, so cherished by both their big brother and their father.

And for a moment, the worries and anxieties that come with pregnancy fade away, replaced by a beautiful anticipation for the future. We're a family, and soon, we'll be one more. The thought sends a thrill coursing through me, and I can't wait to meet the little miracle that will complete our picture.

Excitement crackles in the air as we enter the ultrasound clinic. Bryan supports me with one arm and Cooper, bouncing with barely contained energy, is hanging on his other arm. The prospect of finally finding out the baby's gender has us all on edge.

"Alright, champ, are you ready to know if Mommy is having a boy or a girl?" Bryan asks Cooper, ruffling his hair playfully.

Cooper grins, his eyes gleaming with anticipation. "Yes!"

The white walls of the ultrasound room feel as cold and impersonal as the paper gown I wear. My heart thumps a frantic rhythm against my ribs, a counterpoint to the steady whir of the ultrasound machine.

Bryan squeezes my hand, his touch a warm anchor in the sea of anxiety. Cooper, perched on a stool beside us, bounces with barely contained excitement, his eyes glued to the screen where a grainy black and white image flickers.

The technician, a woman with a name tag that reads "Fran," smiles reassuringly. "Alright, let's get a good look at your little one," she says, her voice calm and professional. She spreads a cold gel across my abdomen, sending a shiver down my spine. The probe presses against my skin, smooth and cool.

On the screen, a dark, formless blob swims into view. It pulses rhythmically, a tiny echo of the life growing within me. Fran expertly navigates the probe, revealing more details—the curve of a spine, the delicate flutter of a limb. The grainy image, once abstract, begins to take shape, transforming from a medical mystery into a glimpse of a tiny human being.

"There you go," Fran says, pointing to a specific area of the image. "That's a good indicator of the baby's sex."

Bryan and I lean closer, our eyes straining to decipher the fuzzy image. Cooper, ever the impatient one, pipes up, "Is it a boy? Am I going to have a little brother?"

Bryan chuckles, his voice barely a whisper. "We'll see, champ."

Fran zooms in on the area she pointed to. The image flickers, the resolution sharpening slightly. For a moment, all I can see is a mass of indistinct shapes. Then, as Fran adjusts the angle ever so slightly, a revelation.

The air whooshes out of me in a rush I hadn't realized I was holding.

"Well," the technician starts, a knowing smile playing on her lips, "it appears we have a little princess in there!"

A wave of warmth washes over me, a tidal wave of emotion that threatens to overflow. It isn't just the relief of knowing the baby is healthy, it's the dawning realization of the life growing within me, a tiny girl who will change our world forever.

Bryan, his eyes wide with a mixture of surprise and delight, lets out a whoop of joy that echoes through the sterile room. He squeezes my hand so hard it almost hurts, but I don't care. His laughter, unrestrained and infectious, fills the room, a stark contrast to the silence that preceded it.

Cooper, confused by the sudden outburst, furrows his brow. "What's so funny, Dad?"

Bryan, still grinning from ear to ear, bounces Cooper on his knee. "It's a girl, buddy! You're going to have a little sister!"

The news takes a moment to register with Cooper. A slow smile spreads across his face as he watches the image on the screen, his brow furrowed in concentration. The initial disappointment of not having a fort-building buddy melts away, replaced by a tentative curiosity about this new addition to the family.

"A girl?" he finally asks, his voice filled with wonder. "You were right, Dad. She'll be as beautiful as Mom. And I'll teach her to fight."

I can't hold back a laugh; the sound is rich and warm. "Of course, honey," I say, my voice thick with emotion. "Princesses can have the best adventures, too. Think about it—you can be the brave knight who rescues her from a dragon!"

The technician chuckles softly and Cooper grins at the idea. Bryan scoops me up in a hug, his laughter echoing through the room.

"See, Alex!" he exclaims, his voice brimming with excitement. "I told you it would be a girl!"

Still breathless from the hug, I can only manage a bewildered, "What?"

Bryan wipes a joyous tear from his eye and points at me with a mischievous grin. "Remember that crazy bet we made in the car? That if it turns out to be a baby girl, we would have our wedding next weekend— and if it's a boy, we would wed next month?"

A blush creeps up my cheeks as the memory floods back. It was a lighthearted wager, a way to ease the pre-ultrasound jitters. But now, with the confirmation of a baby girl, the bet suddenly takes on a whole new meaning.

As Bryan's playful grin fades, a comfortable silence settles over the room. I settle back, one hand resting on my belly, the other intertwined with Bryan's. The grainy snapshot on the ultrasound screen is a vivid reminder of the new chapter in our future, a future shaped by the daughter we never imagined.

"You know," I begin, my voice soft with wonder, "if someone had told me a year ago that this is where we'd end up, I would've laughed at their face.

Bryan's eyes meet mine, a mixture of love and mischief dancing in their hazel depth. "What, you didn't see yourself carrying our second child while planning our wedding?"

I swat his arm playfully, but can't suppress my smile. "More like I couldn't imagine being this happy. There were moments when I thought we'd never get here."

"But we did," Bryan says, his tone serious now. "Every misunderstanding, every obstacle—we overcame it all."

Cooper, who's been uncharacteristically quiet, pipes up. "Is that why you and Dad are always smiling now?"

Bryan and I exchange a glance, remembering the rocky path that led us here. "Something like that, buddy," Bryan says, ruffling Cooper's hair.

As we leave the clinic, I can't help but think of Grace. She's been my rock through it all, from those uncertain days of my pregnancy with Cooper to now. I make a mental note to call her later—she'll be thrilled about her new niece, even as she teases me about "giving her another munchkin to spoil."

In the car, as Cooper chatters excitedly about his plan for his baby sister, I feel a sense of completeness wash over me. This family we've built, the love we've nurtured—it's more than I even dared to dream of.

Bryan leans closer to me, placing a hand gently on my belly. "Do you hear that, Alex?" he whispers dramatically, his voice full of playfulness.

I catch on and play along. "Hear what?"

Bryan laughs, a rich, infectious sound filling the car. "The sound of wedding bells ringing in the distance!"

"So," he says, a sparkle of mischief in his eyes as he starts the engine, "about that bet, I believe you owe me a wedding, Ms. Collins."

I burst into laughter, the sound full and free. " I suppose I do, Dr. Knight. But don't think this means you're off the hook for a diaper change duty."

Bryan chuckles, a teasing light in his eyes.

"You know," I say, turning to Bryan, "we should start thinking about our wedding plans soon."

Bryan's face lights up. "Absolutely. Any ideas?"

I smile, warmth spreading through me. "Something intimate but elegant. A place that means something to us both."

"Sound perfect," Bryan agrees, his eyes twinkling. "We've got plenty of options. We'll find the right one."

"And we'll make sure Cooper has a special role," I add, glancing back at our son.

Bryan nods, then adds, "I should call Mom when we get home. She'll soon be over the moon about having a granddaughter and a daughter-in-law."

I dip my head in agreement, a small smile playing on my lips as I reflect on how far we've come with Mel. From her initial disapproval to the tearful joy she showed when we announced this pregnancy, it's been a quiet journey.

"Your mom's really softened up, hasn't she? Who would have thought she'd be excited about planning a baby shower?" I squeeze his hand, still amazed by the transformation.

As we drive home, I can't help but marvel at the extraordinary path that led us here—from a fake relationship to real love, from misunderstanding to unshakeable trust. Our journey has been anything but conventional—a secret second chance baby that became our opportunity to build the family we never thought we'd have. Cooper, our unexpected blessing, brought us back together, revealing the depth of our love we've never truly let go.

Whatever challenges lie ahead—sleepless nights with a newborn, the demands of our jobs, the beautiful chaos of raising two children, or just the everyday trials of family life—I know we'll face them together. This new baby, a sister for Cooper, is the final piece of a puzzle we didn't even know we were solving.

After all, the most captivating love stories don't simply end with "happily ever after." They evolve, deepen, and flourish with each passing day. And ours—a tale of secrets revealed and love reignited, with a family built through adversity—is poised for its most thrilling chapter yet.

As I glance at Bryan, his eyes shining with joy and promise, I'm filled with an overwhelming sense of rightness. This is where we belong. This is our happily ever after, not an ending, but a beautiful, ever-unfolding beginning.

THE END

Did Bryan and Alex's chemistry leave you wanting more? I'm sure you'll look forward to my next release—Mark (Bryan's best friend) and Natalie's love story in another medical romance with a twist of suspense.

I would greatly appreciate your honest review. Your feedback will help me reach 200 reviews and guide other romance lovers to new reads. Thank you!

Scan the QR code to leave a review for Secret Second Chance Baby.

Meanwhile, prepare to be captivated by the irresistible romance between Elliot, a guarded billionaire single dad, and Amelia, his spirited next-door neighbor nanny. With undeniable chemistry igniting between them, they must confront their deepest secrets, risking everything for love. Join them on a journey of passion and intrigue in this steamy enemies-to-lovers tale as you read Chapter One of **"Grumpy Billionaire Single Daddy"** on this very next page.

Sneak Peek

♥

Grumpy Billionaire Single Daddy

Falling for my grumpy, arrogant billionaire boss is not on the menu.

Elliot Sinclair is the hottest billionaire architect in town.

Our paths cross at the Symposium, where my cooking skills are tested.

His scathing critique of my food sparks a tension hotter than an oven.

But fate has a twisted sense of humor.

He's my grumpy next-door neighbor who needs a nanny for his daughter.

I need the money for culinary school, so I accept the job.

His little girl melts my heart as I spend more time with her.

But getting involved with the boss is a recipe for disaster.

Yet, every stolen glance, every heated touch, ignites a fire I can't extinguish.

I'm determined to chase my dreams, but he's making me crave so much more.

One forbidden night leads to an unexpected twist.

Now I'm carrying his child, a secret ingredient that could shatter everything.

Scan the QR Code to start reading **Grumpy Billionaire Single Daddy**!

Chapter One

Amelia

My stomach is in knots as I look around the beautifully decorated town hall. I study the guests' faces to see their reactions to my food.

Cooking for a hundred guests at a moment's notice should definitely be added to the list of the top five fastest ways to give a chef a heart attack.

Okay, maybe I'm not a chef . . . yet, but my best friend, Emma, didn't care about that when she roped me into catering the Architect's Annual Symposium after their usual caterer canceled at the last minute.

"You can do this, Ame. Besides, you need the extra money to pay for culinary school," she said in a bid to convince me.

Fair point, I did indeed need the money.

The sound of gagging catches my attention, and I spin around to see my impeccably dressed neighbor, Elliot Sinclair, spitting a mouthful of my pecan pie tart into a napkin.

Elliot and I had never met. On my way to my morning run, I've only ever caught glimpses of him sneaking women out of his mansion via a ladder—which looked more like a trellis.

"God, that's atrocious." His deep baritone voice booms, and he looks at me. "If you're considering having the pecan pie tarts, please don't. I almost lost a tooth biting into it, and if I'm being honest, the cupcakes and mini quiches I tried earlier are quite bland, too."

I try my best to mask the anger welling up inside me. "Is that so?"

He throws the rest of the pecan pie tart into a nearby trash bin. "Yes, it's been an absolute disaster. I hope the chef who made these isn't planning on catering more events. Otherwise, Dr. KC will be smiling to the bank with all the chipped teeth he'll have to fix."

"That would be me. I'm the chef who made the pecan pie and every single meal here tonight with only a few hours' notice. Thanks for the wonderful feedback. I apologize for not meeting your expectations. I have other desserts available that you might enjoy." She says with a calm smile, her tone laced with a hint of sarcasm.

His nose—which is a little curved at the tip—flares at the realization, and I hear him cuss through his perfectly white set of teeth. "Well, I think I'll pass on trying anything else." He responds sharply as I scramble to get away from him, excusing myself to head back to the kitchen.

I slip into the empty seat next to Emma and let out an exasperated huff. "I don't think anyone likes the food very much."

"What the hell are you talking about? Look around, everyone seems to be enjoying their food."

"Not everyone." I search the room until my eyes rest on Elliot, chatting away with a redhead like he didn't just obliterate the little ego I had left.

With the way the redhead is throwing her head back in laughter, God only knows the sweet words he's feeding her. I'm pretty sure she'll be tomorrow morning's trellis candidate. *Ugh!*

Emma's soft but distinct voice breaks through my thoughts. "Who doesn't like your food? Point me in their direction, and they'll be singing your praises in seconds."

I would laugh if I weren't using every ounce of strength I have to stop myself from walking over to Elliot and smacking that gorgeous grin off his symmetrical face.

"Apparently, Elliot Sinclair almost lost a tooth eating my pecan pie tart, and he thinks my cupcakes and mini quiches are bland."

Emma's mouth drops open in an exaggerated gasp. Her love for K-dramas means she overreacts to everything, which is a trait I'm not sure she's aware has become a part of her.

"He didn't say that to your face, did he?"

I roll my eyes. "What do you think? This is all your fault, you know, for making me cater this event and suggesting I move to Harbor Heights."

"Um . . . hello. You needed to get away from your psycho ex-boyfriend. I didn't want to pick up the newspaper one day and read about your body being found in a ditch somewhere. Besides, where else would you have gone?"

"I'm sure Cassandra would've offered to accommodate me if she were around."

"Yeah, right. You and your sister are like fire and water. You would've killed each other in a week."

"True." I fold my arms across my chest. " My cousin Cindy offered to accommodate me, too, in her loft in DC, remember?"

Emma scoffs. "You mean alongside her twenty cats? You'd have probably woken up every day with cat poop in your hair and scratch marks all over your body."

"Beats being told that my food is so horrendous I shouldn't dare cater any events ever again."

"Look." Emma turns till we're face to face. "Elliot is a jerk for saying such mean things to you. and I'll confront him later."

I shake my head vehemently. "Please don't, I mean it. This is not like the time Jimmy Olsen ruined my science project in eighth grade and you made him cry in front of the entire school. You gotta stop fighting my battles."

"Okay, fine, I won't."

"Emma, I'm serious."

"I won't, scouts honor. But trust me when I tell you that you outdid yourself tonight. I'm certain that in a few months' time, you'll be the best-graduating student in your class."

I scrunch my nose in disbelief. "Thanks for the vote of confidence, but you're my best friend. You're supposed to say nice things about my food, so your compliments don't count.

"I get it. But remember, constructive criticism is a chef's best friend. It helps you grow and improve."

I sigh. "You're right. Thanks, Emm. I needed to hear that."

I spare one last glance at Elliot, who is still turning on all the charm in his broad-shouldered and certainly sculpted body for the benefit of the redhead beside him. I steel myself to focus on the task at hand, ensuring every detail is taken care of despite the persistent distraction of Elliot's presence.

Yet, even after the event concludes, his charm remains in my thoughts, casting a shadow over what should have been an otherwise successful evening—a sour note amidst the satisfaction of a job well done.

I hiss, grab my coat, and walk through the oak doors of the town hall. I mutter curses under my breath for choosing to walk home in the chilly February night breeze.

When I get back to the three-bedroom home I share with Emma—one she only has thanks to her hippie parents who decided their idea of retirement was to rent an RV and travel across the country together—I walk straight to my bedroom to change out of the strapless bodycon black gown that is so tight it has been digging into my sides all night.

"Beauty is pain," Emma had said as she persuaded me to wear the dress earlier that evening. I had wanted to rock my jeans and chiffon blouse, but she had given me a look capable of melting ice and told me not to give her a reason to pretend not to know me the entire evening.

Emma had always been the one with an affinity for fashionable clothes. On the other hand, I could wear T-shirts and jeans everywhere if only societal standards didn't frown upon it on certain occasions.

After changing out of the dress, I microwave some leftovers, then head over to the brown sofa in the living room and power up my laptop on the coffee table.

I open Google and type in Elliot Sinclair. His picture pops up, and the first article under it reads: *Twenty-seven-year-old architect Elliot Sinclair changes the game with futuristic museum design.*

The article goes on to mention how he's been an irreplaceable figure in the architecture industry and how he's designed some of the most expensive celebrity homes in America.

Reading about how rich and what a game changer Elliot is isn't doing anything to calm my nerves, so I close my laptop and turn on the TV to watch reruns of *Hell's Kitchen,* my favorite cooking show on Food Network. Gordon Ramsay always elevates my stress levels when I watch him, but *Hell's Kitchen* is one guilty pleasure I'm never letting go of.

The ability of those chefs to overcome whatever Chef Ramsay throws at them and still shine is genuinely inspiring, and the hope it gives me that I, too, can be a great chef someday is one thing I wouldn't trade for anything.

Besides, his yelling and cussing is the one thing that remained constant and familiar when it felt like my entire life was going to shit. Leaving my relationship with my *Psycho Ex*—as Em loved to call him—and upending my life to move to Harbor Heights in the space of three months was all the change I could handle.

But tonight, watching Chef Ramsay give the chefs instructions. I notice that I'm far from interested in anything going on in the kitchen and more consumed with thoughts of Elliot and his comments about my food.

As a chef, the first thing you need to learn is how to handle criticism of your food and not take it personally.

I've probably heard many great Chefs say these words about a million times, but tonight, I finally realized how difficult it is to actually put them into practice.

I'm normally not one to care about people's opinions of me. Mom used to live to criticize my dressing and my choice of men. She wasn't wrong about the latter, but it still hurt to hear her say I was a magnet for losers who were up to no good. We have a much healthier relationship now, but we had to work to get here.

Eventually, after wasting the better part of two years crying and torturing myself over her blunt honesty, I decided I had had enough, and I developed an iron-clad immunity to hurtful words, or so I thought until tonight.

Elliott's words are still searing through my chest like hot iron, even though it's been about an hour since he made his snide comments.

I don't understand how I can let him ruin my night this way. He probably doesn't even know what part of his house his kitchen is in, let alone cook a meal in his entire privileged life. So what could he possibly know about good food?

I try to focus on Chef Ramsay tasting the other chef's unique spin on pot roast, but when I can't get into it, I turn off the TV and decide to go for a run to clear my head. I'm usually more of an early-morning runner, but I'm making an exception tonight.

I change into black leggings and a long-sleeve, moisture-wicking sports top and put on my running shoes, and the moment I walk out the door, I regret my decision to come outside.

Pulling into the driveway of the cream-colored mansion beside our bungalow is Elliott's deep-blue Bentley. I freeze as he parks the car, comes out, and goes around to open the passenger door for, you guessed it, the redhead from the symposium.

"Oops." She lets out a laugh as she stumbles into Elliott's chest, and he steadies her with his arms.

From the slight wobbles in their step, as they walk to his door, I can tell they are a little intoxicated.

When they get to the door, he places his index finger over his lips. Either they don't see me standing on my porch—which is highly unlikely considering how lit up the street is—or they don't care that I'm there.

Either way, they disappear into the house, and my zeal to go for a run disappears with them. I turn around, go back into the house, and slam the door with so much force that I'm surprised it doesn't come flying off its hinges.

The next morning, I am awakened by a creak in the floorboard. For a moment, I think I'm back in Pasadena, and Jeremy has come back from one of his benders again.

Springing up from the bed, I'm about to run into the bathroom and hide when it all comes flooding back to me. I'm in Harbor Heights now, and that psycho doesn't know where I am, so he can't hurt me anymore.

Still, I tiptoe to my bedroom door and peer through the crack in the door, only heaving a sigh of relief when I see it's Emma. "Well, well, if it isn't the woman who had the most fun in Harbor Heights last night."

Emma stops and turns around to face me. "Don't judge me, those architects were really cute, and I couldn't resist. Plus, did you know architects are really good with their hands? Sean did things to me last night that will shake the devil in his boots."

"Good for you, Em. I'm not judging, but next time, a text to let me know you're not coming home will suffice."

"Judging from the empty packets of chips lying around and your open laptop, I doubt I crossed your mind at all last night. You were cyberstalking Elliot, weren't you?"

"You know me too well."

"I do. Now, if you'll excuse me, I need to shut my eyes for an hour or six."

After Emma goes into her bedroom, I decide to take that run, and just like clockwork, I see Elliot helping the redhead out of his window and onto the trellis.

I had often wondered why these women had to leave through the trellis that early in the morning until I caught a glimpse of a child, dressed head to toe in pink, getting into his car one evening.

Emma later confirmed that she was his daughter, but she didn't say much else.

I swear I'm not a bad person, but as I watch the redhead climb down the trellis, I've never wanted anything more than for her to fall and break a limb or four.

Scan the QR code to start reading **"Grumpy Billionaire Single Daddy"** here!

Printed in Great Britain
by Amazon